Praise for

HEART AND SEOUL

"With this charming contemporary, Frederick delivers a dramatic love story while sensitively exploring the thorny issue of interracial adoption. . . . Fans and new readers alike will be hooked on this page-turning tale." —*Publishers Weekly*

"Full of twists and turns, *Heart and Seoul* is an addictive, emotional, and tense read that will keep you hooked from the very beginning, much like a K-drama!" —The Nerd Daily

"Thorough exploration of the complicated emotional impact of transracial adoption." —*Kirkus Reviews*

"*Heart and Seoul* totally stole my heart and soul. . . . There is a universality to much of the story that will ensnare readers!" —The Book Disciple

Praise for Jen Frederick and her novels

"This story is written with breathless intensity, and Frederick portrays the seriousness of anxiety and phobias without reducing her characters to walking collections of diagnoses. The secondary characters add enjoyment, giving readers updates on past starring couples and anticipation for stories to come." —*Publishers Weekly*

"Kudos to Jen Frederick for writing another winner." —Book Binge

"Rife with passion and wonderfully paced romance, *Revealed to Him* asks how much a person is willing to overcome for a once-in-a-lifetime love."   —*BookPage*

"Jen Frederick is an amazing writer and she really has a knack for pulling your heartstrings in the best kind of way."
                                                              —Amorette's Reviews

"A fun, sexy romance that will delight romance readers who enjoy watching the redemption of a seemingly unrepentant hero."
                                                              —Smexy Books

"[*Unspoken*] has everything from heart-wrenching moments to lighthearted intelligent banter and intense, sexy love scenes that will leave you breathless."   —Harlequin Junkie

TITLES BY JEN FREDERICK

Seoulmates

Heart and Seoul

THE HITMAN NOVELS

Last Hope

Last Kiss

Last Hit: Reloaded

Last Breath

Last Gift

Last Hit

SEOULMATES

Jen Frederick

JOVE
NEW YORK

A JOVE BOOK
Published by Berkley
An imprint of Penguin Random House LLC
penguinrandomhouse.com

Copyright © 2022 by Pear Tree LLC
Readers Guide copyright © 2022 by Pear Tree LLC
Penguin Random House supports copyright. Copyright fuels creativity,
encourages diverse voices, promotes free speech, and creates a vibrant culture.
Thank you for buying an authorized edition of this book and for complying
with copyright laws by not reproducing, scanning, or distributing any part of it
in any form without permission. You are supporting writers and allowing
Penguin Random House to continue to publish books for every reader.

A JOVE BOOK, BERKLEY, and the BERKLEY & B colophon are
registered trademarks of Penguin Random House LLC.

Library of Congress Cataloging-in-Publication Data

Names: Frederick, Jen, author.
Title: Seoulmates / Jen Frederick.
Description: First Edition. | New York: Jove, 2022.
Identifiers: LCCN 2021038447 (print) | LCCN 2021038448 (ebook) |
ISBN 9780593100165 (trade paperback) | ISBN 9780593100172 (ebook)
Subjects: GSAFD: Love stories.
Classification: LCC PS3606.R4297 S46 2022 (print) |
LCC PS3606.R4297 (ebook) | DDC 813/.6—dc23
LC record available at https://lccn.loc.gov/2021038447
LC ebook record available at https://lccn.loc.gov/2021038448

First Edition: January 2022

Printed in the United States of America
1st Printing

Book design by Kristin del Rosario

To Lily,

heart of my heart,

may you always walk the flower path

SEOULMATES

CHAPTER ONE

"LUNCHTIME," *BUJANG-NIM*, MY BOSS, ANNOUNCES WITH A clap of his hands. "If you work too hard, you won't be productive this afternoon. Go on. Go on." He gestures for us to move.

Bujang-nim isn't his name. It's Park Hyunwoo, but everyone refers to him as *Bujang-nim*. It signifies his leadership role, and Koreans are about class, station, and seniority above all else.

The three of us, the only women on *Bujang-nim*'s international marketing team, stare at him for a long, silent moment. When I was installed in this department, I was relieved to see two women and had immediate fantasies that Chaeyoung, Soyou, and I would be great friends. Ovary solidarity or something like that. I was wrong. Chaeyoung is unwelcoming and Soyou is outright hostile.

Soyou glares at me as if I made up the concept of lunch to annoy her, while Chaeyoung worries one of the three thin necklaces strung around her neck, the diamond-studded interlocking *C*s catching in the bright fluorescents overhead.

The men in the department went to eat an hour ago. It'll be another hour before they return. Chaeyoung and Soyou generally do not eat lunch. I'm not sure if it's because they're dieting or because their workload is so immense. Everyone here seems to be on a perpetual diet, probably because every social activity revolves around food.

When I first started working in this department six weeks ago, I opted to work through lunch, too. I wanted to prove to everyone that I wasn't a worthless addition given a job because my mother is the CEO. I mean . . . yes, my mother is the CEO, but I'm a hard worker. Back home in Iowa, I never had any complaints about my work product or my work ethic. Here in Korea, at the IF Group, on the seventh floor, it's different.

No one is more keenly aware of my position as the daughter of the CEO than ambitious Soyou. As the silence stretches from awkward to uncomfortable, she pastes on a polite smile and rises. Bowing slightly to *Bujang-nim*, she grabs her purse from the bottom drawer of her desk, surreptitiously kicks Chaeyoung's chair, and then starts toward the elevators. Eating lunch with me is not on her list of pleasant things to do, but she's smart and savvy, which means when the boss says to go to lunch, she's going to lunch, even if it means eating with the devil.

"Come on, Chaeyoung-ie," she says, and after a pause, "and Choi Hara-nim."

I don't think I'm as low as the devil in Soyou's mind, but who knows? Calmly, I get my purse and follow the two to the elevator. I could have declined. I can do anything here. *Bujang-nim* would shine my shoes if I asked it, which is precisely why Soyou hates me, and that's why I can't be mad. I can be hurt and frustrated and annoyed, but I can't be mad. I don't deserve this job, the deference *Bujang-nim* pays me, or the energy drinks the resident ass-kisser, Yoo Minkyu, places next to my monitor every couple of days.

I should decline because a lunch with the three of us is bound to be miserable, like three women who meet after finding out they've all been dating the same man. I guess the situation is not all that dissimilar. We crave the approval of Choi Wansu, and the other two resent that I have the inside track, what with her being my mother.

If I'm the demon, Choi Wansu is my opposite. To most of the women in this company, she's a savior. The IF Group is an anomaly among Korean companies. They don't always hire people from the three biggest universities, known as SKY—Seoul, Korea University, Yonsei. Hell, they don't always require a college education. All they care about is results. Can you do the work you're hired to do? If so, here's your badge and your desk. Go to work.

In this achievement- and effort-based corporate environment, I stand out in an ugly way, given a job solely because of my connections, without proper qualifications or education or experience.

In the elevator car, Soyou launches into some topic that I only partially understand because it's all in Korean and Soyou speaks very fast. Chaeyoung slips the double *C* pendant up to her mouth and listens intently.

I catch a few words about drinking and a man and a bastard. The smaller woman nods, offering nothing but support. They're good friends and their strengths and weaknesses overlap. Chaeyoung sometimes struggles at work. She's clever and witty but often forgetful. Soyou keeps the other woman on track, leaving sticky-note reminders or collecting the woman's phone when she's left it in the bathroom or on a conference room table.

Chaeyoung repays her by springing for lunch and snacks, footing the taxi bill, leaving small gifts, offloading things like designer jewelry in a nonchalant manner so as not to make Soyou feel small. She would not be able to afford even one of Chaeyoung's necklaces.

It's their bond that draws me, but they're closed off, always standing to the side, sitting apart from me. Soyou often uses her taller frame as a shield for the smaller Chaeyoung, as if my laying eyes on Chaeyoung is inappropriate. Even now, Soyou is positioned between us discussing their weekend plans. Then her voice drops and I hear myself being referenced—or at least they're referencing Choi Wansu's daughter. I'm the only daughter she has.

When will they stop fawning over Choi Wansu's daughter?

I don't know.

Her US college isn't a good one. Not Harvard or Stanford or Yale.

She's a nakhasan. Chaeyoung shrugs as if that one word—that word meaning a product of nepotism—explains it all.

I swallow a deep sigh and lean against the wall of the elevator. She's right. It does explain it all. I stare at the back of Soyou's worn black heels, where the scuffed spots are colored in with marker, and shift uncomfortably in the three-inch designer heels Choi Wansu bought for me. If I were in Soyou's knockoff pumps, I'd be mad at me, too.

The doors open and Soyou marches out, her long strides making Chaeyoung have to practically jog to keep up. The taller woman doesn't stop to hail a taxi but makes straight for the convenience store across the street. The two of them will buy a prepackaged salad and a beverage. Soyou prefers iced Americano and Chaeyoung gets the Chilsung Cider lemon-lime flavor. They'll talk in fast Korean that I can't quite understand while eating the dry salads on a bench in the nearby Yongsan Park with the stay-at-home moms, day-care workers, and nannies.

My stomach rumbles. I don't want to eat lettuce and I don't want to sit like an outcast with two coworkers who will spend the next thirty minutes icing me out as they've done for the past six weeks. I grab my phone and shoot a text to my group chat.

ME: I'm eating at the fried pork ball food truck. Meet me if you're hungry.

"I'm going to a food truck to get fried pork balls," I call out to the two women. Chaeyoung halts at the side of the road, and for a half second, I think she might respond. "There's a CU next to it. They sell the salads you like there," I add because I'm foolish and want to be liked. Chaeyoung half turns, but Soyou grabs the woman's arm. The crosswalk light turns green and they're off without either of them looking back.

Embarrassment flames through me and I'm back in second grade listening to the schoolyard taunts of some dumb boy asking why my face is flat and if it's hard to see through my squinty eyes. I press the red silk cord of the necklace I wear at all times and tell myself I am not that kid anymore and my feelings are not hurt.

The phone in my hand buzzes. It's Bomi.

BOMI: I'll meet you there. Jules is with me.

See, I have friends. I reread the message and frown. What is Jules, my former roommate, doing in Yongsan-gu? She doesn't live anywhere near here, nor does she work here. Jules is a flight attendant for a private flight service and lives a fairly exotic life, jetting off to Hong Kong and Singapore and Tokyo nearly every other day. She claims it's super boring and spends many in-air hours crafting fantasies about how she would murder her clients—most of whom are rich old men, or *chaebols*, as they are known in South Korea.

Why couldn't I have clients like your Yujun? she lamented once. *All the* chaebols *I've ever served have been old and wrinkly. You walk out of the airport and into the arms of the only young, decent* chaebol *in this entire country. I should hate you.* She then scowled and shoved a beer into my hand. We're best friends now and we're going to have lunch together. I pocket my phone and make my way toward them and the food. Ten minutes later, I spot Jules and Bomi huddled together on the corner. They break apart as I approach.

"You look like they're beating you up at IF Group," Jules observes.

The private flight attendant is dressed in a pair of high-waisted flared jeans and a midriff long-sleeve top. Her blond hair is split into two braids that dangle over her shoulders. Big hoops complete the look. A little more makeup and maybe a few streaks of color and she might be mistaken for a K-pop idol. Next to her, Bomi, clad in a navy pantsuit and a white shirt, peers at me with concern, her brow wrinkling under her straight bangs.

I wrinkle my nose. "Maybe."

Jules steps close and presses the back of her hand to my forehead. "Are you sick? What kind of response is 'maybe'? You're supposed to say something mean back. That's how our relationship works."

"I'm too tired to bicker with you."

"Cripes. This is dire. Get some soju, Bomi."

Bomi shakes her head because she's smart and wants to keep her job. I am not going back to the office smelling like liquor.

"I can't have soju. It's lunchtime." The smell of fried food wafts over and my stomach rumbles again.

"Talk about no fun. You know this food-truck food is going to kill you," Jules warns, but she follows me over to the truck.

I wave a hello to Yang Ilhwa, the owner, an older woman of an indeterminate age. I say indeterminate because Korean women age differently than Western women. In the city, very few of the fifty- and even sixty-year-olds have wrinkles, but this woman does. Her cheeks sag and there are fine lines at the corners of her mouth and eyes, yet I've seen her carry giant buckets of oil and once even helped her lift a tub of pork cutlets, which I swear weighed fifty pounds or more.

"Ah, it's *jungyohan son-nim*!" she cries out when she spots me.

"Yes, your very important customer." I grin and dip my head. She started calling me *jungyohan son-nim* a couple of weeks ago when I ordered the *yachae twigim*, or the Korean version of tempura vegetables. She always has a huge pile left over at the end of the day, and on a whim, I ordered a bunch. They aren't very good. Her best dish is the fried pork balls stuffed with mozzarella. Second is the cheese-corn cups topped with grated Parmesan and *gochujang*, a sweet and spicy paste, but she's proud of her fried vegetables and so I order them each time I visit. I think I've developed a taste for the dried and fried.

"I get you regular order," she announces. "Here." She pushes three containers of banana milk toward us and ducks out of view to prepare our lunches.

"I'm always surprised at how much English she knows," Bomi murmurs, picking up the drinks and handing them out.

"She used to serve the GIs here," I explain. Yongsan-gu is a district in the heart of Seoul on the banks of the Han River. It used to house a US military garrison, but slowly South Korea reclaimed this area for itself, and a couple of years ago, the American soldiers decamped for a base forty miles south of Seoul. It's prime real estate and easy to see why the Koreans wanted it back.

"That explains it." Jules crumples her empty corn cup and tosses it in the trash can near the truck's front tire, one of the few around since public waste receptacles aren't a thing in Seoul. Yang Ilhwa reappears with three small paper boats of food. Nestled inside a lettuce leaf are four perfectly round, golden-fried pork balls along with battered and fried sweet potato sticks and bell pepper slices. My container has perilla leaves and deep-fried peppers along with a jaunty toothpick flag.

"Thank you!" we chorus like schoolgirls and then gather up our food to go and sit on the curb across from the truck.

"Why do you get the flag?" Jules complains. "I want a flag in my food."

"Because I come here three times a week. I may single-handedly be keeping her in business." I bite into the pork ball and let the crispy fried coating with the gooey cheese and savory meat melt onto my tongue. It tastes perfect, like Iowa State Fair food on a hot August day.

"This food really isn't that good," Jules says, but she gobbles down her portion as if she hasn't eaten in a day.

"Ahn Sangki brought me here. He likes it," I remind them.

"Just because Ahn Sangki is famous doesn't mean he has good taste," Jules fires back.

"I like it. It reminds me of Iowa," Bomi says.

"You aren't an impartial taste tester," Jules says. "Hara could have us eating dirt and you would say that it was the best dirt you've ever tasted."

"I haven't eaten dirt before, so it wouldn't be a lie." But Bomi's cheeks are turning pink because Jules is spot-on.

Bomi spent six months pretending to be my friend in America when she was really spying on me for my biological mother, Choi Wansu. Ever since the truth came out, Bomi has devoted herself to me. I could run a dog over and Bomi would either claim she was driving or bury the evidence. In her eyes, I can do no wrong. I can't say this attitude is all that much better than when she was spying on me, but at least she's open about things now. Maybe another person wouldn't have forgiven her, but I'm lonely. My boyfriend has been shipped overseas, ostensibly on business in Hong Kong and then Singapore, but mostly because he's my stepbrother and my mother finds the idea of the two of us together as repulsive as if we were blood siblings. Plus, it would be bad for business, and nothing in this world seems to be more important to Choi Wansu than IF Group. It's why I'm currently working in the International Marketing Department even though I don't speak much, if any, Korean and I have no marketing experience, but it was either take the job or put the entire company at risk.

I took the job.

"Is it the language?" Bomi asks. "Are you having a hard time with your Korean? I thought your department was supposed to only speak English."

Bomi also works at IF Group, and in close proximity to my mother. If I complain to Bomi about the work conditions, she'll tell Choi Wansu, and then someone, or many someones, will be disciplined or fired. I do not want that. I agreed to work at IF Group to save jobs, not destroy them.

Bomi takes my silence as assent. She pats me on the shoulder. "The planet is round. If you keep walking, eventually you will arrive at your destination. Keep walking, Hara."

I purse my lips. "What if I want to lie down?"

"This is not a country of people who lie down. This is a country of people who run," Jules says.

An image of Chaeyoung jogging after Soyou springs to mind. I shove another pork ball into my mouth. Maybe I do love this food truck so much because it reminds me of Iowa, where people lie down all the time.

CHAPTER TWO

FRIED PORK, MELTED CHEESE, AND VENTING TO MY FRIENDS
lift my mood, but as I drag myself back to the IF Group, a tightness
creeps up my spine. IF Group's fourteen floors cast a dark shadow
across the cement sidewalk. In the late August weather, I should be
hot, but I find myself rubbing my arms for warmth as I wait for
Soyou and Chaeyoung to return from the park. We need to walk
in together to keep up the fiction that we shared lunch.

I tilt my head back and stare up at the top floor. Is Wansu up
there in her white marble edifice staring down at me, wondering
whether I inherited even a jot of her aptitude? The irony is that
neither Yujun nor I are biologically connected to our mothers, yet
we match them. Yujun is as admirable as Wansu. He speaks Korean, English, Japanese, and a smattering of Mandarin. He graduated with a degree from an Ivy League school. He's making deals

with businessmen in Singapore and Hong Kong and Tokyo and even LA. I'm a former copy editor for a home and garden magazine. My skill set includes the ability to make a decent apple pie, understanding the difference between perennials and annuals, and knowing the *AP Stylebook* by heart.

These skills haven't been put to much use here in Seoul.

Before he was banished abroad by Wansu, Yujun took me out to a few places. People gravitate toward him, and not merely because he's gorgeous, but because standing near him is like standing in a ray of sunshine—warm and welcoming. No matter where we went, whether it was a club or a shopping mall or a back-alley café, we invariably ran into someone who knew him. Not only knew him, but wanted to talk to him, be with him, bask in his smile.

"Seoul may seem big," he'd once said, "but it's actually small."

I'm proof of that. I'd come to Seoul on a whim in search of my birth father. I'd arrived too late. He'd died two days before my flight landed, and my first activity in Seoul was his funeral. I hadn't known him. We'd only exchanged a couple of emails after he'd gotten my contact information through a data breach at a DNA matching company for adoptees. I didn't grieve when he died, but there are times, especially after my nightly call with Yujun ends and I can't sleep, when a series of thoughts tumble through my head. What if Wansu hadn't given me up for adoption? What if Lee Jonghyung had married Wansu? What if I'd never gone to America? What if I'd been raised in Korea?

When I'm not careful, the what-ifs can get away from me. I'm not exactly a catastrophizer. I prefer to say that I see the end more clearly than those around me. Jules and I are alike in that respect. We sense disaster, often the worst case, before it strikes. In most other ways, I'm like Bomi—quiet, introverted, measured. It strikes me that Yujun and I have a similar dynamic as Jules and Bomi. Could they be . . . My forehead scrunches together. Those pieces don't fit. Jules is nursing a broken heart and Bomi has never indicated she has a preference, but then, I'd never asked. I don't really know. What if— I stop myself. It's none of my business, and besides, it's time to get back to work. My coworkers pass by me on the sidewalk, and I fall into step behind them.

As we wait at the elevator banks, Chaeyoung says, "Did you have . . . *dwaeji gogi* for lunch?"

It takes me a moment to realize she's talking to me and then another to translate her words into English. "Pork? Yes."

"I saw that DJ Song visited a food truck in Yongsan a couple of weeks ago. He ate pork . . ." She uses the English word this time. The pause wasn't hesitancy to talk to me but confusion as she searched for the right word. ". . . there. You are friends?"

There's a slight eagerness in her tone, a friendliness that I haven't heard from her before. Is it because of Ahn Sangki, aka DJ Song, aka best friend of Yujun, aka my food truck partner, and Chaeyoung would like to meet this celebrity friend of mine? If yes, I am not ashamed to leverage that. He's the one person with whom I've shared my work woes and who would completely approve of me using his fame to get in good with my coworkers.

"Yeah, we're good friends." I try not to appear too enthusiastic. "He loves eating at these places. They're more fun and have lots of variety. You should come with us." I wave my phone. "I can text him right now. We could go tonight if he doesn't have plans."

"Tonight?" She leans toward me.

My fingers tremble with excitement as I type. food truck 7 !!

Ahn Sangki, aka DJ Song, lives on his phone. I receive an immediate response.

SANGKI: 8?

Done. I flip the screen toward Chaeyoung. "Eight tonight."

"Really?"

"Chaeyoung-ah, we have plans tonight," interrupts Soyou. No air conditioner will blow colder than her.

A small line creases Chaeyoung's glass-like forehead. "Plans?"

"Yes." Soyou switches to Korean and I catch a few words like "restaurant" and "sushi." At least she's trying to keep up the charade, even in another language. I respect the effort.

"But DJ Song . . ." Chaeyoung makes a half-hearted protest, but her interest wilts under the glare of Soyou's disapproval. The shorter woman's face falls as she capitulates. "No. I have plans."

Despite her refusal, I settle in at my desk with a glimmer of hope. Maybe I can lure her with Ahn Sangki bait in the future. Tonight, I'll plot with Sangki.

"Have a good lunch?" *Bujang-nim* asks when we return.

"Of course," I reply cheerily.

Chaeyoung gives a quiet yes while Soyou takes her seat in silence. She's still miffed at Chaeyoung's response to me, but I don't care. I'm full of fried meat and buoyed by the small chink in Chaeyoung's armor. I will wear them both down, given enough time. I don't radiate charisma like Yujun but I've been known to tell a funny joke once every six months. I'm willing to pay for dinner. I'm a good listener. These are traits of a good friend, if only the two give me a chance. Hell, I don't even need for us to be friends if we can be happy coworkers.

I text Sangki confirmation that I'll see him later tonight and then apply myself to the translations in my inbox. It's not much. For the first couple of weeks, they had me review all the English text on the website. I fixed errors here and there and then was sent around the different floors to check if all the translated signage made sense. Most of it was fine, except for one fire-safety sign that said you should light yourself on fire before exiting. I texted the signage to Yujun, who explained the Korean warning instructed you to check for fire before using the exit. We both cringed and laughed. That week I felt like I'd earned my paycheck.

Since then, my inbox has seen little action. I email *Bujang-nim* every day for more work, but he rarely replies. When he does respond, sometimes it's to have me run an errand, deliver some paperwork, or even use my downtime to study Korean. That last suggestion felt like an attack even though I don't think he meant it as one. My language skills—or lack thereof—are a sore spot for me.

Bomi said to keep walking, keep trying, and I'll eventually get the hang of Korean, but she didn't say how long that journey would take me. There are some days when I feel like I'm making decent progress, but most of the time I despair of even being able to hold a conversation with a baby. I can understand more than I can read, but I can't form the words to express myself. Language learning is a damnable thing.

The lack of work makes the afternoon drag. All around me keys are clacking, phones are ringing, and conversations are being had about creative assets and campaign verbiage while I stare at my empty inbox. The minute hand moves slower than a snail across a seashell. At this rate, I might fossilize in my chair before the end of the workday.

I send *Bujang-nim* another email, this time in Korean, requesting a new project. When I still receive no response, I open my spam folder to see if I can decipher the *Hangul*. I can't, which lowers my mood further. The fried-food high I floated in on drops to the pit of my stomach. My eyelids feel heavy and my head starts to ache. I pinch the flesh at the base of my thumb to keep myself awake. A phone rings. And rings. And rings again. It stops and then restarts. I hear someone from the next department over yell something about the phone.

A sharp blow to the back of my head has me whipping around. "What the he—"

Soyou, with her headset microphone in front of her mouth, snaps her fingers and points to *Bujang-nim*'s desk. It's his phone that's ringing. Chaeyoung is on a call, too. Does Soyou want me to answer his phone?

Tentatively, I start to rise from my seat, but before I can even clear my chair, Soyou rips off her headset and stomps over to *Bujang-nim*'s desk. She swipes the receiver off the cradle with an angry swoop and barks a Korean greeting into the phone. As the person on the other end talks, Soyou wedges the receiver between her cheek and shoulder and jots down a message.

Bujang-nim appears out of nowhere and I jump to my feet to defend Soyou. "Your phone kept ringing and the voicemail didn't pick it up. I think the noise was bothering the other departments. Soyou wasn't invading your privacy. She wanted to make sure you didn't miss something important."

"I don't need you to explain. I was doing my job," Soyou snaps. She hands the sticky note with the message she recorded to *Bujang-nim* and slams into her chair. Everyone is staring at me with varying expressions of disapproval, including Yoo Minkyu, who leaves bottles of energy drinks next to my monitor along with unsubtle hints that he'd like to meet my mother.

Even *Bujang-nim* frowns at me. "Whenever the phone is ringing, the person who is free should answer it. Even you, Choi Hara-nim."

It's the sharpest he's been with me and so I know I fucked up. My cheeks grow hot. I stand up and bow to him. "I'm sorry," I say in Korean. It's one of the few phrases I can pronounce perfectly because I've had to say it so many times; it should be on my work badge as a warning.

The response I get to the apology isn't what I wanted. *Bujang-nim*'s eyes widen as if he thinks he's committed a grave error. "No. It is nothing, Choi Hara-nim." He pushes me into my seat. "You are doing well. I have a project for you. Wait here and I will send it." He hurries to his seat and rapidly types out a message while I ignore everyone's gazes. I don't have to see them to know that they're staring at me with varying degrees of disgust. That's how I would feel in their position. I'd hate me, too.

A new document appears in my inbox. Relief mixed with frustration swirls in my head as I open the file. Frustration wins the match as the familiar words of a document I edited two weeks ago appear on my screen. I swing my head in *Bujang-nim*'s direction to see if this was intentional, but he gives me a gummy smile and a thumbs-up. I force the corners of my lips up before returning to my screen. I see nothing for a long time. A hot sensation burns at the back of my eyes. I press a knuckle against one lid and then mumble an excuse about needing to go to the bathroom. No one responds because they're too busy doing real work to care what the *nakhasan* is up to. Inside the bathroom stall, I lock the door and lean my head against the tiled wall. I've got to figure out a way to improve my work conditions on my own or I am not going to last here. I allow my eyes to drift shut as the cold tile eases the ache in my head.

The sound of a toilet flushing and a faucet turning on jolts me upright. I must've dozed off. The crisp tones of Soyou's voice ring out above the running water. Some stupid, masochistic side has me opening the audio translator app on my phone.

I hate it. I really hate it. This is supposed to be a feminist workplace but we still have a hannam *manager, and* hannam *coworkers outnumber us,* Soyou rants.

At least we don't have molkas *here,* is Chaeyoung's subdued response.

Small things to be grateful for?

I looked up her US college and it is not highly ranked.

She's the Sajang-nim's *daughter. A* nakhasan. *Sajang-nim is no different than any other* chaebol. *She is sitting in her chair because she slept with the president. Now she installs her abandoned daughter to one day take over.*

Even over Choi Yujun?

Is rice white? He's not Sajang-nim's *real child. Why are our lives like this?*

Is the water cold in the Han today?

The water shuts off. The door slams shut. My head aches again. I want to go home, and not to the marble mausoleum that is Wansu's house up in the mountains but my home in Des Moines. That small one-story brick house with the crabapple trees in the back that shed white flowers in the late spring. Where the white walls of my room are decorated with my mom's and my poor attempts to copy designs we saw on television home shows. In the kitchen with the fake granite countertops and the stainless steel refrigerator where Ellen still hangs the tulip finger painting I did at a Science Center art camp as a five-year-old. *It's got your handprint on it. How can I ever get rid of it?*

Where she and I baked two dozen apple pies one summer in an effort to find the perfect recipe. It's lard in the piecrust, we decided, and Braeburn apples. Where I had friends who didn't call me a *na-khasan*. But then I remember how even at my father Pat's funeral I heard people separating his kids into real—the child that he made with his second wife—and not real—me, whom he adopted and then abandoned because fatherhood was too onerous a task for him.

There are shitty people on both sides of the ocean, and just because Wansu doesn't have a stainless steel refrigerator with my childhood art on it doesn't mean she doesn't care. I know she does. We're in a terribly awkward stage right now where we are afraid of offending each other and so we tiptoe around each other, saying almost nothing, like all my coworkers here at IF Group. They won't say what they really feel in front of me because they don't want to get fired, but I know they are eaten up with justified resentment.

I don't have a solution. All I know is that even though I have two mothers, a brother, and an assortment of new friends, I feel more alone than ever. I thumb the red cord again. I miss Yujun so much.

CHAPTER THREE

"MY ADORABLE HARA." SANGKI' S ARMS ARE STRETCHED WIDE
and I nearly burst into tears as I collapse into his thin frame.
"What's this? Are you crying?" He pats my back awkwardly.

"No," I mumble into his chest. I push away and brush a drop of
wetness off his expensive cream-colored cotton T-shirt. I'm sure the
moisture is rain and not my tears, regardless of the cloudless evening
sky. Seoul's a big city. It's raining somewhere. "I never cried before I
came to Seoul." Now all it takes is one sad song before I'm reaching
for Yujun's Hermès tie, which he once let me dry my tears with.

"It's the pollen. All those cherry blossoms the city has planted
are the problem." He takes a tissue that his manager, Lee Taehyun,
is holding and hands it to me. Mr. Lee is Sangki's ever-present companion. Sangki never goes anywhere without the man, who looks
more like a bodyguard with his all-black outfit and his dark-tinted
sunglasses. When I first started hanging out with Sangki, it felt

odd to always have this other person with us who refused to eat or drink or often even sit down, but the more time I spend with Sangki, the more I realize how indispensable Lee is.

For one, Sangki has a handful of dedicated stalkers, or *sasaengs*, who follow him everywhere—from the studio to broadcast stations to home. Not only do they follow him, but they take photos. Sometimes they use buildings or trees as cover, and once we even saw them hide behind an umbrella on a clear night. Other times, they brazenly point their thousand-dollar lenses in his direction.

He persists in going out, though, refusing to allow a few bad apples to imprison him in his home. "If I didn't have fans, I wouldn't be where I am now," he once explained.

Wansu actively encourages my activities with Sangki, leaving me envelopes of won, Korean money, with "food" neatly written on the outside. From the amount of cash inside, Wansu likely believes we're eating at the expensive restaurants in Cheongdam or Apgujeong, the high-class neighborhoods in the Gangnam district. What Sangki and I are really doing is gorging ourselves at as many cheap food stalls as possible.

Another reason why the manager is always here is because Sangki has a memory that is so bad it rivals Dory's. Half the time he doesn't know what day it is or where he has to be in the next hour. He often doesn't even remember to bring an ID or wallet. If he didn't have a manager, I'm convinced we would find him halfway to Busan picking wild strawberries and living with a local villager who lured him to their home with slices of milk bread.

"It's August. Cherry blossoms bloom in April." I blow my nose and pocket the used tissue. Unlike Yang Ilhwa's pork food truck, there isn't a trash can here.

"Minor details," he scoffs. He eyes the chalkboard menu hung on the side of the truck. "What do you want? Rice cake? Spicy rice cake soup? Corn-cheese balls?"

"Corn-cheese balls. Yang Ilhwa-nim serves corn cheese in a cup. I want to see if this is better." I sound out the Korean words in my head so I can make my order without appearing too dumb. *Tteokbokki. Gukmul tteokbokki—*

"Yang Ilhwa?"

"She's the owner of the fried-pork-ball food truck in Yongsan near IF Group. We went there a month ago after I started working for IF Group, remember?"

Sangki taps his chin. "The one that serves the really bad *yachae twigim*?"

"It's not that bad. I eat there all the time. Almost every day."

"Hara, please," he groans in dismay. "I take you to different delicious places every week, but you return to that food truck? You will get a bad idea of Seoul and become unhappy, and when Yujun comes home, I will hear nothing but complaints from him."

"It reminds me of ho— Iowa," I quickly correct, but it's too late. A flash of pity zips across his face.

"Should we order?" he suggests, without commenting on my slipup. One thing that Sangki and Yujun have in common is good listening skills. They don't badger you for details you're not ready to share, and I really appreciate it. Home for now is Seoul, not Iowa. If I start fantasizing about how good Iowa was, I'll never allow myself to view Seoul as anything but temporary.

Our food comes quickly. Sangki carries the corn and two beers and I follow with the two servings of rice-cake soup to the table that Lee has saved for us. When Sangki sets down his cell phone between us to pick up his chopsticks, I notice a new charm dangling off the case. I touch the familiar blue turtle with my finger.

He has a key chain with this same character. He even wore Crocs one day with the blue turtle buttons.

"You're very fond of Squirtle."

"Not really," he says between bites.

"But you have so much of it. I've seen you wear T-shirts and hats with the mascot. You have shoes with the same design."

"I made an offhand comment on a show once about how Squirtle was cute, and now that's my whole life. All my fans buy me the stuff. At this point, I own more Squirtle stuff than they have at the Nintendo headquarters in Kyoto." He wipes his mouth with a napkin and continues. "You have to be careful. Once I said I didn't like mint chocolate, and now I'm branded as one of the celebs that is an anti. Every article on Naver about mint chocolate calls me part of the *banmichodan*. You know who else is on that team? My nemesis Dave Kim. I can't be on the same side of anything as Dave Kim."

Dave Kim is almost as well-known for being a virulent homophobe as is he for his singing.

"The only solution is to kick Dave Kim out of our anti–mint chocolate army." I take a break from the spicy rice-cake soup to pour some water down my throat. There was no false advertising here. The soup is hot.

"Oh, you hate it, too?"

"I don't have any strong feelings about it, but I'll be an anti with you so that you aren't alone in the squad with Dave Kim."

"That's the spirit." Sangki pumps his fist. "What do you hate? I want to repay the favor."

"Soy— Work." I grimace. I almost said her name out loud. I don't really hate her, do I? I thought I was doing so well in being understanding, but the first thing that I associate with hate and nemeses is Soyou? I'm not in a good place.

"So it is work. I thought so. Tell *oppa* everything," Sangki invites.

I shake my head. I don't want to give voice to my petty feelings. Plus, verbalizing will only give those feelings power. I change the subject. "Yujun says that I can only use *oppa* with him."

Sangki rolls his eyes. "That violates all rules of Korean language. *Oppa* is used for any older male who is close to you. We're friends. You should call me *oppa*. My baby cousin calls me *oppa*." He waits. I stare at him. He sighs in disappointment and returns to his soup. "Fine."

To Sangki, the use would be me acknowledging that we're close friends and that I can rely on him like a big brother, but to Yujun it's a romantic word. "If it makes you feel better, I tried using you as bait for my coworkers today."

"In what way?"

I explain that Chaeyoung was tempted to have dinner with me when she learned that the two of us were friends. "I figured you would approve."

"I do. What else can I offer? Tickets to a show? I have one coming up, you know."

"Yes, the Banpo Music Fest. I bought tickets." Two of them, in case Yujun shows up.

"I could give backstage passes. I'm also performing at the End of the Summer Splash Party at the Banyan Tree this weekend. It's sold out because the social media influencers love this event, but I've a few extra passes."

"This sounds like a party where I'd have to wear a swimsuit. I don't know if I want to make friends with my coworkers that badly," I groan.

"It'll be fun." He nudges my shoulder with his. "Some of Yujun's friends will go, and if that would be uncomfortable, you could sit with Taehyun-ie over there."

"Yujun has friends other than you and me? That's not acceptable," I joke. "If I get desperate, I'll call you."

"Deal."

After we seal our agreement with a pinkie shake, we finish our meal. The fried corn balls taste like cheese-filled croquettes and they are miles better than the cheese-corn cups at the food truck near work, but I tell myself it's because it's fried. Everything tastes better fried.

After Sangki and I devour our dinner like a pair of animals that haven't been fed in a week, I snap a photo of the food truck and send it to Yujun.

ME: This was good. We should eat here when you get back.

I don't get an immediate reply, so I tuck my phone away and give Sangki a shake of my head. He fake pouts and texts his own message to Yujun. I sometimes wonder if Sangki and I exacerbate our longing for Yujun by spending time together. The two of us missing him is why we started hanging out. Sangki said it was his duty as Yujun's closest friend, but having spent six weeks with Sangki, I've come to realize that our connection is the man himself. When we're together, it almost feels like we can summon a solid manifestation of Yujun. Almost.

Thinking about him makes my heart ache. The red string of fate he says has connected us since before we were born has wound itself so tightly around my heart that sometimes the pain of missing him becomes a physical hurt. It's best to focus on other things. I buy two more beers and return to Sangki.

"I know that *nakhasan* is nepotism, but what is *hannam*? There's a Hannam district. Does it mean rich people?"

Sangki's eyebrows crash together as he takes the beer. "Did someone call you a *hannam*?"

"No. Chaeyoung called the other office workers *hannams*."

"She meant the men. *Hannam* is short for *hannam choong*, or Korean male parasite, and it is an insult basically meaning misogynist."

"I'll remember that for the future. How about *molka*?"

His mild confusion turns to alarm. "How do you know that word?"

"Is it a curse word?"

"No. It means secret videotaping and generally of a person in their private time. If that's happening at your office, you better report that to your mom."

"Actually, Chaeyoung and Soyou were saying that the absence of *molkas* was the one good thing about the office in between the nepotism and the misogyny."

Sangki grimaces. "*Aigoo.* That's not good. That's like me saying that at least the *sasaengs* leave me presents."

I pop open my beer and glance over to the small huddle of fans about twenty yards away. Feeling cranky, I point my phone camera in their direction. One of them turns away, but the other two stare defiantly.

Sangki nudges me to leave them alone. "How are you getting along with Yujun's mother?"

One other curious cultural difference is that in Korea, people refer to others by relationship status. It's not Choi Wansu, but Yujun's mother. It's not Park Hyunwoo, my boss, but *Bujang-nim*, because those words identify that person's placement in your life. To Sangki and all the other people who know the Chois, Wansu is

Yujun's mother. That's my problem. That's why I'm sitting here with Sangki and not with Yujun and Sangki. That's why Yujun is in another country and has been for the last six weeks. That's why life is so very awkward at home. Choi Wansu is my mother, my boyfriend's mother, and my real boss. In the six weeks since we've been alone together, she and I haven't made much progress on the relationship front.

Whereas I know that Ellen gets upset easily, cries often, laughs loudly, and forgives readily, Wansu is a mystery. She only knows me from reports my adoptive mother sent her over the years. I only know her from passing comments Yujun has made.

I set my phone in my lap. "It's going."

Sangki makes a small noise of encouragement. "Choi Yujun's mother isn't known for her warmth."

"It's not that, actually. It's that she keeps giving me things. I have a whole room full of bags from Louis Vuitton, Dior, Chanel. I think I could fund a small school with the things she's bought for me in the past six weeks. Our relationship can't be leather goods and fancy clothes."

"It could."

"What do you mean by that?"

"Some people's relationships are like that. Their parents buy things to make them happy or quiet or compliant."

"Let me rephrase, then. I don't want it to be like that. I know we can't be Ellen and Hara, but I don't want it to be sponsor and Hara."

He grimaces. "Don't use 'sponsor.'"

"Why not?"

"Because it means someone who pays for things in exchange for sex."

"Oh. Yeah, no. Not that."

"What are some things you would do with Ellen?"

"We watched home decorating shows together. We picked wild-flowers once illegally to make these art pieces we'd seen a decorator do."

"I can't see Choi Yujun's mother doing that."

I think for a minute. "How about knitting? Mom and I took a knitting class together." But the minute I suggest the craft, I know it's not right. Sangki and I look at each other and then shake our heads. Choi Wansu is not a knitter.

"Sometimes we cooked or baked."

"Yujun's mother doesn't cook."

No. She has a full-time chef and housekeeper.

"Why don't you make something for her?" Sangki suggests.

"Like a wildflower painting?"

"No. Like food. You eat with her nearly every night. Why don't you cook dinner for her?"

"I . . . guess? I'm not like a real chef."

"Anything you make will be good. I once boiled eggs and my mom said they were the best she'd ever tasted. She raved over me for at least five minutes and even went so far as to say that I had golden hands—which means someone who is really good at something."

"Those must've been some good eggs."

He chuckles and shakes his head, the little hoops in his ears swaying slightly. "She was so enthusiastic that I became suspicious. After she went to read, I snuck into the kitchen and looked in the trash. The eggs were there."

"You hadn't tried them?"

"Nope. I didn't trust myself."

"So you're saying that Wansu will lie to make me feel better." I tug on the sleeves of my sweater.

"No. I'm saying that it's the effort that counts. Mom was thrilled that I'd cooked for her, and Wansu will be happy that you did the same. In the end, they're complimenting your effort, not the results."

"I can boil eggs, Sangki."

"There you go." He pats me on the back. "You're already ahead of the game."

CHAPTER FOUR

"WHAT DO YOU THINK OF ME COOKING DINNER FOR YOUR mom?" It's nearly midnight and Yujun has yawned three times since he answered the phone, but he refuses to hang up. Every night, we have a video call no matter how late it is. There's a callus developing in the junction of my index and middle fingers where the charger cord rubs. I'm going to be useless tomorrow, but I figure it doesn't matter since my inbox will be empty.

"Our mom?" he says.

I crinkle my nose. I hate being reminded that we share a mother.

"Not our mom," he corrects. "*Eomeo-nim*." He uses the formal Korean version of the word "mother" as if that makes a difference. "I think she would like that. What are you making and why haven't you cooked for me?"

"First, you've been away for six weeks, and second, there was no cooking allowed at Jules's apartment. You grilled on the back porch and that was it." When I first came to Seoul, I sublet a room in a house halfway up what always felt like a small mountain in the north part of the city. It was rented by three teachers and Jules, my flight attendant friend. We ordered in almost every night, and the few things that the girls cooked for themselves were *ramyeon*, a soup made with *mandu*—or what we would call potstickers—and *tteokbokki*, a spicy dish made with a rice cake shaped like a penne pasta noodle.

"You must not have had a dirty kitchen."

"A what?" I hadn't heard of that before.

"It's a second kitchen. Some are wet kitchens that are all tiled and you can hose down. Other people call it a dirty kitchen, but it's where the real cooking is done, with meat and fish, and where the kimchi is made. Has no one given you a tour of the house?" He arches a well-groomed eyebrow.

"Wansu did, but I don't remember a second kitchen. I feel like that's something I wouldn't forget." I prop the phone against the pillow next to me. If I close my eyes and listen to his voice, I can pretend he's here in bed, an arm's length away.

"It's tucked away. Only Mrs. Ji uses it." He sighs and looks up at the ceiling. "I miss her cooking." The sheets rustle as he rolls on his side.

The lower part of my body clenches at the sound. I've only slept with Yujun once, and my sweet memories of that night are mixed up with the bitter ones. That day, I'd found out that his beloved stepmother was my biological mother, who had abandoned me when I was a few weeks old.

I ran away from her, that knowledge, the pain, fell into the Han River, and limped back to Jules's apartment. Yujun was there, and I shut away the knowledge of how he was inextricably tied to Wansu and took what pleasure I could find in that moment. I needed the comfort and he provided it, with his hands and mouth and body.

I want a repeat where I'm not seeking to assuage any feeling other than pure lust.

"Does she always cook Western food?" Wansu and I eat together frequently. Every morning, we down a terrible wheatgrass smoothie. It's Wansu's morning meal, and during that first awkward meeting at the table, as opposed to all the awkward mealtimes that followed, she asked what I wanted to eat. Not to be a bother, I replied stupidly that I would have what she was having.

She gave me a dubious look and offered cereal. Bomi later told me that the staff had to go all the way to Itaewon to buy the box at an international store that catered to expats and diplomats. The following day, I adamantly declared my love for Wansu's green drink. I thought it would be some Korean delicacy, but instead it's a kale, pineapple, mango, and strawberry smoothie with a protein scoop full of all the essential vitamins a woman needs. Wansu was oddly excited to explain this to me, and for that reason, I have downed that disgusting thing every day for the past six weeks.

I do not feel any healthier today than I did when I started drinking the kale smoothie, but that may be because I'm consuming copious amounts of fried chicken, *hotteok*—a flattened and fried patty of dough with melted sugar in the center—batter-fried hot dogs sometimes topped with sugared apples, and fish cakes. And, of course, my beloved fried pork balls.

In the evenings, if I'm not out with Sangki discovering another food truck or hanging with Jules and Bomi, I'm at the walnut dinner table with Wansu eating a meal made by the chef slash housekeeper, Mrs. Ji. The food served is fantastic, but it's decidedly Western—pasta, grilled lemon chicken with a side of roasted potatoes, buttered scallops with asparagus spears, creamy mushroom soup with homemade croutons. I'm beginning to wonder if Wansu even owns chopsticks.

"No. Not really. She makes a great radish soybean paste stew. I love it in the winter, and her pork-potato *jeon* is also delicious. *Jeon* is a Korean pancake," he starts to explain, but he doesn't need to. I'm familiar with the savory fritter.

"I love *jeon*. Sangki and I went to a food truck at the Gwangjang Market last week. They made about ten different kinds. I liked the scallion ones the best." They were thicker than most of the *jeons* I've seen in the basement department store food halls or in the restaurants.

"How was the spicy stew tonight?"

"Very good. What did you have?"

He yawns and turns his face away from the camera to hide his tiredness. "The team ordered Singapore noodles. They were good, but I'm tired of Chinese food. I want to come home and eat Korean food with you."

"I want that, too." I want him home with me.

A soft smile curves the corners of his lips up. "Do you miss me, Hara?"

"Yes."

"You don't say it much."

"Because I sound needy and desperate."

"I must sound the same, then, as I tell you this every night."

"No. It sounds cool when you say it."

"Ah, but I am needy and desperate." His voice drops. "It has been forty-five days since I've had you."

A dozen, no, a hundred images fly through my mind. Yujun at the airport in the suit. Yujun waiting outside the Airbnb in jeans and a simple white shirt. Yujun in crisp wool slacks and a sunny yellow T-shirt rolled at the sleeves. Yujun in nothing but sweat and skin, his biceps flexing as he lowers his body down and inside me. I close my eyes as if that can shut down my imagination, but it only gets worse. In the darkness, with the sound of his breathing on the phone, it's as if he's here with me, stroking me, kissing me, loving me. I'm overwhelmed and don't want him to see it. It's too humiliating.

"I think I need to go," I croak. "Big day tomorrow. Lots of work." The excuses tumble out of me.

The smile turns slightly smug, but he only nods. "I miss you, *aegiya*."

I miss you, too, babe.

I don't sleep well. Who could after that?

AS I PREDICTED, I am barely functioning the next day, but it also doesn't matter. I have no new work. *Bujang-nim* is out at meetings, so I sit at my desk and blearily study Korean. My walk across the world is taking a long time. I decide to leave at five, and while it's technically the end of the workday, a twinge of guilt pricks my conscience as the rest of the team remains in the office bent over their respective projects.

I have my own project—Project Get Closer to Choi Wansu. We met for the first time a few weeks ago when I stormed into her office and demanded to know if she was my biological mother. She admitted it without hesitation. She followed her confession with a less-than-grand gesture of asking how much money I wanted. That hurt a lot. It also hurt to find out that the boy I'd fallen in love with was the child she chose to parent over me, the child she'd given birth to. That pain was compounded by learning that my adoptive mother, Ellen, had actually been in contact with Wansu since I was twelve. Thirteen years of betrayal and lies is a lot to get over in six weeks.

I could've held on to my bitterness and trauma, but I didn't have time. The press learned of my existence, and Wansu and Yujun's family business, a multimillion-dollar enterprise that employs hundreds of people, was suddenly in danger. Years ago, when Yujun's father fell into a coma after a heart attack, Wansu stepped forward to take charge of the business, and in doing so she began to make changes. She championed women's causes. She accepted awards for furthering the advancement of women. She gave money to and sat on the boards of adoption organizations, all the while never telling anyone she had given her own child up twenty-five years ago.

I could have left Seoul, returned to Iowa, and allowed her, Yujun, and IF Group to burn to the ground.

I stayed. I stayed, but not for completely altruistic reasons. Yes, I wanted to know Wansu better and I wouldn't be able to sleep in my bed back in America knowing I'd put so many people out of work, but I also stayed because of Yujun. And Sangki and Jules and Bomi and even Wansu.

I had come here looking for belonging and I'd found people I cared about. Wansu is one of them. As much as I resent her and am still hurt by what she did, I cannot deny that I might've made a similar decision in her shoes. When she found out she was pregnant, she was only one of at least five women my biological father had been sleeping with. Her parents were strict, and her father—

Well, Wansu hasn't come out and said this, but I got the impression he would've harmed her if he knew the truth. And she tried. For six weeks, she tried to care for me, but she couldn't manage. She had no education, and other than an innate adeptness for language, she had no skills to get a job, so she left me by a police station and waited forty-two minutes until a policeman came out for a smoke break and found me.

I can stew in the bad memories or lift up my feet and walk forward. I'm choosing to do the latter, but the path ahead is not without thorns. We still step quietly around each other, selecting our words with care. She speaks to me with gifts; I speak to her with service. I hurry to bring the food to the table. I jump up to clear the plates. I go to work every day at IF Group even though I'm beginning to dread waking up in the morning because of it.

All Koreans are big on gifts. I understand that showing up to a person's house without a gift is one of the biggest social sins out there, but Wansu is overdoing it. In the large house in northern Seoul that Wansu calls home, I've been allotted a bedroom, an attached sitting room, and another room that is lined with closets that are nearly empty and a floor overflowing with designer bags. On an almost daily basis, she arrives home with a new purchase. "I saw this on my way to a meeting" or "My assistant said this is trending" or "An actress wore it in an ad" were all excuses that accompanied these gifts. The price of the gifts, the overwhelming number of them, makes me uneasy, and I've only unpacked a tiny fraction of them. I want us to have more of a relationship than one that is marked by luxury goods.

Yet, what have I done to extend myself, to put myself out there so she can get to know me? Not much. Cooking dinner for her seems like the least thing I can do.

Sangki suggested I cook for Wansu, but he didn't say what dish. Yujun had a few favorites he mentioned last night, which means he must've eaten them frequently at dinners with Wansu. Why would he bring them up otherwise? I decide to cook the radish soybean paste stew and pork-potato *jeon*.

Using a translation app, I copy down the ingredients and stop at a market near the office. I have no problem in the produce section. Korean radishes are easily recognizable, as are scallions and onions. Potatoes are the same everywhere. The dried kelp and anchovies for the dashi broth present a bit of a challenge, but I find a soup base in the refrigerated section. It's the soybean paste aisle that stumps me. The sheer selection and variety are intimidating. There have to be at least fifteen different brands, and each brand has multiple versions. Obviously this would be no problem if I could read Korean, because back home the soup aisle looks much like this, with rows of red-and-white cans offering various versions of tomato soup.

After picking up and setting down a half dozen containers, I opt for a red container with a gold seal on it. The gold must mean it's great. It probably won an award for best soybean paste in the country. It probably says recommended by ninety-nine out of a hundred Koreans on the label. I stick it in my basket and head to the meat department to find ground pork for the *jeon*. Once I have all my ingredients, I check out. The clerk says nothing as he checks me out, which I appreciate.

I try not speaking to anyone I don't know if I can help it. My limited command of the language is embarrassing, and even if I can get past the initial "hello" and "how are you doing," the next-level conversations stump me. A person could be asking me either how the weather is or if I am going to eat the poop on the ground and it'd sound the same to me.

Even with the taxi driver, instead of saying the address, I show him a screenshot from my phone. I've tried to say the address in the past, but there must be something wrong with my pronunciation because I'm often met with an *Ihae mothaetseumnida*, or "I don't understand."

Mrs. Ji is surprised to see me when I arrive. "You home early."

"Yes." I lift my two bags of groceries. "I'm going to cook dinner tonight so you can go home early as well."

One of her eyebrows shoots upward and the other scrunches down. "You cook?"

In the face of this alarm, I try to reassure her. "Yes. Soybean paste soup and *jeon*." When Mrs. Ji doesn't move, I try to think of the Korean words. "*Mu doenjang guk. Jeon. Dwaeji gogi jeon.*"

"You make?"

"Yes. I make."

"I'm cook." She reaches for the bags, which I swing away from her.

"No. I want to cook for Wansu tonight. Yujun said you have another kitchen? Should I use that? Point me in the right direction."

She shakes her head violently. "No. No. I cook. I cook everything."

I fear we are about to get into a wrestling match over the groceries. "Just this once. I want to do this for Wansu. I promise I won't poison her."

CHAPTER FIVE

"I ALMOST KILLED WANSU TONIGHT." MY FACE IS IN THE PIL-
low. I'm too embarrassed to look into the camera.

"*Eomeo-nim*," he corrects.

"I almost killed *Eomeo-nim* tonight."

"I don't think that's possible. Were you driving?"

"I appreciate you thinking that it's something involving heavy
machinery and not my cooking."

"Ahhhh." He suddenly remembers our conversation. "Do you
want to tell me what happened?"

"You know how the *gochujang* and soybean paste are packaged
in the same plastic tubs?"

"Oh."

"Yes."

"Did you taste it before you served it?"

"Yes, but I thought it was supposed to be that spicy and I was unused to it because I grew up eating spaghetti rather than soybean stew." I flip over to my side and scrunch up my face pitifully. "I put so much red pepper paste into the soup that I felt like I had fire coming out of my ears. Wansu—*Eomeo-nim*," I say as Yujun opens his mouth to remind me I keep using the wrong identifier, "took one bite and started choking. I jumped up and tried to give her the Heimlich because I thought she had a radish lodged in her throat, but her breathing problems were a reaction to all the spice. She had to tap my arm five times before I realized I was actually preventing her from breathing rather than dislodging a foreign object. It was one of the more humiliating experiences of my life."

Yujun clears his throat, stretches his neck, rubs a hand across his eyes, presses his lips together.

"Let it out." I sigh.

Laughter bursts out like a waterfall. I drum my fingers against the mattress while he gets the giggles out of his system. Near tears when he finally gathers himself, he swipes a knuckle under each eye and apologizes. "*Mianhae.*"

My heart instantly melts. Yujun makes an effort to always speak English when I'm around. Even when we ran into people here in Seoul, he would greet the others in English, a subtle push for them to speak in my language as well. English proficiency is a mark of an educated Korean, he's told me. Most of his acquaintances know enough to hold a conversation. But despite this kind and inclusive gesture, he slips up when he's tired or his defenses are low. I love hearing him talk in Korean. It's a beautiful language, full of imagery. I mean, how can you not love a language where the word for fish is *mul gogi*? The literal translation is "water meat."

"You're forgiven. I guess the bright side is that the dish wasn't too hard to make, and if I hadn't mixed up the soybean paste and the *gochujang*, it would've been delicious." Before I'd added the spice, it had good flavor, with nicely cooked radishes that weren't too mushy, and a savory base.

"You'll have to make it for me when I come home."

"I will."

Home. The word lingers between us. "Home" should be a banned word for us. Using it reminds us of what we don't have. How we are oceans apart.

"I should get some rest," I say.

"Me too. Good night, Hara."

"Good night." After he hangs up, I stare at the ceiling and wonder why he didn't call me *aegiya* this time. Maybe Wansu is the only one who sees the end clearly and she's trying to prevent a disaster. I fling an arm over my eyes and try to push those negative thoughts out. Yujun and I were both tired. That's all. Don't make more out of it than it is, I chide myself. I turn my phone on and scroll to a photo that we took together at the river. Both our eyes are closed, but we're smiling. He told me I had a beautiful eye smile. I trace the upside-down crescents of his eyes and then mine.

It will all work out, I can hear him saying. I clutch the red silk cord in my fist and fall asleep.

OVER OUR KALE breakfast smoothie, I repeat my apology to Wansu. "I'm sorry about dinner last night."

"It is nothing. I should be used to spicy foods, but as I grow older, I find I like more bland flavors. It is more my fault than yours."

"Is that why we eat mostly Western food? Because I like Korean food and I can use chopsticks. I don't need a fork."

Wansu sets her glass down onto the coaster next to a beautiful china plate that has blue cherubs chasing each other around the edges. The plate is empty. It's there for looks. "Are you unhappy with the meals, Hara? You should have said something earlier. Mrs. Ji can make anything you like." She raises her arm to summon the cook, but I reach out and touch her arm.

"No. Please don't." A hot flush of embarrassment spreads from my chest to my cheeks. "Everything she has made has been delicious. Obviously better than mine. I was only saying that if you were making Western food because you thought that was what I preferred, I wanted to tell you that I like Korean food, too, and you don't have to use forks and spoons as I know how to use chopsticks. Mom—I mean Ellen—has had me using them since I was a baby. I had these ones that had animal heads at the end to hold the sticks together, like a shark and an elephant."

I shut up then because I am babbling. Wansu lowers her arm. "Ellen took very good care of you."

"Yes. She loves me." I groan internally at the way I phrased that—as if I think Wansu doesn't love me.

Her lips tighten a fraction. "I care as well."

"I know." I couldn't have handled this worse. Having two mothers is a minefield. I don't know what I was thinking when I got on the plane to come here. Actually, I do. I was running away from the hurt caused by my adoptive dad, his remarriage, his "real" child, and his death. Searching for my biological dad made sense in the moment, but I'd been focused on the discovery, not the aftermath. It's ironic because I always hated those adoption reunion shows because they only focused on the singular moment of reunification rather than the hard work of sorting through the hurricane of emotions that come with facing the person who abandoned you.

She reaches into her briefcase, which is sitting next to her chair, and pulls out a dark blue folder. It looks like a bound business proposal. One thing about Wansu that I can appreciate is that feelings do not get in the way of business. I sit up in interest. Am I getting a project to work on?

She slides the portfolio across the table. "Here. I put this together for you. I did not teach you how to use chopsticks or aid your studies. I attended not one softball game or one doctor visit. We cannot go back in time and change those things, but I can provide for your future."

How intriguing. I open the proposal eagerly, but instead of a business plan there's a glossy photo paper-clipped to a sheet of paper that looks like a résumé. In the photo, a young man wearing a blue suit and sporting a red-striped tie leans against a granite wall. His black hair is swept back away from his forehead and he has large, double-lidded eyes that look surgically enhanced and a high nose bridge. He's conventionally attractive in the way that social media influencers are attractive—nice to look at but without an ounce of the charisma Yujun has.

Kim Seonpyung is twenty-seven; "international age" is added in parentheses. He attended Korea University and graduated in the top 1 percent. He comes from the Andong clan, which is in a North Gyoengsang province. I have no idea where that is or what that means, but there's another helpful parenthetical that says the Andong clan dates back to the Joseon dynasty, with three royals in the lineage. I wrinkle my nose. Is that . . . Bomi's handwriting? Nice of her to give me a warning. She's supposed to be on my side.

Kim Seonpyung, Soon-ie to his friends, Bomi unhelpfully notes, is a lawyer and works at the best firm in Seoul, Kim & Kang, in the contracts division. He plays the cello and guitar, and his blood type is AB, which is a really good match for my blood type, B. How does Bomi know my blood type? Did Ellen include that tidbit in the monthly reports she sent to Wansu behind my back for thirteen years?

I close the folder and look toward Wansu with useless hope. "Are you hiring someone for the marketing division? Because I don't know that a contract lawyer would be a good fit."

"No. Kim Seonpyung is very good catch. An *emchina*. A young man that all mothers hope to have as a son-in-law. You could meet him this weekend. Tomorrow it will be beautiful. I believe the weatherman said in the seventies with very little air pollution."

I scrape my teeth over my bottom lip in frustration. I'm fully aware she does not want me dating Yujun, but setting me up with some random guy I've never met seems too much.

"No disrespect, but if you like him, then you should da—" I cut myself off before I say something really callous. Her husband is upstairs in this house in his makeshift hospital bed, hooked up to monitors and machines that are keeping him alive. I rein in my temper and try again. "I'm not interested. I know you don't approve of Yujun's and my relationship, but it exists. I'm not going to date anyone else."

Wansu's face hardens. "You and Yujun cannot be together. The sooner you accept this truth, the sooner you both will be happier."

Maybe I should've poisoned her last night. People say neardeath experiences can soften hearts. "If you wanted the Nation's Son-in-Law, Ahn Sangki is right there."

Wansu's eyebrows arch. "Ahn Sangki will not marry you."

My back bristles. Does she think I'm not good enough for him?

"And not because of what you are thinking. It is well-known that Ahn Sangki prefers men."

My jaw drops. Sangki never came out to me, but he didn't have to. It was easy enough for me to guess where his affections lie because he looks at Yujun the same way I look at Yujun. "How did you know? Does Yujun know?"

"Everyone knows, Hara, including Yujun. How could he not? Those two are close as brothers."

Does he also know that Sangki is in love with him?

"Ahn Sangki is a very nice young man, but he will not be anyone's son-in-law. I do not recommend that you date any other celebrity either. They are not known for their fidelity or their long-lasting relationships. If, after meeting with Kim Seonpyung, you find that he is not a good match for you, there are others. In fact, I can provide you with several candidates. Text me what you would like for dinner. I can provide you with a list of restaurants that would be suitable for first dates." She rises from the table, hooks her briefcase with her hand, and strides out of the dining room toward the front door.

I push the half-drunk smoothie to the side and pick up my phone to text Bomi, who has some answering to do.

ME: Traitor!

BOMI: She gave you the dating profiles?

ME: You did more than one?

BOMI: Ten. I did ten of them. I wanted to tell you but I knew you would be mad

ME: Yes! I am mad. You could've at least warned me

BOMI: I was going to at the food truck but you were already 😟 . . . Sorry.

She sends me an apple emoji. I drop the phone to the table and shake my fist at the screen. An apology is not cutting it. A horrifying thought occurs to me. If Wansu is sending me dating profiles, she must be doing the same to Yujun. I hadn't even thought that Yujun might be cheating on me. He calls me every night. I've watched him fall asleep on the phone. During the day he attends business meetings. At least . . . I think he does. Doubt creeps into my thoughts like black smoke.

I fumble with the phone again. My fingers tremble slightly as I type out, Are you going on blind dates?

I hold my breath waiting for a reply, but none comes. It's so early. Is he in a meeting? *Or in someone else's bed?*

It's a good thing I don't have anything going on at work because nothing would've been accomplished. I can't concentrate for shit and I spend every other minute looking at my phone. Around mid-morning, I actually power down my phone, telling myself he'll text when I least expect it. That self-restraint lasts all of ten minutes. I finally get a response close to lunch.

YUJUN: No?

No? With a question mark? What kind of answer is that? I jump up from my chair, mumble an excuse about using the bathroom, which is unnecessary since no one is paying attention to me anyway, and scurry to the stairwell. I open the door to find it already occupied by another IF Group employee talking on her mobile. She glares and shoos me off.

The bathroom doesn't have the best signal, but it's the one place I can be guaranteed a moment of privacy. I slam the door of the stall shut and dial Yujun. It rings and rings and then I get a text message.

YUJUN: In a mtg sorry call u ltr 🖤 u

Phone in hand, I drive my thumbs into my temples. I am not a melodramatic person. I don't cry—often. I don't lose my temper. I don't have tantrums, but at this moment I want to throw my phone on the floor, jump on top of it until the screen is crushed, run outside, and scream until all the tension is released. I send Whatever your plans are tonight I need you to cancel them and then immediately wish I could retract it, but it's too late. The bubbles in the group chat are already moving.

JULES: ???

BOMI: Are you okay? Are you here at work? I'll come down

SANGKI: plans canceled

Seeing everyone's sympathy and worry over this stupid moment of insecurity makes me feel even worse.

ME: nvm ignore this

JULES: Shut up. Let's meet up at Casa Corona. They have private booths. You or Ahn Sangki are paying. I can't afford that place on my flight attendant salary

BOMI: I can't afford it either

I'm not getting out of this.

ME: I'll pay

Technically, Wansu is paying.

BOMI: Is this about the dating

JULES: What dating? why didn't u tell me? Choi Yujun's
mother is dating someone?

BOMI: Of course she isn't!!! Choi Yujun's father is still alive

JULES: Sorry! I was confused by your mention of dating.
Who's dating

BOMI: Hara.

SANGKI: you're dating? Does Choi Yujun know this?

I bang my head against the bathroom wall. Look at the mess
I've created.

ME: No one is dating anyone.

ME: I hope

A flurry of question marks follow but I don't want to lay out my
embarrassing laundry for anyone to reread later. Text messages
should expire after a certain number of days. I flip to my chat log
with Yujun, still listed in my contacts as simply "Yujun from
Seoul."

YUJUN: I miss u

YUJUN: Look at this cute dog

YUJUN: I walked by this waterway and there were two
ducks under the bridge. I tried to take a photo but the
male, the colorful one, must have thought he was in danger
or didn't like another male staring at his girl. He flapped
his wings and they disappeared under the bridge. I
thought of you. I thought of us.

He attached a photo of the red silk cord and the jade duck that
hung around his neck. I press my matching silk cord into my collarbone. Messages should be immortalized, I decide, never expir-
ing, always enduring.

ME: Come home to me, please.

CHAPTER SIX

CASA CORONA IS A ROOFTOP BAR AND GRILL IN ITAEWON, A
neighborhood adjacent to Yongsan. Back when the US had a major
presence in Seoul city, the Itaewon streets would be filled with
American GIs. Bomi said that Itaewon used to be a place where no
good Koreans would go. It had a seedy nightlife and an even seed-
ier underbelly of illegal sex, drugs, and contraband goods. The
neighborhood has been gentrified in the last twenty years. Gone
are the American soldiers and the cheap shops that lined the
streets. In their place are fancy restaurants, nightclubs, and boutique stores. A little west is the very exclusive UN Village in
Hannam-dong, a neighborhood where only the rich and powerful
live. Sangki has an apartment in the UN Village as do many celebrities.

There is no private room on the deck of Casa Corona, but Jules
has staked out prime real estate in one of the canopied booths away

from the glass railing that wraps around three sides of the rooftop. Bomi and I wend our way past the rattan tables and chairs to Jules's side.

"Is Ahn Sangki-nim coming?" she asks as we slide onto the cushions next to her. The table already has a small ice bucket with beer bottles, a bottle of tequila, and four shot glasses. "I came early and got this because we can close the drapes." She points to the long cream linen curtains that are tied to wooden posts.

"He's coming," I confirm. "Let me text him."

But it's unnecessary, as he is stepping off the elevator. Dressed in all black with a cap over his dyed-blond hair and sunglasses over his eyes, Sangki has an aura. Eyes swivel in his direction and whispers start to ripple across the crowded bar as patrons try to guess who he is. He spots us right away and quickly crosses the room. Mr. Lee closes the curtains before Jules can get out of her seat.

"He's so efficient," she says, offering a beer to Sangki.

"It's not his first time at the rodeo." I move over so that Sangki can take a seat.

"I don't know what that means. Explain. Please." He takes the beer.

"It means you—or rather Mr. Lee—isn't inexperienced. Have you seen a rodeo?"

He frowns. "I don't think so?"

Bomi shakes her head. "Was there one in Iowa?" She looks disappointed that she missed something vitally American.

"Not really. At the state fair, there are elements of the rodeo, like roping calves and barrel racing, but those are horse show events. At a real rodeo—and I'm saying this like I've attended when I haven't—it's a whole festival. The clowns and steer wrestling and the bull riding are at rodeos."

I go on to explain this in more detail, describing only what I've seen on television. Bomi and Sangki are fascinated by this, while Jules is more interested in ordering food.

"We should go," Sangki declares. "Is there one in LA? There's a Rodeo Drive, right?"

I laugh a little at the thought of a rodeo taking place in the middle of Beverly Hills. "They're pronounced differently. *Ro-day-oh* Drive is the fancy shopping district in Beverly Hills, and *row-dee-oh* is the show with the horses and cowboys. You have to go to Texas to see a real rodeo."

"Let's go to Texas. When Yujun gets back, we'll plan something. He'd love a rodeo."

"He would." He would buy a huge hat, look gorgeous, and make a dozen friends in the space of an hour.

"I can't afford to go to Texas," Bomi says in a small voice.

"Me either. And if I'm flying back to the States, I have to visit my family, which is on the other side of the country. We can go to Jeju or you can stow aboard one of my trips to Singapore," Jules invites.

Bomi gives her a grateful smile and the two touch their knees together, slightly, almost imperceptibly. I would've missed it had I not been watching, but now I feel like I've witnessed something I shouldn't have. It also makes me feel even lonelier because these two have found each other and my love might be going on blind dates with Singaporeans.

Sangki catches my eye and arches an eyebrow toward the other two. I merely shrug. They'll share when they're ready.

"What was the emergency, Hara?" Sangki asks.

"Can we pretend that I didn't have a meltdown earlier and we decided to get together because we missed each other and wanted to have a drink and some nachos?"

"We can, but you aren't drinking," he points out.

I grab the tequila bottle on the table and pour four shots. "It's everything."

I turn to the side and toss the shot back. The booze slides down smooth and then strikes when it hits the subway fish cake in my stomach—the only thing I've had today. I pour myself another shot and then another. Jules covers my glass before I can finish a fourth.

"Define 'everything.'"

I tighten my grip on the neck of the bottle. "It's work. I don't think I'll ever shake being a nepotism hire. It's the slow progress of my Korean. It's Wansu's matchmaking and blind dates. It's Yujun being gone. It's not knowing if Yujun is getting the same dating profiles. It's that this tequila is not making me drunk fast enough."

"That is a lot." Jules plucks the liquor from my hand and pours the shot herself.

I drink with gratitude. "The other day, *Bujang-nim*'s phone was ringing. Everyone was busy but me. I figured that voicemail would kick in, but—"

"But you were supposed to answer it and everyone thought you were arrogant because you refused to help your superior out," Jules finishes.

"Yes. How did you know?"

"Because in the US, people use their work lines for personal shit all the time, but in Korea, that would be grounds for termination and no one ever does it. If the phone's ringing, it's a business call. You gotta pick up."

I make a face. "That information would've been helpful last week."

"I guess it's on-the-job training," Jules quips. "But let's back the truck up. You're dating? I thought you and Yujun were." She interlocks her fingers and makes a jabbing motion.

Sangki starts coughing. Bomi averts her eyes.

This time I cover Jules's hands. "Please never do this again or we will have to ban you from our get-togethers."

"This was my idea."

"I know, and it's going to be very sad to see you standing in the street as we get drunk in here, but you brought it on yourself."

"She's right." Sangki cracks open another bottle. "You can't do that again. I'm traumatized."

"I guess we're all pretending like we've never seen or heard of sex before." Jules scrunches her lips together in annoyance.

I release her fingers and reach for a piece of dried squid—something I would've never eaten back home because it sounds terrible, but it's actually chewy and salty, which is really a perfect pairing for the sharp bite of the tequila.

"Wansu does not approve of Yujun and me as a couple—"

"No one approves of you two as a couple," Jules interjects.

"Shhh," Sangki puts his finger to his lips. "Let Hara tell us the story." He pins his bright brown eyes on me. "You are the most entertainment we've had in ages."

"Speak for yourself. I'm very entertaining," Jules boasts.

Bomi nods encouragingly. I don't know if I should be worried that Bomi is in the fresh crush stage, where she finds every outrageous thing Jules does quaint and funny, or delighted that the two have found each other.

I opt for the latter because at least someone is happy. I refill all of our glasses and then down both mine and Jules's. Sangki moves the empty glasses to the side.

"I support you and Yujun," he says.

Jules rolls her eyes. "I will, too."

We all look to Bomi, who flushes under the attention.

"Kim Bomi?" Sangki prods.

"I support you as well," she says, and hurriedly picks up her drink so she can hide her unease under the guise of politeness as she turns to the side and covers her face to drink.

In her hesitation, her answer is obvious. Even Jules picks up on it. "How can you, of all people, disapprove of this?"

The subtext is clear. How can Bomi, who is in a relationship that Korean society does not acknowledge as appropriate, be judgmental of another relationship that Korean society does not support?

Bomi rolls the empty glass between her hands. "Family means everything here. Even though the country makes it legal for people of the same clan to marry each other, the changed laws have not affected the hearts of the people. Some won't talk to you after they find you have the same clan name as theirs. While there are no laws that keep Hara and Yujun apart, traditions will. When it is time to hold *jesa* during Chuseok and honor the ancestors, Yujun will be invited but Hara will not. At a wedding of his cousin or the baptism of a niece, Hara will again be left out. Maybe that life is okay for some, but Hara came here to Seoul to find her family." Bomi sets down her glass and turns to me with an urgent look in her eyes. "Choi Wansu did not send Yujun away or prepare dating profiles for you because she does not think you are good enough for Yujun or that he is not good enough for you. She does it because she loves you and does not want to see you in pain."

"Are you saying that my choice here is either Yujun or be an outcast in the Choi family or maybe even society?"

"No," say Jules and Sangki, but I keep my eyes on Bomi, who nods sadly.

"It is a hard answer to give, just as *Sajang-nim* is risking that you will not love her because of the actions she takes now, but it is better now to steer you in a different direction before your boat strikes the iceberg. You may only see a small portion of the danger and dismiss it, but underneath there is an unmovable mountain."

"Is that how you really feel?" Jules demands.

Bomi hesitates before giving a short nod. A hurt sound escapes from Jules. She gathers her purse and stands. "I'm finished for the night. One more drink will ruin me."

As she walks out without a look back, we all know it's not the alcohol that she's talking about.

I turn to Bomi. "I thought you hated Chuseok. You said that you had to cook twenty dishes while all the men in your family did the ancestral rites, and after they ate, you had to clean."

"I do hate Chuseok, but I'm a female and Yujun is the eldest son of an eldest son. Choi Wansu has hosted the Korean thanksgiving for the entire family ever since I can remember. Choi Yujun has always loved it, hasn't he?" She looks pointedly at Sangki, who is busy staring at the label on the tequila bottle.

"Sangki?" I prompt.

He doesn't want to answer, but Bomi and I aren't moving on. "Yes, he enjoys it. He's an extrovert! He loves people. He loves his family. He has little cousins that he adores and he gives them special gifts at Chuseok, but no one in the Choi family is going to refuse to come to Choi Wansu's home because Yujun-ie is dating someone inappropriate." He squeezes my shoulder. "It'll be fine. Don't worry."

But, of course, I worry.

Later that night I FaceTime Ellen.

"Mom, I miss you." A wave of homesickness sweeps over me when her face appears on my screen. Life was simpler back in Iowa. One mother. No stepbrothers. A father who ignored me. Friends who bickered and said occasionally unintentionally racist things. Okay. Maybe home wasn't that great.

"Darling, darling, I miss you, too." She waves and smiles. "How is your Korean going?"

"Not great."

"I read that your brain stops learning languages after the age of ten or so. Something about how your brain needs to be rewired."

"Is there a machine I can be hooked up to?"

"I'm sure it's going much better than you think. You never give yourself enough credit."

I'm tired of talking about myself. "What are you doing today?"

"I'm going to the farmers' market to buy flowers and the fixings for pico de gallo. Louise is coming over this afternoon and we're going to weed the garden and then cut out quilting squares."

"Since when do you quilt?"

"I'm learning! Louise makes these gorgeous ones. She even won a ribbon at the fair. I'm going to make one for Wansu. Do you think she'll like it? What colors should I do?"

I close my eyes and try to picture a multicolored quilt in this contemporary shrine. "Black and white?"

"Pshaw. That's so boring. Why don't you go around and take some photos of the home and of her clothes. Whatever color she wears the most is her favorite."

"Black and white. Sometimes red." I yawn.

"What time is it there? I can never remember. Let me look at my phone. I added Seoul to my world clock." Her voice gets more distant as she pulls the phone away from her mouth to check the time.

"It's eleven."

"Eleven!" Her face returns to the screen. "Go to bed, Hara. You look tired and you'll be exhausted at work tomorrow."

"It's Friday." And I'm waiting for Yujun to call.

"Still, you should be going to bed at a reasonable time and not sleeping in even on the weekends. I love you, darling. Good night!"

I hang up and place the phone on my pillow and wait for Yujun to call. The device is maddeningly silent. To make the time pass, I pick up a book that I've been reading to Yujun's father, but that doesn't hold my interest. I scroll through YouTube and watch street-food vendors make everything from chocolate-covered waffles to bread shaped like bears and filled with cream. I fall asleep hungry, the phone clutched in one hand and the jade duck in the other.

CHAPTER SEVEN

WHEN I WAKE THE NEXT MORNING, I SMELL BACON, AND SUD-
denly I'm back in Iowa with Ellen cooking breakfast in the kitchen.
I close my eyes and try to tug back that comfort space, but the sun-
light bouncing off the marble wall opposite my bed brings me back
to reality. My bedroom back in Iowa has white plaster walls with
two small wildflower prints my mom and I made together my se-
nior year. Mom had watched this home decorating show where
two designers competed to have the homeowners stay or move. It
was Mom's favorite, and almost always the designer who renovated
the existing home won due to some sentimental hook. In this particular episode, the designer pressed petals from the homeowner's
wedding bouquet onto a giant canvas and hung it over the mantel
in their old home. The resulting work was an abstract depiction of
a bird rising from a nest of flowers that looked as if it was explod-

ing. The bride burst into tears and the groom bit his lip and stared at the ceiling for a good ten seconds, which does not seem like a long time, but is an eternity on television. I was really moved. Of course, the couple chose to keep their renovated home.

Watching that romantic moment didn't stir any desire for marriage in me, but I did think that using flowers to create an abstract piece of art was brilliant. Mom agreed. The main problem was that we didn't have a flower garden and buying blooms at the grocery store didn't hold the same charm.

The next weekend, we trekked to Brown's Woods, a forest preserve of almost five hundred acres, and picked wildflowers along the path. It's illegal to do this, but Mom didn't have the patience to grow plants and I was born with a brown, withering thumb. I killed a cactus and three succulents in college. Mom wasn't much better, and after a few years of trying to nurture a rubber tree, which a local greenhouse said would survive even the most forgetful of owners, she finally gave up and bought semi-fake artificial plant decorations. We didn't realize we were supposed to spray them with water once every couple of weeks until the leaves dried out and turned brown. In other words, we weren't winning any horticulture awards at the state fair.

I'm not proud of my ineptness, but we agreed we were better off paying whatever fine for the wildflowers should we get caught than using the few weeds in our backyard as the centerpiece of our art project. We didn't get in trouble but neither did our resulting works look anywhere as good as the designer's piece on television. I guess it was karmic retribution or the fact that the designer had a special eye for design and my mom is a homemaker and I'm—or was—a copy editor for a magazine. More simply put, there's a reason the designer had a television show that Mom and I watched from the sofa in our small brick two-bedroom home with its pale yellow walls and its half-country, half-rustic decor.

At that time, there wasn't anything in my life that warranted a small- or big-screen adaptation. A few months ago, I was Hara Wilson, a twenty-five-year-old adopted Korean American living in Iowa with my mother, Ellen, while estranged from my father, Pat, who had been dipping his wick in the well of a woman not much older than me. He fathered a "real" kid and then died. For some reason, even though we hadn't had much of a relationship since I was twelve or so, I had an identity crisis, which resulted in me running off to Seoul, South Korea, in search of my biological father. I landed in Korea two days after Lee Jonghyung died.

A person shouldn't have to attend more than one funeral for a parent in a calendar year. That should be a cosmic law. It's too much for any single individual to process. I once read that insurance money allows people to not make hasty decisions following someone's death. The beneficiary can press pause in their lives instead of selling everything that their loved one owned in order to feed themselves. Unfortunately, there's no such thing as emotional insurance that allows you to put your heart into deep freeze so your head can make rational choices free of all the grief and confusion that death brings, and because of this I am now working at a Korean company while not being able to speak the language and sleeping in a giant room with more marble than you'd find in a hotel lobby.

I don't live in Iowa and I don't have one mom anymore. I have two of them. Choi Wansu doesn't look like she's ever seen a glue stick or hiked in the woods or broken the law. Her home is modern and minimalistic, with marble floors and marble walls and marble pedestals upon which precise and perfect bonsais rest. My bedroom isn't merely a bedroom but a small suite of rooms.

I drag my tired body out of bed and wonder if Yujun is going to break up with me over the telephone or whether he'll make a special trip back home to do it. Wansu will be happy. Her gambit worked. She sent Yujun away and he found someone else. I don't know how else to interpret his silence. I didn't get another text message and he didn't call me last night. It must be over between the two of us.

I choke back tears as I brush my teeth. A flash of red in the bathroom mirror catches my eye. I reach under the neckline of my sleep shirt and tug on the silk cord until the jade duck pendant is free. Yujun gave me this the night before he was sent away. Ducks mate for life. The jade is a symbol of health and fortune—a mystical stone that wards off evil spirits. The red cord is the physical manifestation of our bond. Pre-destiny is what he'd say. He believes in these things. He's romantic and lovely and charming and I miss him so, so much. I squeeze the jade duck until the beak bites into my skin. He was busy and fell asleep. That's all. I'm catastrophizing even when I swore I wasn't that person.

As I shuffle toward the door to the sitting room, the smell of bacon becomes even stronger. I feel a strange wave of homesickness and almost turn around to text my mother—the Iowan one—before I remind myself of the time difference. It's past bedtime for Ellen but she told me she sleeps with her phone now so that she can wake up if I text her, which means I never text her when I think she is sleeping.

It strikes me that the smell of any kind of food, let alone meat, is odd given my room is so far from the kitchen. Is the house on fire? I jerk open the door and nearly bean myself on the edge of a tray.

"Good morning." A sparkling smile, a deep dimple, and gorgeous brown eyes greet me.

"Yujun," I gasp.

The smile deepens and so does the divot. My knees get watery but I can't launch myself into his arms because of the stupid breakfast tray. I tug the tray out of his hands and nearly sprint to the table in the seating area of my bedroom. When I turn around, hands free, he's there, gathering me in his arms.

Our mouths meet. My fingers find the buttons of his shirt. He tugs the collar of my sleep shirt far enough away to expose my collarbone and the red string of the necklace he gave me before he left. His thumb presses the string into my skin hard enough that I can feel the silk cord making an indent. I welcome the slight pain. I welcome him. He breaths into my mouth, a sigh of relief or acknowledgment. I feel the same way having him here in the same space. My head is filled with giddiness, glee, and lust. He walks me backward until my calves hit the edge of the sofa. I fold and let his momentum push me into the cushions.

His heavy weight presses me down. I don't have much to take off but we spend a good minute wrestling him free of his shirt, undershirt, pants, socks, and underwear until it's his bare skin flush against my bare skin. He slips inside me easily. I've been waiting for him and my body is always ready for his intrusion. I scrape my fingers over the broad expanse of his shoulder blades, down his spine, and to his ass. He groans, his chest rumbling like a big cat against my sensitive breasts. It's a luxurious, erotic feeling that I want to capture and bottle to take out in times when we are not together, which seem all too often.

I close my eyes and try to capture the moment, try to memorize his mouth against my neck, the muscle movement of his back as he thrusts forward, the sensation of the thick head of his shaft driving against my million nerve endings, but soon, too soon, my own need overcomes me and thinking becomes a thing of the past.

I surface, gasping and sweaty. Emotion chokes me, fills my throat, makes me shake like a drug addict coming off a dangerous high. I used to never cry and now I find myself on the edge all too often. My cheeks will get chapped at this rate.

"Shhh," Yujun from Seoul whispers against my skin. He shifts into a sitting position and pulls me into the cradle of his embrace. "Don't move," he cautions, and reaches between us to untangle the silk cords of our matching jade duck necklaces. Ducks mate for life. I clutch the tiny jade bird in my fist and wrap my other arm around his neck, wondering if I can stay here forever.

He fishes a blanket off the back of the sofa and throws it over us. "I'm exhausted," he says.

I sink into him, burrowing like a kitten into the one warm spot in the entire marble mausoleum. This is where I want to be at all times, in the circle of his arms with the warm scent of his skin filling my lungs, and the rumble of his chest under my ear. I don't even register what he's saying. The sound, the feel, is enough. I rub my cheek against his chest like a cat against a scratching pole.

Then horror turns my blood cold and I shoot upright. "Where's Wansu?"

He pulls me back against him. "She's at the office. I called her from the airport to let her know the Singapore office has some questions for her and that I've written everything in a report that I was leaving on her desk."

I collapse. "Then you left."

"Knowing that she would come straightaway." He nuzzles my neck. "I may have taken advantage of her."

"You are workaholics."

"Perhaps." He moves on from my neck to lave my collarbone. I cup the back of his head. "How much time do we have?"

"Enough."

His head moves lower still. I knew he'd come back. This was home.

CHAPTER EIGHT

"DON'T EAT THAT. EVERYTHING'S COLD." YUJUN TRIES TO TAKE the tray away from me, but I block him with my body.

"No. You made this."

"This is like when you made the stew for *Eomeo-nim*." He reaches again, and this time I slide farther down the sofa.

"It's not. This is actually good." Yes, the eggs are runny, the toast is slightly burnt, and the bacon isn't crispy, but I am *not* complaining. I keep shoveling the food into my mouth, scooping the eggs onto the toast and swallowing the bacon in two gulps.

Yujun gives up, leaning back against the sofa with a sigh. He picks up his phone and starts to scroll through the news.

"You know Iowa is famous for their hogs," I tell him between bites.

"I did not know that." He strokes a hand down my robe-covered spine as he clicks on one article. I don't know what he's reading since it's in Korean, but it could be the horoscope for all I care. He's here. That's what matters. He's back in his pants and his shirt, with the white dress shirt unbuttoned enough that the shadow of his chest is visible. It's sexy as hell. I turn my attention back to the eggs and remind myself that I had sex twice. One more time and my vagina will close up forever from the overuse.

"Yes. We have hog lots and meat-processing plants. A lot of immigrants work there because the jobs are so hard and no one really wants to work them."

He puts his phone down. "That's very similar to here. How else are Korea and Iowa alike?"

"The climate is the same. We have roughly the same kind of weather—cold, snowy winters and hot summers. No real air pollution like you have here, but the hog-lot smell can be terrible. Des Moines is actually an insurance town, though. One of the largest in the world."

"I did not know that either. We should visit there. You, me, and *Eomma*."

For a moment, I think of Wansu in Iowa, walking around in her cream-colored power suits and her sharply cut bob. We could drive around the small downtown of Des Moines for an hour and not run into another Asian. Would she feel out of place for even a moment, or is her personal confidence so powerful that she would not experience one ounce of loss of self? Probably the latter. It's hard for me to think of Wansu shaken about anything. She passed down her surety to Choi Yujun, whereas I ended up with a basket of nerves and a bundle of insecurities. Nurture versus nature is playing itself out in this mansion in Seoul.

"Ellen would love that, but our home isn't very big. No marble anywhere."

"I'm sure it's wonderful. I'd like to see where you grew up, Hara. Where you went to school. Where you worked. Meet your friends." His hand drifts up to cup the back of my head. "I want to know everything there is to know about you."

I'm melting inside but I'm afraid to let him see it. I'm afraid of our future and I'm afraid to get hurt, so I allow myself a strained smile and a nod. "It might not be what you expect, so don't get too excited."

He doesn't say anything but cradles my head in his palm while he reads. He's a steady presence in this not-so-familiar place. I want to crawl onto his lap and inside his shirt, inside his heart. It's safe there. That's where my home is.

As I rub my cheek against his palm like a cat, my eyes catch on his expensive Rolex. I double-check the time against the analog iron clock on the wall, and sure enough the black arrows tell me it's past eight. "Oh my God. Is it that time already? I'm late!" Even though it's Saturday, I have an appointment to keep. I jump to my feet and race into the bedroom and then the bathroom to quickly rebrush my teeth. I can't have egg in my mouth all day.

He stretches and I get momentarily distracted by the show of skin and tight muscle in the opening of his shirt. I give myself a mental shake and brush by him to my dressing room. I stumble over a new bag that Wansu must've dropped off when I wasn't paying attention.

Yujun follows and leans against the doorframe, slightly out of my view so as to give me a bit of privacy. I appreciate it. I'm not as comfortable in my bare skin as he is in his. If I had his toned body with the ridged abs and solid pecs, I might walk around nude as well.

I throw on a pair of slacks and an oversize shirt. It's warmer

upstairs where Yujun's father is. I guess they keep it that way because he can't regulate his own body temperature. I spritz a tiny bit
of perfume on and then fluff up my hair. It's kind of a mess, but I
don't have time to shower and redo my hair. Choi Yusuk will
survive.

"What is the big appointment and should I get dressed?" He's
surveying my outfit, trying to decipher my plans.

I run my hand over my throat and wish I'd told him earlier. We
had texted and chatted frequently, but the topic of his father never
came up. Instead our exchanges seemed to be more of a running
account of my adventures in food-truck land and him complaining
that Singapore was hot. At one degree north of the equator, Singapore is an endless summer. There wasn't a good time for me to in-
sert that I was spending mornings with his father, but now that
omission seems glaring. "I read to your father."

Yujun's eyebrows arch high. "Choi Yusuk?"

"Yes, that's him." My lover only has the one. "I'm late." I barrel
forward. Yujun follows, asking questions as we go.

"When did you start reading to my father?"

"About two weeks ago. Wansu suggested it."

"*Eomma* does as well. And watches dramas. Dramas are her
vice."

"Why does everyone say that?" No one talks about dramas at
the office. There are only loud complaints about how trot, a type of
music popular among the over-forty crowd here, is overtaking every show. Trot and idols and dramas. No one seems to like them—
or, at least, they profess not to like them. Trot is for old people and
idols for teens and dramas for bored housewives. Bomi tells me
that there are very few bored housewives. Korean households, like
those in most advanced countries, are two-income these days,

which is putting a strain on women because they now have two jobs—the office one and the household one.

"They're coded as entertainment for women—romances and melodramas—so men pretend they haven't seen them, and if the majority of your coworkers are men and you want to fit in, then you say you watched Son Heungmin and Ryu Hyunjin and occasionally you can admit to watching a crime drama or something pertaining to *jopoks*."

Son is a soccer player and Ryu a baseball player, but *jopok* is a new one. "*Jopoks?*"

"Mobster movies."

I file the word away. "You watch dramas. You said you watched a couple of them." We climb the stairs to the second floor and turn to the right. Choi Yusuk is installed in a large room directly above mine.

"I didn't say I agreed with the stereotype. Some dramas are great and some are terrible." He shrugs. "*Eomma* likes the very terrible, very melodramatic ones, but that's between you and me and my father." He pushes the door to his father's room open.

The nurse aide who watches Choi Yusuk during the day rises to her feet and gives a low bow, which I know is for Yujun because I usually only get a nod.

"Thank you, *ganhosa-nim*. We will call you when we are finished." Yujun dismisses the nurse aide easily.

Park Sooyoung bows again and disappears out the double doors without another word. Choi Yusuk rests in a king-size bed with a headboard that is big and grand enough to decorate a presidential suite. It's made of mahogany, and the lion's head, tree branches, and pine cones were all carved by hand by an artisan in Germany. It was a gift, Wansu told me, from a famous German furniture maker to

Choi Yusuk's father for a favor done. What favor, Wansu isn't sure, or she's not sharing with me. When Choi Yusuk passes on, this massive wooden piece will become Yujun's. I cannot envision Yujun propped against the dark wood with his dimples bracketed by wooden pine cones. Choi Yusuk's bed is from two generations ago, while Yujun, from his slacks, which are precisely hemmed at his anklebone, to his well-groomed eyebrows, is thoroughly modern.

"Is your bed a platform style?" I blurt out, wanting to believe I know him.

Yujun cocks his head, wondering where this question suddenly came from. "Yes?"

Mentally, I pump my fist at my accuracy. "I thought so."

A wicked grin spreads across his face, his left dimple deepening past the puddle stage into the bottomless well. I want to poke it, kiss it, swim in his happy look forever.

"Spent a lot of time thinking about me in my bed, have you?"

I could play coy, but why? "I have."

He runs his tongue along his lower teeth and arches an eyebrow high. "I have yellow pillows."

Why does that sound erotic? His hand snakes out to wrap around my waist, but I scoot out of reach. "Not in your dad's room," I whisper in a half-joking, half-serious tone.

He gusts out a small sigh but joins me at the bedside, dragging a chair over. I wince at the sound of the wood scraping against the marble. Yujun's casual familiarity with his home speaks of his comfort level with this kind of wealth. I'm still adjusting.

"What are we reading?" he asks.

"Korean folktales. In English, though."

He sits down and waits for me to begin. I hesitate. It's wonderful having Yujun back and I do want to spend every waking minute with him, but maybe not for the next hour or so. Reading aloud is much like acting out a story, and I don't know that I can do it in front of him. I might as well sit at the dining room table naked. That's how uncomfortable I would feel. "I can't read with you in here, Yujun. I will be too self-conscious."

"Really?" He's surprised.

"Yes, really. My tongue already feels thick and my throat's closing so—" I make a shooing gesture. "Off you go."

"I was gone for six weeks, Hara. I want to spend time with you."

"I want the same thing, but I can't." I'm whispering now, as if Choi Yusuk can hear me. I mean, I think he can hear me, which is why I read to him in the mornings and Wansu spends every evening in here, but I don't know what he comprehends. Maybe he understands it all and is now internally frowning as he pieces together what my little argument with his son means.

"Pretend I'm not here." Yujun crosses his arms and stretches out his long legs, looking like he doesn't plan to leave for the next five days.

"Because it's so easy to ignore a six-foot man. Please, Yujun," I plead.

Reluctantly and slowly, he rises from the chair, giving me plenty of opportunity to stop him. I don't and he finally caves. "I'll wait outside."

"Sorry about that, *Sae Appa*," I whisper after Yujun closes the door, using the Korean words that Wansu taught me. They mean "stepfather," she said, and that's how she wanted me to address him. I straighten the covers and pull the blanket under his chin. I always worry about him being cold.

Yujun once told me that he put his father in this bed after they'd argued about the direction of IF Group. Choi Yusuk did not support the changes Yujun and Choi Wansu wanted to make. They argued and Choi Yusuk had a stroke. His condition deteriorated until he slipped into unconsciousness three years ago. He's a traditionalist, Wansu said, and a traditional Korean man had a certain way of thinking. If he were awake, I don't think I'd be in this house, and so even after these two weeks, I'm still on edge when I'm at Choi Yusuk's bedside.

"Is it okay that I'm here? Would you give Yujun and me your blessing if you were awake? Would you allow me space at your dinner table? Would you eat food I cooked during Chuseok? Would you permit Yujun to love me?"

CHAPTER NINE

SAE APPA HAS NO ANSWERS FOR ME. THERE'S NOTHING BUT the sound of his breathing machine, the *click, click, click* of the heart monitor, and the quiet hum of the heater. I rub my cold hands together and open the book I've been reading. It's a collection of Korean fairy tales. I'm on the story of "Sim Cheong." "Sim Cheong" is a traditional Korean folktale, one of the five *pansori*, a Korean opera, that have survived through the centuries. So much of the *pansori* is steeped in mysticism that it is hard to know where the human ends and the dragon begins. This particular *pansori* is about filial piety.

"Sim Cheong" is sad—emo, black-eyeliner, long-bangs sad. Sim Bongsa, Sim the Blind, loses his wife upon his daughter's birth and gradually begins to lose his eyesight. When his daughter is thirteen, Sim Bongsa is begging in the street, crying about his blindness. A monk passing by overhears these complaints, which Sim

Bongsa has made many times before. Tired, the monk makes an offer. For a grand price of three hundred bags of rice, the temple will offer up prayers to Buddha for Sim Bongsa's sight to be returned. Sim is so poor that even one bag of rice would be a luxury, but he foolishly agrees to this insane bargain. When Sim Cheong hears of the deal that her father has struck with the monks, she weeps, for she knows that the temple bargain cannot be met.

The following day she learns that sailors have landed in search of a virgin to sacrifice to the King of the Sea, who is tormenting the ships with storms. For three hundred bags of rice, Sim Cheong agrees to be that sacrifice. She is thrown into the sea, and the prayers of the monks, if they were actually made, result in no change to her father. He remains blind and now childless.

The Sea King takes pity on Sim Cheong, and because of her enduring loyalty to her father, he rewards her by placing her in a lotus blossom and sending her to the top of the sea. The sailors who cast her out discover the giant blossom and haul the flower aboard to take back to the king. In the palace, the blossom petals unfurl to reveal Sim Cheong. The king falls instantly in love—lust, more likely—and asks for her hand in marriage. Sim Cheong agrees but requires that a wedding banquet be held for all the blind. Sim Cheong waits until her father arrives at the palace grounds and calls out to him. In this moment, Sim Bongsa's eyes are healed, and with his new vision, he is able to see his daughter for the first time.

I finish the story and drum my fingers against the paperback. A traditionalist like Choi Yusuk would like this story. Sacrifice everything for your parents, including your life, and you will be richly rewarded. I wonder if Yujun knows this story. He must since it is so famous, but it isn't controlling his life. I need to learn from that.

Wansu will relent, eventually. My coworkers will see that I'm a hard worker who deserves a job, and when the other women go to the bathroom, they'll invite me to join them. After the *hweshik*—company dinner—which we all hate, we'll skip out on the second round of drinks at a different bar, shove the drunk men into a taxi, and escape to a *noraebang*, where we will sing our favorite idol songs, pretend we are onstage, and drink until *we* have to be poured into taxis. It will be fun and bonding and we will laugh about how they all thought I was this nepotistic hire but I'm really a decent person whom they are so happy to have as a coworker. Soyou especially won't have a pinched expression around her mouth when I call her *sunbae-nim*. Hell, she might even invite me to call her *sunbae*, dropping the honorarium *-nim*.

I finish reading a passage in the book, tuck the folded sticky note I use as a bookmark between the pages, and stow the collection away in the bedside drawer, refusing to admit how sad my fantasies are. I fuss with the covers again.

Sae Appa, your son is so handsome and good. You would be so proud of him. He's open-minded, sweet, and good at his job. You raised him right. Your ancestors are cheering you on. You should wake and see what he has done, and Wansu misses you. She comes here every night. I hope you enjoy the dramas.

I pat the side of the bed because it feels wrong to touch him, even his hand. He hasn't given me permission to do so. I wonder again about Wansu. She doesn't have many friends that I've seen. We haven't had a house party or even a single guest in the six weeks I've lived with her. She spends her nights with her unconscious husband watching melodramas. Her mornings are given to tending a collection of small bonsais and reading.

Ellen watches game shows and reality television, and if the circumstances were reversed and Yujun was Ellen's son, she would've had a party the second night and invited everyone within a fifty-mile radius. She goes to pottery parties, martini nights, knitting socials. She's dragged me to dozens of these events, where I slink to the back, drink copious wine, and find my way home with a dubious craft that sits on a shelf collecting dust for months until I finally stow it away with the sweatshirts from college that I can't seem to get rid of even though I never wear them.

Since I moved in, only Wansu and I have ever sat at the large walnut table that seats twelve, and every night after dinner, Wansu retires to this room and this man. And then there's Yujun. We've never really discussed his father, which is my fault. I've been so focused on my own drama that I haven't made time for him. I need to do better.

Outside the bedroom, Yujun is seated on a bench that wasn't there before. "My legs were tired," he says by way of explanation.

"Did you wait here the entire time?"

"I said I would. I didn't want to break my promise again." He stands and tucks my hand into the crook of his arm, leading me toward the stairs.

The last time he told me he'd be waiting was right after I discovered Choi Wansu was my biological mother. I went to her office to confront her and ran into Yujun. He'd said he would wait for me while I confronted Wansu, but when that first disastrous meeting had concluded, he was gone. He had been called away to see his father.

My apology is long overdue. "I'm sorry that I didn't tell you before I was spending time with your dad."

At the first step down, he stops and turns. We're almost eye to eye. "Why would you need to apologize for that?"

"Because it feels like something you should've known, and I

wasn't trying to hide it, but it felt awkward to bring it up." Because your dad's unconscious and can't give his consent to me, the interloper, being in his room.

"It's fine. It really is, and I'm not merely saying that." He tugs me down for a quick kiss. "*Eomma* is on her way home. This will have to last until tonight." He wipes his finger across my wet lips. The touch is fleeting but I feel it everywhere. "Come and keep me company while I unpack."

I let it go. Yujun believes this is my home now as well. It's not. His rooms are on the opposite side of the house, far away from mine. It's different over here—warmer and more inviting. When Wansu gave me the tour, she opened the door to his room for all of a half second. I caught a glimpse of wood and carpet before I was hustled back into the living room.

The floors are mahogany and the walls are painted a dark blue. A large king-size platform bed rests on a raised floor. On the level below is a large-screen television, a black velvet sectional, and a desk. Around the corner is a small eat-in kitchenette with a sink, microwave, and hot plate and doors leading to his en suite bathroom and a dressing room full of sneakers, hats, and enough jackets for every day of the month. A large suitcase rests open on a bench.

"What story are you on?" he asks as he begins to unpack.

"'Sim Cheong.'"

"'Sim Cheong'?" He hoots. "Going for the traditionals. Let me sum them all up for you. Be selfless, put your family first, and you will be rewarded. Have you read the goblin one?"

"As in the great and lonely god?" There's a dreamy K-drama based on the story of a goblin god.

"No. The one about the two brothers. I won't spoil it for you since you haven't reached it."

"I'll get there eventually. I found the book in the English section at Kyobo in Gwanghwamun." Above his desk is a shelf lined with trophies. I don't know what they're for, but he has a lot of them. "Bomi says that there is a Korean version, but I didn't want to torture your father with my terrible pronunciation. I did buy some children's books. Maybe when I finish with the Korean folktales, I'll move on to one of those."

"I've read *Where's Halmoni?* to my cousins a dozen times. You should try that one." His voice fades in and out as he moves around in his dressing room.

"I will." Some of the trophies appear to be academic ones since there are books or pens etched into the crystal and metal.

"Don't look." A large hand covers my eyes. "This is an *eomeonim*'s shelf."

A mother's shelf? That makes sense. I pull his hand down to rest on my shoulder—a comforting weight. "I love it. Tell me what each one is for."

He leans forward and rests his chin on my head. "We are a competitive people. Every show on television is a competition. If two men meet at the crosswalk, they will instinctively speed up, trying to beat the other man across while appearing not to care."

"What I'm hearing you say is that one of these trophies is for speed walking."

"They are for his exemplary achievements in football, mathematics, language, and living as a dutiful citizen." Wansu's voice is like a whip slicing the air and striking us apart.

Yujun jerks upright and backs away at the same moment I'm

leaping out of the circle of his embrace. My foot catches on the corner of Yujun's desk and I start to topple over like the last bowling pin teetering on the edge of the pin deck waiting to fall into the gutter. Yujun's hand shoots out, catches my arm, and hauls me upright.

We're both breathless when we turn to face Wansu. She walks toward us, her face expressionless as usual. We're all going to pretend Yujun was not hugging me, I guess. In Wansu's head, we're siblings. I can't reconcile that. Yujun is the man I met at the airport, who took me to the top of Namsan, kissed me by the river, and held my hand when I was breaking apart. He is not my brother.

"This one"—she points to a gold medal suspended above a walnut base and encased in glass—"is for placing first in the Korean Math Olympiad, and this one"—a trophy with a scroll and ink pen—"is for English language proficiency."

Behind his mother's—my mother's—back, he winks at me. There's a lot of pride in Wansu's voice and Yujun basks in her praise, not at all uncomfortable with this recitation of his high school glory. If it was me and Ellen, I'd be under the desk, red as a cherry. Wansu raised Yujun to be bold and confident, to not shrink under pressure, and to not apologize for who he is and what he wants. Ellen raised me to persevere, but quietly. Don't be boastful; let your actions speak. Give of yourself to be given in return. Let others have a turn.

Would Wansu have raised me differently or would Ellen's mothering have changed if I was a boy? I don't think that has anything to do with how we were raised. Choi Yujun is an extrovert and I'm an introvert. Wansu's an introvert like me. I guess it's part of my DNA.

"I think Hara has heard enough," Yujun interrupts his mother's recitation of his brilliance.

"Then let's eat lunch." She heads for the door, but the open closet doors catch her eye. "Are you unpacking here?"

"I thought I'd stay here for a while. I know you missed me." I'm not sure if he's talking to me or Wansu. He walks to the door of his bedroom and gestures for us to move. "We don't want to make Mrs. Ji wait. She'll be unhappy if the food is cold."

Wansu hesitates but, after a brief internal battle, decides not to fight this one. I follow. At twenty-five, I should date who I want, love who I want, live how I want. I don't want to be Sim Cheong.

CHAPTER TEN

LUNCH IS UNCOMFORTABLE, BUT NOT FOR THE REASONS I thought it would be. I thought we would be awkward, silent, with nothing but the sounds of our forks clashing against the china, as is ordinarily the case when Wansu and I eat together, but instead, she and Yujun can't stop talking.

"You did well on your trips. Yujun-ah was able to achieve all his goals. He came home with two signed contracts and several new leads. It was very fruitful." Wansu beams, and by that I mean the corners of her mouth have ticked up two degrees. "And Team Manager Park tells me that you are doing well in your position, Hara. He finds your work to be exemplary."

Bujang-nim's a big fat liar. I smile tight and give a diplomatic response. "He's good to work for."

He is great to work for because he expects nothing, never scolds me when I screw up, and always has a ready compliment.

"You'll have to come with me next time, Hara," Yujun invites. "The food in Singapore is amazing. I went to the Keppel Road market and got *bak kut teh*. Remember that place, *Eomma*? Henry Lui brought us there."

"I do remember. It's delicious." She frowns at the pasta, peas, and lemon chicken on her plate.

"I ate two servings and would've had one more, but the chili crabs were calling for me." Yujun has demolished his serving and is working on buttering a roll.

"Did you eat many of those?" Wansu's voice is warm and loving as she listens to her son list all the food he stuffed himself with on his business trip. He sounds like he did more eating than business-ing, but his lean frame doesn't show it.

"Too many. Finished it off with mango *tau huay*."

"The cold kind?"

"Yes. It was that kind of night."

"As it always is in Singapore," murmurs Wansu.

Their ease, their shared memories, are showing me that they're a unit in a way I hadn't envisioned before. I'm happy they have this, like I have with Ellen, but I won't lie. There's a sliver of resentment, too, because I overthink every interaction I have with Wansu, questioning whether I'm wording even a compliment appropriately.

But I can push the peas around my plate or jump in. I jump in. "I've never had any of this food, and now I want to eat it all."

"*Bak kut teh* is a pork bone broth soup," Yujun explains. "There are some places in Seoul that serve Singaporean food, although, *bak kut teh* is more Hong Kong cuisine."

I had never heard of it, but Koreans love their soup. Almost no meal is complete without a bowl of soup, often served at the end before the fruit. Even Wansu's Western meals will include some sort of soup, even if it is only a broth with a few green onions and peppers floating in the liquid. "Is it like *seolleongtang*?" One of the food trucks serves cups of ox-bone soup ladled out of a huge iron cauldron.

"Sort of, but a different flavor. *Seolleongtang* has a milky color from the boiling of the bones, whereas *bak kut teh* broth is made like a tea with a spice packet. Everyone makes it differently."

The chicken is beginning to taste like rubber. "Like *banchan* and *limoncello*."

A wide smile breaks across Yujun's face, like the sun shoving itself out between two clouds. "Exactly like *limoncello*."

"What is this?" Wansu is the one who feels left out now.

"When I took Hara out to eat, I told her every restaurant has its own *banchan* like Italian chefs have their own *limoncello*." Yujun will never allow someone to feel excluded.

The mention of my date with Yujun dims Wansu's pleasure, and her lips flatten. I clench the back of my teeth together. Yujun pretends nothing is amiss.

"Should we go to the Banyan Tree tonight?" he suggests. "Sangki is doing a short set. We could invite Bomi and your friends from the Airbnb."

Wansu and I are the two clouds in Yujun's life, squeezing the sunshine behind our dark glowers. I resolve to do better. "For the Summer Splash thing? I forgot that was tonight, but yeah, that sounds like fun. Now that you're back I won't have to sit with Mr. Lee."

"Mr. Lee? Oh, you mean Sangki's manager. I don't think he ever sits, does he?"

"Only in the car."

We share a small smile, which goes on for too long, because

Wansu clears her throat. "It will be nice for Yujun to introduce you to some of his friends. Perhaps you should invite Lee Sikook."

Yujun cops immediately to Wansu's plans. "Lee Sikook is dating Ryu Sooyeon these days."

Wansu spears a piece of a cantaloupe. "Is that right? They would make a nice couple. Ryu is a pharmacist, isn't she? And Lee is a biochemist. What about—"

"I don't think anyone you would like will be at this party, *Eomma*. It's an influencer crowd."

"I see." The edges of her nose flare in obvious disgust. The influencer crowd must not be one she approves of.

Yujun is unperturbed. "We will have fun." He pulls out his phone. "I'll text Sangki and let him know to put our names on the list. Who else?"

"Bomi and Jules."

"Kim Bomi?" Wansu interjects with a narrowed glance. "My Kim Bomi? That is not a crowd to which she belongs."

"It'll be fun for her and Hara. It's not like either of them are going to start a YouTube channel. Are you?" He looks to me.

I shake my head vehemently. "No. Never." While I watch a lot of videos, I can't imagine starring in one myself.

"There." He nods to his mother. "No one is joining the influencer crowd. We are going to have drinks, eat food, and listen to good music."

And that was that.

"YOU DON'T SEEM to be in a party mood," I murmur to Jules over the noise. "Maybe this was a bad idea. We should've invited your other roommates."

I pull the calf-length sheer sweater closer around my frame and tuck my wedge-clad feet against the leg of the black stained rattan bench. Half the girls here are wearing less than me, but fancy pool parties are outside of my experience, which was mostly bars with sticky floors and dozens of big screens blasting the latest Hawkeye or Cyclone sporting event.

Since we arrived, Yujun has been mobbed by a bunch of people who exclaimed that he had been gone a decade. Right now, he's on the other side of the banquette having an in-depth discussion about the flight of international businesses from Hong Kong to places like Shanghai and Seoul due to the political unrest. It's an interesting topic, but while it started in English, they've unconsciously slipped into Korean.

"They already had plans." She's glum, too, but not because she's self-conscious about her severe black one-piece with the large circle cutouts on the sides.

"Are you and Bomi fighting?" The other girl had quickly turned down Yujun's invite.

Jules sends me a suspicious look. "Did she say something to you?"

"About you two dating or you two fighting?"

"Both."

"No."

"How did you figure it out, then? We've been so careful."

I fiddle with the umbrella in my piña colada. "Your knees touched."

"Huh?"

"The other night at Casa Corona, your knees touched."

"Bullshit. There's no way you guessed we were seeing each other from our knees touching. Bomi must've said something."

"Nope. I figured it out. Sangki, too. You guys looked like a couple."

"You and Ahn Sangki-nim look like a couple," Jules shoots back. "And you aren't one."

I laugh out loud at this. "We do not."

"Whatever." She huffs out a sigh but it's obvious Sangki and I have zero chemistry. We're friends and anyone looking at us would know that, just like anyone looking at Yujun, whose hand didn't leave my back until his friends pulled him away, knows that we do not act like siblings. "I think she's avoiding me because I got mad and walked out of Casa Corona, but what was I going to do? Listen to her declare that being with me will ruin her life?"

"That's not what I heard her saying. She was warning me to be careful."

"She was warning both of us. She was saying that a relationship with me is as impossible as a relationship between you and Yujun, which isn't even true. There's no law that prohibits you two from being a couple, whereas Bomi and I could be fired for indecency if it got out that we were dating."

My eyebrows fly up. "Wansu would fire Bomi over that?"

"Theoretically, although I don't know where Choi Yujun's mom stands on it, to be honest. But most older Koreans are against it. Younger ones say that they aren't, but there are plenty of people with prejudices who don't like to admit it."

I've run into that at home just being Korean in America. The people you least expect think certain ways about you because of how you look or whom you love.

"The thing is that it's all about family here," Jules continues. "Take Chuseok. It's centered around honoring the ancestors and it's a big deal. The women start to prepare a week in advance. You have to make certain dishes and even place particular foods on different parts of the table. There's a rule about how many times you bow and when you're supposed to drink the special rice wine.

"They hold these *charyes* twice a year. Once at Chuseok and once at Seollal, the Lunar New Year. *Gijesa* is held on the anniversary of the dead person and they even observe *sije*, a ceremony held seasonally. This country's traditions are all built around the family and the continuation of the family. If her family learned she likes girls, they might try to take her siblings away. Her brother is the eldest son, and he's supposed to carry on all the family traditions."

"Are you trying to convince me or yourself here?"

Jules drops her face to her hand. Her blond braids fall forward and I brush them aside before one falls into a salsa dish. "I don't know. Bomi takes care of her sister and brother, so her relatives shouldn't judge her. But I guess even if the majority accepted our relationship, it wouldn't work out. We're so different. Bomi would never come to a party like this."

"Why not?"

"Because this isn't her type of crowd. This is a fast crowd and one the older Koreans don't approve of. In a lot of ways, Bomi is old-fashioned. She likes to dress conservatively, is afraid to show a little skin. She would not wear this." Jules points to the cutouts in her sexy black one-piece.

"She doesn't seem to mind how you dress or act or talk."

Jules's lower lip pushes forward slightly. "I know."

She really adores Bomi.

"What are you two discussing so intently?" Yujun is alone finally. He leans back and stretches an arm across the top of the rattan love seat. The buttons of his loose-fitting cream embroidered shirt have given up at the midway point. Both the red silk cord of his necklace and the jade duck are visible, nestled between two hard, defined pecs. Mouthwatering, really.

"Swimsuits," I answer when I roll my tongue back into my mouth.

"*Mukbangs*," Jules says.

"Chuseok," I add. I'm not sure if Jules wants to share what's going on in her life, and it's not my story to tell.

At the mention of the upcoming holiday, Yujun's face hardens slightly. My own gut tightens as my friends' words swirl in my head. *When it is time to hold* jesa *during Chuseok and honor the ancestors, Yujun will be invited but Hara will not. At a wedding of his cousin or the baptism of a niece, Hara will be left out again. . . . Choi Yujun is an extrovert. He loves people. He loves his family.*

Maybe I should be the one worrying about Chuseok, not Jules.

Yujun has other ideas. "Are you spending it with anyone, Jules-nim?"

He's always so formal with Jules—well, with anyone other than Sangki and me.

"My roommates and I get together with some other expats and have Thanksgiving buffet at Route 66."

"If you wish to do something different, you can come to our Chuseok. We won't even make you cook."

"I'll think about it." Jules stands up. "I'm getting in the water. There's no way that I'm here at Summer Splash and I'm not getting wet. I didn't buy a special swimsuit for nothing." She hauls me to my feet. "Come on. I'm not going in alone."

We dance in the water, drink too many piña coladas, laugh loudly—so loudly that the girls next to us start giving us sour side-eyes, but I don't care. For one, they're wearing heels in the pool so how can they be annoyed with us, and for two, when Sangki throws merch into the pool, an autographed T-shirt wrapped tight with rubber bands hits Jules in the face and knocks her off the unicorn floatie. How can I not laugh at that?

When Sangki's set is over, we drag ourselves out of the pool and wrap up with the complimentary towels provided. Despite the mid-August heat, it's chilly at night, especially here near Namsan. Sangki joins our table, and a roving photographer from the club snaps a few photos for publicity. Sangki and Yujun put their heads together and scrunch up their eyes in a way that I wouldn't have been comfortable doing back home, but on them and in this setting, it looks adorable.

"We should go on a cable car ride," Sangki suggests after the photographer leaves.

"No." I huddle around a new drink; this time it's pink and fruity. A chunk of ice hits the back of my wisdom tooth and I wince from the sensation.

"She's afraid it's going to crash," Yujun explains. He reaches past my face to grab a glazed chicken skewer. His sleeves are rolled up and I get a nice flash of skin. Bare chest, exposed forearms, thick thighs cozied next to mine, his glossy black hair hanging over his eyes. It's wonderful. Whoever invented pool parties is right up there with Einstein and his theories of relativity. Absolute geniuses.

"Have we ever had a cable car fall at Namsan?" wonders Sangki.

Yujun shakes his head. "Not that I can remember."

"There was a crash at the platform because the operator didn't put the brakes on. Rumor has it he was staring at his phone. No serious injuries." Sangki tips his beer back.

"And what if the operator is busy looking at his phone and accidentally speeds the car up and it flies off the cable, plummeting to the ground?"

Yujun muffles a laugh while Jules rolls her eyes. "Then you hope in your next life, you're rewarded with something special for the trauma you endured in this one."

CHAPTER ELEVEN

"SHOULD WE GO HOME OR WOULD YOU LIKE TO SEE MY apartment?"

Yujun has turned on the heat even though it's August. Pool parties are fun in the moment, but when your ass is covered in damp Lycra for most of the night, the romance of the concept wears off. I pull the towel that Yujun paid for close around my frame and wonder if the shiver is from excitement or cold. "Apartment."

"Let me text *Eomma*."

It's nearly midnight. "You think she's awake?"

"She is, and even if she's not, I don't want her to worry."

He's so thoughtful, and even that comes off as incredibly sexy. I'm really gone. Under the towel, I clasp my hands together so I don't attack him while he's driving. The traffic is light and it takes us no time to get from Namsan down to Yongsan, where Yujun's place is. The apartment complex is close enough to IF Group that

Yujun could walk, but not so close that I can see the river—at least not from the ground.

He tucks me close to his side as we ride the elevator up to the ninth floor.

"Don't expect too much. It's small," he says.

It could be a box and I wouldn't care. We're together. That's all that matters; besides, Yujun's concept of space is skewed. He grew up in a mansion, but as he leads me into his place, I realize it *is* small. The room is square, with the bedroom area partitioned off with smoky glass walls to give the illusion of more space. Once you pass the shoewell and entrance closets that are standard in every Korean apartment, there's a door on the left leading to the bathroom. On the right are floor-to-ceiling wardrobes that give way to a tidy galley kitchen with a two-burner cooktop, a small but fancy-looking oven, and a sink. I presume there's a refrigerator somewhere behind one of the cabinet doors. Approximately twenty feet from the end of the bed is a set of large windows overlooking a twenty-floor-tall office building.

The walls that aren't lined with cabinets and wardrobes are papered with wheat-colored grass cloth. The cabinet fronts are stained a brown-black and the floor is a dark wood, too. It reminds me a little of his rooms back at Wansu's house. Between the bed and the panel of windows, a singular long black leather sofa sits. There are no yellow pillows, but it's not white like Wansu's either.

"I feel misled," I declare, looking out the windows at the city streetlights below.

"In what way?" Yujun fills a kettle with water and sets it on a burner.

"You said there were yellow pillows."

He tilts his head toward the center of the room. "On the bed."

The apartment is small enough that it only takes me a few strides to decide that he's confused about the color wheel. "These are off-white."

"Lemon yellow. That's what the package said. Hungry? I'm going to make some *ramyeon*."

"I'd love some."

"Do you want spicy pork or spicy chicken?" He holds up two packages.

"Chicken."

"Egg?"

"Yes, please."

He presses on a cabinet door and it swings open to reveal a small refrigerator. "Cheese?"

"Yes, please." Yujun introduced me to cheese ramyeon before he left and it was surprisingly delicious. "Can I help?"

"No. It's *ramyeon*, and even Wansu can make that."

"Why even Wansu?"

"She's a disaster in the kitchen. My dad used to make fun of her—how she could do everything from speaking four languages to solving complex math equations in her head, but put her in the kitchen and she immediately becomes less helpful than a toddler." He digs a few more things out of the refrigerator and plucks a knife off a magnet strip on the side of the cabinet. "Mrs. Ji taught me a few basics before I went to college and I picked up a few skills in the army. The Korean military teaches you how to shoot a gun, find a land mine, and cook a stew. You can pull out a couple of seat mats, though. It's in the last entry closet. We'll eat at the table." He gestures to the wood and marble coffee table in front of the sofa.

As I'm squeezing by him, he drops a kiss on the top of my fore-head and a flush of heat zips from my crown to my toes. This is a domestic scene. He's cooking. I'm setting the table. The bed with its off-white, not at all yellow, pillows is a few feet away. Anticipa-tion hums inside me.

"There are also chopsticks and table mats in a drawer under the table," he adds as I carry the floor pillows over to the window. I love that I'm getting an actual visual of how Yujun spends his evenings when he's home from work. He throws a pillow on the floor in front of the sofa, heats up some water for a bowl of *ramyeon*, and then . . . well, I'm not sure what he does after that, but I'm going to learn.

Moments later he joins me, setting down two trays—one for each of us. There are little plates of kimchi, soybeans, and soy sauce cucumbers, a small covered dish decorated with painted flowers along the edges, and the bowl of *ramyeon* trimmed with green on-ion sprinkled over a slice of American cheese. I straighten my chopsticks and poke at the cheese. "We're big on cheese in Amer-ica. How is it that we never thought of this combo before?"

Yujun's twin dimples appear on his cheeks before he digs in. "I'm not sure. The GIs introduced processed cheese to us during the Korean War. Someone put it on *ramyeon* and the rest is history. Eat up before the noodles get swollen."

I watch as Yujun pierces the cheese with his chopsticks and lifts his noodle-laden chopsticks to his mouth. The melted yellow cheese glides down the noodles like drops of thick rain. He closes his eyes and makes a small moaning sound that echoes in parts of my body that are hungry for something other than food.

I slurp down my own noodles until all that's left in my bowl is a cheesy broth with small bits of green onion and maybe a tiny bit of egg.

He watches with approval, and as I finish the meal, he gestures toward the skyline outside the windows. "Do you know what Yongsan stands for?"

"No."

"Yongsan means 'Dragon Mountain.' *Yong* is 'dragon' and you know that *san* is 'mountain.'"

"Right, like Namsan or Bukhansan."

His left dimple appears. "Exactly. Back in like AD 90, Korea was divided into three kingdoms. The central kingdom was Baekje. During King Giru's reign, a sighting of two dragons flying over the Han was recorded, and thus this region was named Yongsan, shielded in the rear by Namsan and protected in the front by the Han. Or you can believe that the mountains look somewhat like a crooked dragon."

By the scornful way he refers to the second explanation, you can tell he views the latter as sorry and sad and only suitable for those who have no heart. Yujun is the man who gave me a jade duck on a red cord and said that ducks mate for life or die. He's a romantic. Who likes cheese on his *ramyeon*.

"The dragon is our most mythical creature because it is virtually indestructible. Its body is covered in scaled armor. It has claws and horns. It can fly, jump, climb, and no one can escape its wrath. The king's throne is *yongjwa*, or 'chair of the dragon,' and his clothing was known as *yongpo*, 'the clothing of the dragon.' Any sign of the dragon is revered. Almost all of the subway station names reference some part of Korean history. Like Seongsu means 'Holy Water.' There was a stream in that area that was so pure you could drink directly from the source, so it became the town with holy water."

I shove my bowl aside and lean back against the base of the sofa. "That's it? Is that all you know?" I tease.

He launches into a full etymological discussion of the other subway stops. Banghak is for a crane and Nokcheon is for a deer that bathed in a stream after a natural disaster. Dolgoji means skewer made of stone and represents the black rocks on the range of Mount Cheonjang. And as he talks, I explore—not the apartment or the recesses of his medicine cabinet—but him. I test the steel of his thigh, the warmth of the skin of the back of his hand, the tender region along his collarbone exposed by the open neckline of his shirt.

He pauses after Boramae, the falcon that represents the air force, whose academy used to be situated at the current Boramae Park.

"Don't stop," I whisper against the shell of his ear.

He goes on, but I don't hear him over the swell of desire that has filled my head and infused my body. His hand comes up to hover at my waist, as if he's unsure if he moves whether I'll stop, but I won't. I'm learning him. I'm learning that licking the curve of his inner ear makes him shudder and that his pec will jump under my palm. I'm learning that his eyelashes are longer than I recall and that his thick hair is kept in check by a slight undercut, unnoticeable unless you brush the outer strands aside. I'm learning that his smell is like sunshine and forest and comfort and need, all of it wrapped up in one heady scent. I'm learning that his patience can be snapped.

He stands abruptly and scoops me into his arms. Two strides

and I'm on the bed. He slaps his hand on a button near the night-stand and the soft whirring of a motor engages as the curtains slide shut.

"Fancy," I murmur.

"Necessary," he replies.

I have a fleeting thought about who else he's had on this bed making those curtains necessary but shove that out of my head because it doesn't matter who he's had in the past. I'm here now. I twine my arms around his neck and pull him to me. His hand on my waist, his mouth on my neck, his heavy frame pressing me into the mattress—those are the meaningful things.

This moment is different from the others. We've had sex in an Airbnb room, a frantic near coupling in an office restroom, a for-bidden encounter in his mother's—my mother's—house, but here there is no time limit, no worry about interlopers, no heavy thoughts, just him and me, skin to skin, mouth to mouth.

I sink deeply into the feelings, into him. When there is only Yujun and me, the outside world and its constraints and rules and expectations do not exist. I open my legs and pull him into my body, matching his urgent strokes with thrusts of my own. He kisses me or I kiss him. It's hard to say. Neither of us lasts long, not this first round. Our hunger is equal and our need is unquenched. It's been too long and so almost before we descend from the moun-taintop we begin the climb again, our limbs never untangling, our skin never separating. We moan and laugh and sigh, fingers dig-ging deep into thighs and shoulders. His mouth is everywhere, from my jaw and my breasts and my knees and the soft spot on my inner thighs to the even softer spot between my legs.

His tongue does wicked things that curl my toes and I repay him a thousandfold, taking his length into my mouth, swallowing him deep. I lose all my inhibitions and ride him mercilessly, until he's the one begging for release. I kiss his dimples, the ones that grow deep enough to drown in when he's at his happiest. We collapse onto the mattress full of sweat and tender feelings. As I drift into neverland, he whispers in drowsy, deep Korean that he missed me, that he loves me, that he's home.

CHAPTER TWELVE

ON MONDAY, CARRYING TWO COFFEES, I TAKE THE ELEVATOR to the fourteenth floor instead of getting off on the seventh. One of my privileges as Wansu's daughter is that there is no place I can't go, including Bomi's desk in the Research and Development Department. It's still early and there's almost no one present, except for my friend, who is diligently bent over her work. Of course she would be here early.

"Hara, is everything all right?" She stands up immediately and rushes to my side. "Should I call Wansu? Don't you ride to work with her?"

"Not always and not today. I came early." I hand her one of the drinks. "I need you to come save me for lunch. *Bujang-nim* is always telling me and the other two women in my office to eat together, but I think they've got plans, so please don't make me look like a loser who has to eat on her own."

"I eat on my own."

"I'm not calling you names or anything," I tease.

Bomi bestows a small smile. "I'll meet you in the lobby a little after one?"

"Yes. We are going to the pork truck again." I wave bye and head down the hall toward Yujun's office.

"Hara!" Bomi whines.

"I know you love it," I call to her and disappear around the corner. After that errand is finished, I bounce down to the seventh floor and settle in to work.

Even though I am still proofing the document that I proofed two weeks ago, the anticipation of seeing Bomi for lunch helps the morning go by quickly. That and the occasional text I get from Yujun informing me that he arrived at the office, that he appreciated the iced Americano that I left there, and that he's happy to be back in Korea.

No one is happier than me.

ME: I'm having lunch with Bomi today

YUJUN: What about me? 😠

ME: I left you the iced Americano what more do you want

YUJUN: 😔

ME: It's a workday! Don't answer that

YUJUN: LOL

For the sake of my sanity, he moves on.

YUJUN: it's my turn to take you to eat without sangki. save your Friday night

ME: Saved!

I'm giddy.

"Did you get good news?"

I'm momentarily silenced by surprise at Chaeyoung's question. I glance at the desk next to mine where Soyou usually sits and discover it's empty. I was so absorbed in my texting that I didn't realize she'd left.

"Yes. I did. I"—don't want to tell Chaeyoung I'm going on a date with Yujun because she might find it off-putting or more evidence of my nepotism hire—"got a notice that there was a sale on a pair of earrings I liked."

"They must be very pretty."

"Very. Silver with dangling pearls." As my mouth moves indiscriminately, the rest of my brain is telling me to shut up because finding these is going to be a real bitch if Chaeyoung asks to see them.

"Was the Summer Splash Party fun?"

The light bulb goes on. She must've seen photos of me at the event. "It was. Sangki got us in because the tickets have been sold out for a while, he said."

"Yes. They sell out in seconds." She snaps her fingers and the jewels embedded in her nails twinkle.

"You should come with us next time."

"It was the last one."

"There's the Banpo Music Fest," I suggest.

"Maybe." She starts to swivel away.

Desperately, I throw out, "I have backstage passes."

She turns back. "From DJ Song?"

I blank and then remember that's Sangki's stage name. "Yes. From him."

"Could I bring a frie—" She cuts off and her eyes fly to a space over my shoulder.

Soyou must be back. Chaeyoung resumes typing as if she wasn't trying to finagle celebrity perks from me ten seconds ago. I rub a finger across my eyebrow in frustration and counsel myself to take this slow. If I start walking across the earth, at some point I'll make it around the entire world. This is the second time that Chaeyoung has initiated a conversation with me, which means she's thawing. I'm at least a mile into our journey to becoming frenemies. By the end of the year, maybe she'll gather up enough courage to speak to me when Soyou is around. It's progress.

"You seem happy today," Bomi observes as we make our way to the pork truck.

"The sun is out but it's not too hot. There's no pollution warning. Yujun is back." I can't keep the grin off my face. "You should've come with us to the pool party. It was fun even though I had to wear a swimsuit. There were girls there wearing heels in the pool!"

"It's a glamorous group. I saw a lot of photos on Instagram."

"The Banpo Music Fest is soon. Why don't you come with me?"

"Maybe I will."

There's no line to the food truck, and Yang Ilhwa greets me with a wave of her metal spatula. As usual, we don't even have to place our order anymore. I bite into the crunchy fried croquette immediately.

"Mmm. These are so good, *Imo*." I wipe a crumb off the corner of my mouth. "Did I tell you I almost killed Wansu last weekend?"

Bomi chokes on her croquette. "What?" she asks with watery eyes.

I hand her a napkin and explain how I mixed up the *gochujang* and soybean paste. Yang Ilhwa stops cooking to listen to the story. "*Aigoo*." She shakes her head. "You come here and I teach you how to cook."

"It's a deal, *Imo*. Tell me the time and date."

"Anytime. I am here all day. You come."

"I will. Thanks for the food."

She leans over and places another pork ball in my paper tray. "You good girl. Eat well."

The small praise makes me glow.

"You shouldn't have promised because now she will expect you," Bomi warns as we take a seat on the curb.

"Good. I plan to. Even if I have to take a day off"—as if my real work schedule is so crushing—"I'll do it. She seems lonely. Gosh, I'm thirsty. I'll be right back."

I run into the convenience store and buy two iced Americanos with pretty idol boys on the label.

"I can't drink this," she jokes as she takes the drink from me. "I'm in the fandom of their competitor."

"After you drink it, stomp on the can and it'll be like crushing them."

She considers it for a half second and then agrees.

"I saw in the advertisements for the Banpo Music Fest that there are a lot of families that attend. Do you want to bring your brother and sister?" She doesn't answer right away and I can guess what she's thinking. "I don't know if Jules will be coming, if that's what is making you hesitate."

"Oh." It's a small sound with a little bit of pain and a lot of guilt.

"You don't have to make up your mind today. It's not for another couple of weeks."

"It's because I care about her that I don't think we should see each other," Bomi bursts out.

"Okay." I open my drink.

"I didn't think about the consequences, only that she was lovely and fun and I liked how I felt when I was with her."

"That sounds great, though."

"But then when you asked about Yujun, I realized that I could never have an open relationship with her. You know what happened in her last relationship? Her boyfriend hid her away like she was a bad secret and then dumped her for a Korean girl. I realized that I can't do that to her again." Bomi's lip quivers, but she inhales deeply and swallows the lump in her throat. "This is not America, where same-sex relationships are accepted. This is Korea, and even if it were legal, which it is not, there are many families that would not approve. I am responsible for my *dongsaengs*. They will need education and jobs and marriage in the future. I am not the right one for Jules. I'm sorry."

God. I place an arm around my friend's shoulders. "You do not need to apologize." At least, not to me. "But in our circle, you would be welcome. Whatever you decide, you're welcome."

She sniffles and nods, tucking her small frame against mine. Our iced Americanos are forgotten and our lunch grows cold. Neither of us is hungry anymore. We get to our feet and trudge back to IF Group. I don't understand why things that bring happiness to our lives are always a battle. It's unfair, like how all the delicious-tasting food such as chocolate and ice cream and French fries are bad for you and the things that are good for you are kale smoothies and riced cauliflower.

At five, I leave even though my coworkers are still hunched over their desks. Before I go, I order dinner to be delivered for the team under Chaeyoung's name. The delivery system here is so efficient that I cross paths with the black bean noodle delivery person as he is entering into the lobby and I'm exiting.

At home, Mrs. Ji flutters around me as I prep the ingredients for dinner. The soup base of rice water and anchovy, kelp, dried mushroom, and pepper packet simmers while I julienne the radish. Mrs. Ji shows me how to strain the soybean paste into the soup base so that the broth is clear and clean. She pulls out two spoons for a taste test. The broth is light at first, but when it hits the middle of my mouth, the depth of the flavors sinks in. I love it but I need an impartial opinion.

Mrs. Ji is expressionless as she folds the liquid over her tongue, allowing the broth to rest in her mouth like a wine. When she finally swallows, I'm on the balls of my feet in anticipation of her judgment. Her simple and slow nod of approval sends my spirit skyrocketing.

The aromatic broth steams around the kitchen, reminding me of the times when I was young and Ellen cooked Korean food for me, before I grew dumb and ashamed of my heritage. My childhood wasn't solely bacon and corn; it was also kimchi and seaweed soup and *japchae* and bulgogi.

Heat pricks my eyes and I honestly don't know if it's emotion or the soup. I press the back of my hand to my eyelids and keep moving, scooping out the mushrooms, slicing them thin. The *jeon* mixture is next. As I mix the batter, Mrs. Ji heats the earthenware for the soup. We don't talk—at all—but there's no need to. Our language right now is cooking. When the *jeon* batter is ready, Mrs. Ji has a frypan with oil prepared. I thank her and she gives me another brief nod. She's not beaming but she's lost the worried expression. She no longer believes I'm out to poison the family she's

been taking care of since long before I arrived. While I fry the fritters, she tosses radish and mushrooms into the soup.

We move together as a team, readying the small side dishes and
then ladling the soup into the heated stone bowls.

Yujun wanders in as I plate the *jeon*. "This smells amazing. Did
you make it?"

"With Mrs. Ji's help."

"*Ani.*" She shakes her head. "She did all work. I watch only."

"She helped," I repeat.

Yujun's dimple pops out. He's delighted I'm getting along with
Mrs. Ji. "Can I do anything?"

"Go change. We'll be ready in ten minutes."

"Yes, Captain." He gives me a smart salute and then escapes before the dish towel I throw in his direction lands.

By the time dinner is completely ready, Wansu is at the table
wearing a soft blue silk pant set while Yujun is in jeans and a long-
sleeve faded green cashmere sweater with the sleeves pushed up to
his elbows.

The individual stone bowls are so hot that the soup is still bub-
bling when we set them on the table.

Yujun rubs his hands together in anticipation. "Smells delicious. *Masitgyeda.*"

The *banchan* is a mix of my *jeon* and seasoned soybeans and
scallions and Mrs. Ji's *gamja jorin*, baby potatoes she roasted first
and then braised with soy sauce, rice wine, and brown sugar. The
soup is the main course along with marinated and grilled *galbi*.

Wansu's approach is more measured, maybe even hesitant, as if
she can't quite shake off the bad memory of the other night when I
nearly killed her with the *gochujang* I'd added to the stew. I pretend
not to care, but I will be crushed if she doesn't like it.

"It's good, Samo-nim. I tasted it myself," Mrs. Ji encourages Wansu, using the term "lady of the house," as Mrs. Ji always does.

I almost want to cry at this visible sign of support. Yujun gives Mrs. Ji a thumbs-up on my behalf before she retires to the kitchen.

"I am sure it is delicious. I was waiting for the soup to cool down." Wansu dips her spoon into the bowl and takes a small taste. When the spice doesn't blow the back of her head off, she takes a large one and then another. Her stern mouth lifts slightly and she gives me a gentle nod of approval. "Very good. The flavors are very good . . . very Korean."

If I have stars in my eyes, everyone look away. "Thank you."

Yujun is beaming; both dimples are showing. This time when the table falls silent and the sounds are only brass spoons against fired clay, I don't feel any discomfort. It's a companionable silence and it doesn't last long. Soon, Yujun is talking about the pool party, sharing a funny story about how Sangki almost fell into the water trying to avoid a flamingo floatie and that I saved him by grabbing his shirt, only for it to rip. Wansu smiles, which is the equivalent of a laugh from her, and even though I spend the night alone, I go to sleep happy. Yujun is only down the hall. Wansu lost the tightness around her mouth that seemed like it would be permanent. There's only one small pebble in my happiness shoe, and that's the situation between Bomi and Jules. That will work itself out. I fall asleep dreaming up new things to make. Maybe an apple pie. I'm really good at apple pies.

CHAPTER THIRTEEN

Wear sneakers, **YUJUN TEXTS ME ON FRIDAY.**

> ME: This sounds athletic. You know I'm no good at those
> things.
>
> YUJUN: You've said so but I have not seen any evidence
>
> ME: Is this a test
>
> YUJUN: It will be fun

Anything with Yujun is fun. Jumping out of a plane would be
fun with him, and I'm scared of heights.

Yujun's surprise date is at a virtual reality arcade. There are private rooms for group activities but we stick to the main space, filled
with rows of simulated racing machines and experience pods. A

staff person straps me to a waist-high railing shaped in a half circle and Yujun helps me don a pair of goggles and special gloves. Because of my fear of heights, I opt to swim on the ocean floor. Yujun skydives. He tries to get me to jump with him but the VR is too real and I refuse to do anything more adventurous than a hot-air balloon. Even that has me clinging to him. He laughs in my ear, the small puffs of air reassuring me that I won't fall, that he's holding me.

"How long will you be like this?" he teases. "We will not be able to ride on the Namsan cable car."

"Has this been a goal of yours?" I stare up at the fake fire powering the fake balloon instead of the fake ground that looks a thousand miles below my feet.

"That cable car has never failed."

"There's always a first time."

He laughs again and hugs me. "Then we fall together."

"You'd be right about that. I have no plans on going up in that tin can with anyone else."

"There's also a few paragliding places." There's a big smile on his face and his left dimple is so deep that I could fall into it and never come out.

"I will watch you from the ground and take a thousand pictures. You're welcome."

His chest shakes with his happiness. I lean in, resting my cheek against that solid surface. Hearing him laugh, feeling his warmth, I can almost make myself believe that this will all work out. Yujun takes one more solo flight trip while I eat a snack and watch him sway on his platform. He should look foolish with his arms outstretched, leaning left and right as he simulates flight motions, but he is one of those people who can get away with doing anything. It might be because his frame is lean and long and he has a certain elegance in movement. It could be my love-tainted vision. Possibly both.

His face is all smiles, dimpled cheeks, and bright eyes when he's finished. "Hungry?" he asks after we return the equipment.

"Yes." I wasn't really, but a meal means more time with him and I will never turn that down.

"Should we take the metro? I know you love it."

I do. It makes me feel like a Seoulite, navigating the subway system, eating food from the vendors in the underground, buying twenty-thousand-won shoes and one-thousand-won socks. These are things ordinary people in Seoul do, and there's nothing more that I long for than to feel ordinary here in this big city that gave birth to me.

Yujun holds my hand and sneaks a quick kiss. Hand-holding and matching outfits and couple rings are common, but a kiss in a public place is not. I guess it's the one out-of-the-ordinary thing I enjoy. We take the 6 train and get off at the World Cup Stadium Station exit. It takes about thirty minutes to get to Nanji Hangang Park but it's a nice night, and I am, as Yujun requested, wearing tennis shoes.

"This used to be a garbage fill, but it was rebuilt. There's a camping site and a marina. You can set up your own tent or rent one," he explains as we cross over the bridge and approach the park. The Nanji Hangang Park is more like a campground. The ground is packed hard and covered mostly in dirt, with only a few green areas carefully tended in between the sandy roads. Yujun points out a graffitied concrete skate bowl and a field of huge reeds to the east. Below us the tent city dots a grassy expanse that is separated from the riverbank by a wide paved boulevard. The tents are mostly small ones—the kind that you have to crawl to get inside, and as I watch, some of them are moving in a recognizable rhythm.

"Are they . . . ?" I trail off.

Yujun winks at me. "Teenagers. Some adults but mostly teens, who, for obvious reasons, need some privacy. The tents are supposed to have two sides open, and some parks, like the Yeouido one, make you take down the tent after seven."

"Really?" I hope Yujun and I are never so desperate for privacy that we rent a tent here at the river for some conjugal action. I'd cry. "Please tell me we aren't here to rent a tent."

"I have the apartment, Hara." He's amused.

"Right. Right." As if I could forget. My dream is to hide in that small jewel box of an apartment and pretend that he is not Choi Yujun, stepson of Choi Wansu, and I am not Choi Hara, daughter of Choi Wansu. "I never did get the view of the Han."

Yujun chuckles. "That was in the advertisement, but you can only see it if you stand on the toilet seat and stick your neck out of the window to the southwest. I bought it because it is close to IF Group, and when I work late, it takes too long to get home. *Eomma*'s place is still home to me. Even before you came, I would spend many nights there and most weekends."

"Your dad is there," I add. "When I got my own place after college, I was lonely, too. And I worried about my mom, Ellen, being alone. I worry about that now, to be honest. She's back in Des Moines all by herself."

"Living here would be too foreign for her, wouldn't it?" He squeezes my hand.

"I think so. The language barrier is a lot." Plus, Ellen said she didn't feel comfortable because she stood out, the only white woman in the midst of millions of Koreans.

"How come there are no barges on the river? It's almost always empty." The main waterway closest to me is the Mississippi River and it is full of tugboats and barges moving cargo up and down the north-south commerce artery.

"It's zoned for residential traffic only because it's connected to North Korea. The river starts in the Kumgang Mountains, joins another river to form the Han. About fifteen years ago, Seoul decided it would try to create a"—he pauses, searching for the right word—"greenbelt?"

"Yes, greenbelt. I know what that is."

"The government decided to create many greenbelts to encourage Seoulites to enjoy the outdoors and to help with pollution, as it is very bad here."

Air quality is of constant concern to Seoulites. Every home has an air purifier. There are several in the office. The government sends us text alerts to wear masks outside if the air quality is poor, but tonight, the sky is clear, the air is fine, and Yujun's hand covers mine. Honestly, I'd be out here in a sandstorm if it meant I could be with him.

His stomach grumbles, reminding me of why we came here in the first place. "This way." He pulls me down a walkway to a concrete boulevard that's lit up by streetlamps and lights from various vendors.

My eyes land on a familiar vision. "A food truck. In fact, I think it's the Yongsan pork lady."

"There are restaurants here."

"I can't skip a food truck, Yujun. It's part of my civic duty to help small-business owners."

His dimple winks into view. "Okay. I, too, am a proud citizen of the Republic of Korea. Let us do our patriotic duty."

We hurry over and get in line. To my delight, it is indeed Yang Ilhwa from Yongsan. I wave to her and she waves back in recognition.

"You know each other?"

"She parks in an alley not too far from IF Group. I've eaten there a few times." A few dozen times. "The pork balls are very good."

"I didn't know there was a food truck over in that area."

We order a whole tray of the fried food, including a new dish with crispy pork belly, which Yang Ilhwa slathers with parsley and some kind of creamy hot sauce. It basically tastes like a form of bacon-wrapped cheese curds in all of its melty, salty goodness. I devour five of them, while Yujun massacres the rest of the container.

"These are good," he exclaims. "I haven't had them before, but it's like *tonkatsu* but stuffed with cheese."

"Yes." *Tonkatsu* is fried pork cutlet. It's funny how we both have our different food frames of reference for the same types of flavors. When he's done, we find a dessert stall serving powdered sugar doughnuts and banana milk in cartons no bigger than a fist. Walking away from the stall, we narrowly avoid a pack of teens careening down the cement on skateboards. They run into an older couple and the man curses at them. The kids shout something at him, one of them bows, and they all run off. But for the language difference, it could've taken place at the Riverwalk in Des Moines. Okay, but for the language, the fact that these are all Koreans, and the size of this park, this could be the same. We are not so different, Des Moines and Seoul.

"You have some sugar," Yujun starts to say but decides he might as well take care of me. He leans down until his face is a whisper away from mine and brushes the back of his pinkie along my cheek. His knuckle catches against the corner of my lip, and while it shouldn't, that brief touch makes my whole body clench. I sway toward him, my hand finding purchase at his waist. I'm so close I can feel the swift inhale of his breath and then a slow, painful hiss of release. "Hara—"

"Choi Yujun-nim?"

Both our heads pop up in response. I guess we are tent desperate despite what we proclaimed earlier. I take a step away from him, putting a safe distance between me and temptation before turning to see who addressed us. It's a man and a woman, about our age. He's wearing jeans rolled up slightly above his ankles, a pair of expensive tennis shoes designed to look dirty, and a T-shirt with a designer logo emblazoned across his chest, matching the one on his shoes. Over it, he has a loose-fitting black blazer. The woman has a similar blazer, but underneath is a white dress with little blue and pink bouquets embroidered all over. On her feet are a pair of snowy white tennis shoes with the same logo that's on his shoes and shirt. Her handbag is also a designer brand.

"Kim Seokhoon-nim." Yujun dips his head. "It has been a long time. Have you been well?"

"Yes." Kim bows in return and eyes me speculatively. *Who is this girl he does not know holding the hand of someone he does?* he silently questions.

"This is Hara Wilson. Hara, Kim Soekhoon and Park Soomin. They are old friends." Yujun makes the introductions.

The girl stiffens at my name. She recognizes me—not me personally, but whatever was on the forums or in the press that trended for days right before I took the job at IF Group—she remembers. He does, too.

"Oh, this is your sister . . ." His eyes fall to our clasped hands.

Yujun's fingers flex around mine, an angry gesture. And, I, who hate confrontation, jerk my hand away and shove my fingers into the pockets of my pants. The girl backs away, clearly not wanting to greet me. She tugs at the arm of her male friend. The guy makes a half shrug and says, "Sorry," in Korean, and he walks away, too.

Yujun is furious. I can feel the heat of his anger radiating from him in waves. He takes a step toward the couple. I haul him back with two hands. "No. Don't."

"It's not okay," he seethes. "That bastard's father went to jail for tax fraud and embezzlement, but they can't be polite and greet you."

I knew that it wasn't okay, but I also knew that Yujun couldn't force someone to accept me, not by punching them or with words.

CHAPTER FOURTEEN

I CAN'T KEEP LAST NIGHT'S ENCOUNTER OUT OF MY HEAD. THE part where the girl physically recoiled keeps replaying over and over.

While there are no laws that keep Hara and Yujun apart, traditions will. . . . Choi Wansu did not send Yujun away or prepare dating profiles for you because she does not think you are good enough for Yujun or that he is not good enough for you. She does it because she loves you and does not want to see you in pain. . . . I realized that I could never have an open relationship with her. You know what happened in her last relationship? Her boyfriend hid her away like she was a bad secret and then dumped her for a Korean girl. I realized that I can't do that to her again.

I can't imagine a relationship where one person is the source of constant embarrassment and pain for the other. How would that work? It wouldn't.

I stare at my screensaver. I need a distraction. There must be something I can do. I'm going to have to have a frank talk with *Bujang-nim*, and if there is truly nothing for me to do, then I need to move to another division. I don't know what that would be. Maybe I could monitor the security cameras. That wouldn't require language skills.

He's not at his desk this morning. When his phone rings, I jump up and answer it before anyone else even raises their head. To my everlasting joy, the person on the other end speaks English. They're from LA and want to know when the marketing materials for an upcoming trade show will be delivered.

"I'll leave a note and we will get back to you right away."

The phone rings again almost before the receiver is fully settled. This time the speaker is Korean and I don't understand a word. In halting, horribly pronounced Korean, I ask for their name and number. The answer comes fast and I'm sure I get it wrong. I repeat it, but before I can get out the last digit, the person has hung up.

Chaeyoung makes a disgusted noise. Guess we won't be moving into frenemy territory soon. She must've lost her desire to cozy up to celebrities.

I shoot her a glare. "If you have something to say, say it." She glares back but remains silent. "I thought so."

I stomp over to my desk and stare at Soyou's empty chair. She's been gone for a while. I wonder where she is. *Bujang-nim* shows up about ten minutes later. All fired up, I ask him for more work.

He brushes a hand across his chin. "I sent you a project."

"I worked on that two weeks ago."

His eyes fall to the awkwardly penned *Hangul* on the sticky note. "I'll get back to you. In the meantime, you could study your Korean."

Chaeyoung snickers.

I clench my fingers into fists and push my nails into my palms to control my flaring temper. She'll meet Ahn Sangki over my dead body. Cheeks burning, I lift my chin. "Sure. I'll do that."

Back at my desk, I pull out a notebook and start lettering the *Hangul* characters. Soyou appears, looking uncharacteristically mussed. Her usually tidy hair looks as if she's run her fingers through it several times in frustration, and her skirt is askew. It's the sign of a bad morning. I've been there, and if we were closer, I'd slide her a chocolate bar or maybe send her a funny gif, but we're not, so I keep my hands and thoughts to myself. She shucks her slightly scuffed heels and shoves her feet into her office slippers—the ones most employees wear at their desks. When she slumps into her chair, her shirt pulls to one side, revealing a bruise on her collarbone. Strict Soyou making out with someone in the bathroom at IF Group strikes me as unusual, but it's definitely a hickey. The security guards are sort of hot. Maybe she's hooking up with one of them. Even so, I'm sure she would be mortified if she knew what she was revealing.

I tap my fingers against my desk, telling myself that Soyou hates me and would not ask me for help if I was the only person standing between her and a speeding train. I last five minutes before scratching myself in the very same spot, hoping that my actions will prompt her to check herself, but she doesn't look my way even once. I scuffle my feet against the floor and make loud throat-clearing noises. When she finally glares at me, I pat my collarbone. Her eyes flare in some kind of recognition. A slam of her desk drawer and a muttered curse later, she's off to the bathroom. When she returns, her shirt is buttoned all the way up to her neck.

I pull out my phone and restart my Korean lesson. I'm conjugating verbs now. Every ten minutes or so, I check my inbox, but it remains stubbornly empty. I'm not even getting Korean spam. Saturated with grammar rules, my head starts to ache. When you're not busy, time slows to a crawl. The minute hand never moves. Your eyelids get heavy even if you've had hours and hours of sleep. I press the tips of my fingers into my sockets and shout silently to wake up. I might be a drag on this team, but I can't be caught sleeping, literally.

Salvation comes in the form of Yujun, who sends me a text around eleven.

YUJUN: Take a coffee break. I'm in the stairwell.

I smush my lips together to hide a smile and tuck my phone into my pocket.

"*Keopi?*" I ask and make a motion with my fingers of running an errand. For the first time today, people talk to me.

"I'll have an iced Americano. Two packets of sugar," one calls.

"I'll have the same. No sugar," says Yoo.

Chaeyoung looks up, but when she sees that Soyou is ignoring me, she puts her head down. No one else makes a request.

Yujun is leaning against the stair rail when I arrive. I almost launch myself into his arms, remembering at the last minute the security camera. I back away and jerk my head toward the flashing red light. Yujun curses under his breath. He shoves his hands in his pockets.

"I won't be home until late tonight. My department wants to have a team dinner to celebrate my return. I offered the company credit card, but they insist that I come."

"It's not a problem," I say with false brightness, as if my entire day isn't ruined.

"Come here." He reaches for me.

With a finger upward, I remind him of the security camera.

"I don't care. Come here."

I resist for a half second and then cave because it's been a long morning and I need this. I press my cheek against his hard chest and listen to his heart for a beat of five and then ten. "I need to get coffee," I mumble against his shirtfront.

"I need to go back to my desk."

His cell phone rings. Neither of us moves. It rings again.

"I have to go." He sounds reluctant.

"Me, too." I take one deep breath and step back.

He clenches his jaw. I press my lips together tight.

His hands fist and then he bounds up the stairs, taking them two at a time, his speed saying that if he doesn't leave now, he'll never go. When I can't hear his footsteps anymore, I run the errand. Two Americanos, iced. Two sugar packets. I get back to the office and deliver the drinks.

"Where's yours?" asks Chaeyoung.

"Drank it before I got here."

"Hmmph."

It's the last thing anyone says to me all day.

CHAPTER FIFTEEN

WANSU AND I SHARE A COMPLETELY SILENT DINNER OF braised chicken, buttered brussels sprouts, kimchi, and chicken broth dressed with fresh scallions. I'm sure it's delicious, as all Mrs. Ji's dishes are, but my appetite is nonexistent these days.

"Are you unwell?" Wansu asks.

I shake my head. "Not hungry. I had a big lunch," I lie. I didn't eat anything.

"Is there a particular dish you would like Mrs. Ji to make for you?"

I force a brussels sprout into my mouth. I manage to eat enough that Wansu doesn't comment again. After dinner, she retires to watch melodramas with Choi Yusuk and I call Ellen from my bedroom.

"How are you!" She greets me with a smile and a wave. "I miss you!"

"You should come back." I stare at her pretty face. Sometimes I think about my life pre-Seoul, when I knew only Ellen as my mother. Ignorance really was bliss.

"Oh no, honey, is it the language thing again? It will come to you."

"No. I mean, yes, it's that, but it's everything. I keep thinking I made a mistake."

She makes a clucking noise. "You can do it, honey. I believe in you."

"Thanks." I make a face to let her know I'm not really grateful for this encouragement.

Ellen laughs. "Is this about the blind date?"

"You know about this?" I drop onto the sofa in shock.

"Yes, of course. Wansu asked me what you liked in a man."

Yujun is what I like in a man. Dimpled, charming, the kind to hold your hand at the river and dry your tears with a silk tie while also kissing you deep enough that you feel it in your toes.

"Wansu?"

"Yes. We keep in touch regularly. I downloaded KakaoTalk for her." Ellen sounds so pleased.

"You and Wansu."

"Don't act so surprised. We're your mothers. Why wouldn't we stay in contact? We've communicated regularly for years."

Is she referring to the monthly reports she sent to Wansu without me knowing? "You stopped those when I turned twenty-five."

"Yes, but that's in the past." She waves her hand as if her and Wansu's secrets are as insubstantial as air.

"I wish you would have told me that you were talking."

"Why?"

I try not to allow my irritation to show on my face but it leaks out in my tone. "Because this is about me."

Ellen clucks her tongue. "Not everything involves you. Yes, you're our daughter and you take up a lot of conversation time, but sometimes we discuss other things. I asked her for skin-care recommendations. She wondered if I could send her wool socks that the nuns knit up in eastern Iowa. We're trying to get to know each other, be friends. This is about her feelings of guilt and my feelings of inferiority. I could never get pregnant. Pat left me. She raised a child not her own." Heavy stuff. "Sometimes Wansu will talk about her job and her love life."

"Her love life?" My voice rises an octave.

"Honey, it's hard for Wansu. Her husband has been in this state for three years. He did not have a DNR and his son has never expressed any desire to let him go. She's lonely. You shouldn't tell her I said that, though."

This new information floors me, and I don't know how to respond. Ellen either doesn't notice or takes pity on me.

"Did I tell you that I'm learning how to cook vegan food? Barbara—you remember Barbara from when Pat worked at the brokerage house? She came to the funeral. Anyway, Barbara is coming over with her daughter. Her daughter is your age or close to it. She's twenty-seven. She left her husband, who was seeing a church lobbyist behind her back. Can you believe it? Sarah, that's her name, moved back in with her mom because the house was a gift from his parents and apparently he gets to keep it because it was from his parents? I'm not really sure how all that works anymore. These laws change so fast. I'm rambling. Tell me about the young man."

It's only because I have years of practice that I'm still with Ellen after this freight train of topics. "He's a lawyer."

"That's very promising."

"He hates kids," I lie. I do not need Ellen and Wansu ganging up on me over this blind-date thing.

"I don't believe you. Wansu would not choose someone who didn't like kids. She wants grandchildren, you know."

I press a hand against my tummy. "Grandchildren?" I squeak.

"Maybe not from this man, but someday from someone."

"I don't even know if I want kids."

Ellen falls silent for a moment.

"That's your right," she finally says. "No one needs to have children."

"Right." I suck in a deep breath. I want to be honest here. I don't want to hide. "And if I did want to have a relationship right now, it wouldn't be with this stranger. I have feelings for Yujun."

"Yes. I know. You were in quite a state after the board meeting."

I blush. After word got out Choi Wansu, staunch advocate of adoption rights and single motherhood, had abandoned a child that was then adopted by a foreigner, IF Group's future looked perilous. There was a demonstration in front of the building in Yongsan. Bomi had an egg thrown at her head. Wansu called an emergency meeting of the board of directors, introduced me, and said that she was formally recognizing me as her daughter. Yujun and I lost our minds for a second, panicked, and nearly had sex in an IF Group bathroom. I sort of wish we had. It was the last time Yujun and I were alone before Wansu shipped him overseas for six weeks.

"I'm your mother," she adds, as if this explains her embarrassing knowledge. "I know things are hard for you, but I also believe in you. Don't make things more complicated than necessary."

My jaw hardens. "You mean Yujun."

"You're very closed off, Hara. You are afraid of being hurt because you suffered that big wound when you were a tiny baby and your psyche remembers it. Some part of you thinks you aren't lovable, but you are! I love you. Wansu loves you. Pat loved you in his own way. Yes, he ran away to the golf course and another woman, but he truly did love you. He cried when we met the plane that brought you to America. I wrote it in your baby book, do you remember?"

Now that she says it, I do. "I thought you made that up."

"No. It was the truth. I swear on my mother's grave. And Wansu's ex-partner—"

"Lee Jonghyung."

"Yes, him. Lee would've loved you, too, if he'd known about you. His first response when he found out he had a child was to request to meet you. So listen to me. You're lovable. Don't tie yourself to the first person who says those words because you think he's the only one who will ever love you."

CHAPTER SIXTEEN

I WAKE UP TO A TEXT FROM YUJUN THAT HE'S GOING DOWN TO Busan for the day.

> YUJUN: I'll be back for dinner.

Only dinnertime arrives and it is only Wansu.

"No Yujun?" I take my seat. There are forks and spoons on the table.

"He's negotiating a new contract with our shipping partners now that we have the new international business. It is likely we will not see much of him for the next few days." She pops a spear of asparagus in her mouth, but the cover of food doesn't hide her smugness. I was surprised she remained silent when we didn't return from the pool party until the next morning, but she was playing the long game. Her belief is that distance and time will

break us apart more effectively than her constant parental disapproval.

If I didn't know better, if it wouldn't have been too big a coinci-
dence and too hard to have pulled off, I would blame the river park
incident on her. Ellen is in on this with her, and the thought of
these two women conspiring behind my back to direct my life in a
certain way makes me want to scream. I clench the metal handle of
the fork so tight that it leaves marks.

I don't eat and Wansu doesn't comment. After dinner, she goes
upstairs and I pace in my room, waiting for Yujun to return home.
I fall asleep and wake up in the middle of the night to see that I
missed three messages.

YUJUN: Sorry

YUJUN: Don't wait

YUJUN: Love you

Uncaring what Wansu might say, I run down to his room, only
to find it vacant and the bed untouched. He must be at his apartment. I drag both hands down my face in frustration and loneli-
ness. Sleep does not come again that night.

"YOU DON'T LOOK good," Yang Ilhwa observes as she hands me
my paper boat of food.

"I haven't eaten since lunch yesterday. It's a hungry face." I
skipped out on the morning kale smoothie and went straight to the
office hoping to meet Yujun there.

Coffee, I'd asked in a text as I rode up the elevator to the fourteenth floor.

Sorry sorry sorry am still in Busan cant talk luv u 🖤 🖤 🖤 🖤 🖤 🖤 🍵 was his response.

"You should always eat. Eat is good," Yang Ilhwa orders. "You hungry and do no good."

She's not wrong. I don't think I've had a decent meal since the park. That encounter has really messed me up. That and Ellen's accusation that I've latched onto Yujun because I believe he's the only one who loves me. First of all, how could anyone look at that man and think I was settling? A woman at the airport crashed into a sign because she couldn't stop staring at him. Second, even if he wasn't gorgeous, he'd have a line of people waiting to sit at his table because he's so fun and kind and decent. I'm punching above my weight class with Yujun.

I'm not hitching my wagon to him because he's the only one who has said he loves me. I love Yujun because he's a good listener, because he's funny, because he's kind, because his dimples are two bottomless wells of happiness, because he's fucking good in bed and he looks like a god. I don't know why he loves me, but it cannot be a surprise as to why I love him. I can't believe this is even questioned by Ellen.

I'm not even sad. I'm angry. Give me a little credit here.

I eat two bites of my lunch, but even that leaves my stomach upset. I rub a hand across my face. I need a break from life. I need to do something mindless and entertaining.

"*Son-nim, irioseyo!*" calls Yang Ilhwa. Customer, come here. She motions for me to her side.

I crumple the uneaten food inside the paper tray and stuff the mess in my purse and then jog across the street. "Yes?"

She hands me a fizzy milky yogurt drink. Usually she charges the equivalent of two dollars for this can. "Free," she says. "Very refreshing. Then, after work, you go to *noraebang* and sing. Lets out lots of *bunno*. Anger." She pats her chest.

A *noraebang*. God, what a good idea. A private soundproofed room where I can scream my head off and no one will know? "That's a perfect idea, *Imo-nim*."

"Don't go alone. Bring good friend. You have one?" She taps another can. "Your American friend."

"Jules." She's come with me here a couple of times. "Yes. She would go." Jules would definitely encourage me to scream. I take my drink, bowing to Yang Ilhwa, and then run off toward IF Group, fumbling out a text.

Tonight? Jules replies.

ME: Yes

JULES: Why not. Ok if anna n Mel come?

I hesitate. Anna and Mel are Jules's roommates, and since I moved out, I don't have much contact with them, but they know my story. They helped me find Choi Wansu.

ME: Sure

JULES: I'll reserve a room. Where do you want to go?

ME: Close to your place is fine as long as you call the cab home for me

Most of the cab drivers are decent, but there are some, particularly late at night, who have no patience for a Korean girl who can't speak the language well. I've had more than one refuse me service.

JULES: will txt you the deets

In the afternoon, I get a message from Yujun.

YUJUN: I feel like I'm always saying I'm sorry these days and I am sorry but I've said it so many times the word has no meaning. I miss you. This will all work out. Once these projects are finished and the contracts are signed we will have more time. The holidays are coming. We'll do something special, just the two of us.

The holidays, meaning Chuseok, are over a month away. I guess it's not that long, in the grand scheme of things.

ME: I will block the long weekend off for you. I miss you too. Love you.

I add the *Hangul* version for extra sincerity. I let Wansu know that I won't be home until late. Spitefully, I don't tell her what I'm doing. I hope she thinks I'm having mad sex with Yujun at his apartment, but she probably knows he's working. Hell, she could be sitting next to him in some conference room right now.

Am I jealous of my birth mother? Is that what I've been reduced to?

The thing is, before the encounter in the park, I sort of thought Wansu was overreacting. She's protective of IF Group, in part, I think, because she married into the company. From what little I know, there was conflict between the way that Wansu thought the company should be run and the way Choi Yusuk believed it should be run. Yujun backed Wansu over his father. Yujun doesn't regret this but he feels burdened by guilt. He said once that the argument they had put Choi Yusuk in the condition he is in now.

Objectively, I don't think Yujun believes he caused his father's stroke and slide into a comatose state, but one's head isn't always in control. In his heart, Yujun carries grief over this mess, which is why he works himself to the bone. If the company is successful, then he can justify his behavior. If the company fails, then his bold stance, his non-"Sim Cheong" behavior, would have been for nothing.

"Turn the music off," Jules orders.

I look up from the binder of karaoke songs in my lap to see Jules, Anna, and Mel staring at me—or in the case of Jules, glaring. "Are you waiting for me to pick a song?" I blindly point at one of the selections. "Here. I'll sing this one."

"'Ohmona'? That's a trot song from"—she lifts the sheet closer to her face because the room is dark and it's hard to read with only strobe lights spinning around—"2007. Do you even know it?"

I barely know what trot is other than it's hugely popular now. Every station has at least one trot musical show on every night. "There'll be lyrics on the screen."

Jules snatches the binder from my hands and tosses it aside. "You haven't been with us the whole night." She knocks a fist lightly against the side of my head. "What's going on in there?"

"Did you have a bad day at work?" Anna asks.

"Right. Very busy. Work is piling up." I nod repeatedly.

Jules snorts, as she knows this is a big lie. "It's about Yujun."

She sits back with her arms folded across her chest like she knew I was going to be in this position at some point.

"It's not about him. Not exactly."

None of them look like they believe me.

"Do you guys think I'm closed off?"

All three nod simultaneously.

"How can you say that?"

"You didn't tell us why you came to Korea. When you left for your father's funeral, you kept that to yourself, too," Anna reminds me.

"I asked for you all to help me find my birth mother! How is that closed off?"

"Only because you suck at Korean," Jules retorts.

"Fine. I'm closed off." I fold my arms across my chest.

"See?" Jules points at my posture.

I throw my hands to my sides. "Whatever. Let me ask this. If you had a chance with Yujun, would you take it?"

"Yes."

"No question."

"Jules?" I prompt, since she hasn't answered.

She makes a face. "If I didn't like someone else, then yes."

Anna and Mel show no signs of surprise at Jules's admission. She must've told them she was seeing Bomi.

"Speaking of Bomi," I begin.

"No, we were speaking of you and Yujun and your emotional constipation. Let some of it out before you explode," Jules says in exasperation.

"That's a stunningly bad visual." I shudder.

"You know what? I'm not pushing anymore. If you don't want to talk about it—"

"I was shunned last weekend," I burst out.

Jules puts down the remote. "What do you mean?"

I tell them about the park. "This is a place where manners are important. I have to turn to the side to drink my soju when I'm sitting next to Sangki because he's older. This girl would not bow or shake my hand but actually backed up like I had a communicable disease. She was *disgusted*." I drag the last word out as if it's ten syllables. "Yujun wants it all. He wants his friends, his family, his successful company. He wants us. I want that, too, but there seem to be a lot of people who think we're foul. What if that kind of distaste is transferable and eventually Yujun thinks I'm icky?"

"There are bitches and assholes everywhere," Jules said. "If Yujun wants to make it work and you want to make it work, then it will happen."

"Do you really believe that?" Because she had stormed out of the bar when Bomi talked about the obstacles to the two of them dating.

"If you're referring to me and Bomi, the situation is entirely different. She doesn't want to be with me."

"That's not true. She wants to be with you but she can't be open about it, not with her family."

"Would you be willing to live like that with Yujun? You'd never be able to marry him or have kids. You'd always be known as his sister, and someday he'd get tired of that and find a woman he could have a normal, ordinary life with."

"I thought you said that if Yujun and I want to make it work then it will."

"But Bomi doesn't want to make it work," Jules nearly shouts. "That's why it's not happening for me, but if you give up, it's because you didn't try hard enough. If you want to be with Yujun, then fuck everyone else. He doesn't have younger siblings like Bomi." Jules reaches over and grabs the songbook. "Yujun's friend must be one of those strict traditionalists who is offended her rich friend isn't hooking up with one of her rich friends. Anyone would be offensive to her."

Is it as easy as Jules says? My choice is binary? To be with him or not be with him? If it is that simple, then I know what the answer is. "I want to be with Yujun."

"Great." She punches a number into the *noraebang* remote with more force than necessary and then tosses it to Mel, who, along with Anna, has been quietly watching this exchange from the sidelines.

"Oh, and about your work situation." Jules is not done. "They are mad at you because you're a nepotism hire. Even if you spoke fluent Korean, you'd still be Choi Wansu's daughter and all of the good and bad that flows from it would exist. It's not the language barrier; it's your circumstances, and so you either do nothing and be depressed or do something."

"Like what?"

"I don't know, but if you're miserable and you do nothing, you're complicit in your own misery. Take some action. If it gets worse, then quit. If it gets better, keep going."

What had Yujun told me the other night? *The dragon is our most mythical creature because it is virtually indestructible. Its body is covered in scaled armor. It has claws and horns. It can fly, jump, climb, and no one can escape its wrath.*

I need to be the dragon or, at least, a small lizard.

CHAPTER SEVENTEEN

IF GROUP IS IMPORTANT TO BOTH YUJUN AND WANSU. SO long as the company is healthy and successful, their decisions can't really be questioned. Yujun is working his ass off and I'm at my desk conjugating verbs. There are a lot of things I don't have control over, but my own work product is not one of them. Jules is right. Complaining about my situation does no good—not for me, not for Yujun, and not for IF Group. I resolve to change. No more passively waiting around for projects. No more allowing Soyou to hate on me for merely existing. I will contribute and be useful. Should IF Group falter, it gives Wansu more reason to be against us, but if the company is stable, then her arguments hold less water.

"What if we do a team-building exercise?" I suggest at our next weekly meeting, where *Bujang-nim* reviews our current projects (I have none) and sets new goals for the week.

"Team . . . building?" he repeats. It's not a term with which he's familiar.

"Team building?" Soyou curls her lip up. She not only knows what this means but already hates it.

I ignore her and focus on my boss. "I'm not sure if there's a different term here in Korea, but in the US we call it team building. It's to help a group of coworkers get closer and improve communication so that they function better as a team. In my last job, we all signed up to do the first leg of RAGBRAI. That's where thousands of bicyclists from across the country ride their bikes from one side of the state to the other. It's short for Register's Annual Great Bike Ride Across Iowa. The bike trail along the Han River is over thirteen kilometers and we could bike for a while, eat together, and . . ." I hadn't thought about exactly what we'd do. I figured I'd bring up the idea and someone would jump in with other details, but they're all staring at me as if I have horns growing out of my head. I did vow last night to be a dragon, so I press on. "And we could all share one thing that we like about each other and one thing that might surprise everyone."

"I heard in Japan they do bathhouse building exercises. We could all go to a public bath together," suggests Yoo, the kiss-up.

"I'm not going to a bathhouse with you," spits Soyou. "That's sexual harassment."

Yoo stiffens and sniffs. "There are no public bathhouses that are mixed gender. It would be separate. The idea is that skin to skin breaks down barriers."

I would rather jump in front of a white K-drama truck, the kind that always ends the life of a character you love at the most inopportune moment, than get naked with my coworkers. From the expressions on Soyou's and Chaeyoung's faces, they are in fervent agreement.

"We could build something." I try again. "Like a house of cards, and we could vote who has the best one."

"This is a great idea. *Daebak.*" *Bujang-nim* puts his thumbs up. "We will all contribute one idea that can be done in a conference room or in this area, and afterward, I will give you the credit card and you can enjoy a *hweshik* without me since I know that is the trend these days. Right? The trend?"

I have no idea but almost all the staff except for Yoo is nodding so, of course, I nod, too.

"Good. You have ten minutes to come up with an idea and put it here on the board." He places the dry-erase marker on the tray in front of the whiteboard. No one moves. So be it. It was my idea. I'll be the first.

I walk up and write "card" and "house" in *Hangul.* I don't know the exact way to say "house of cards," but this gets my point across. I draw a little house, too, for the hell of it. Yoo rises and writes down *jjimjilbang* for "bathhouse," and he draws a little picture as well, but of a person's head covered in spa towels with the ends wrapped in Princess Leia–like rolls over each ear.

Yoo's entry prompts Soyou to rush over. She doesn't cross his suggestion out, but you know she wants to. She writes down *myeongsang*, which isn't a word I'm familiar with, but she draws a picture, too. Hers is of a figure meditating, and I smother a smile because it's actually a super-clever way of avoiding a team-bonding experience. Chaeyoung is next. She writes in English "share a playlist" and next to it puts a musical note. Im Donguk, who I've seen bike to work, suggests hiking, and his symbol is a pair of tennis shoes. One after the other, the rest of the team offers suggestions with tiny little icons next to them. The sight of all those drawings in a row below mine is lifting my heart and my spirit. A tiny candle of hope lights. Maybe my work situation is salvageable and my own passivity lent itself to the tension in this department. I should've found my inner dragon before.

Bujang-nim wants to narrow the list of activities to five. He suggests we play rock paper scissors, which is the traditional Korean way of solving every dispute. I'm terrible at this and lose immediately. Soyou is, of course, amazing and wins. We start with meditation. Afterward, we will exchange a three-song playlist with the person on our right and listen to the songs. The next activity will be trash-can basketball. Teams will be chosen by the office desk arrangement. The five closest to *Bujang-nim* will be the blue team and the five farthest away will be the red team—the colors of the Korean flag. The fourth activity he announces is coffeehouse shuffle. We each have to drink someone else's favorite coffee. The final one is house of cards.

"But she didn't win," Soyou protests.

"All the others require us to leave the building and we should stay here. Start the meditation while I go and get the coffee." He hands her a legal pad. "Write down your order."

The meditation exercise should have been the easiest team exercise to complete. It required no interaction from anyone, which is why Soyou recommended it. But not one minute into the breathing exercises, Yoo starts laughing. Someone else farts and the whole team falls apart. At minute four, it's obvious no one is going to find transcendental peace today. Soyou gets to her feet and grabs her phone. "Let's do the playlists instead."

My knowledge of Korean music isn't vast, but there are a couple of female soloists I love, so I select the two most recent songs from those artists and then scroll through the music and add three older songs to make it appear that I'm not a complete bandwagoner. The person on my right is Bong Hyoseob, one of the quietest members of the team. He's not talked to me since I joined, but he doesn't talk much at all, not in the office or at team dinners, so I don't feel any anxiety when I share the link to the playlist. When it pops up on his phone, he silently opens it and proceeds to hit play. What he thinks of my music choices isn't clear, and I'm not at all interested in his approval of my musical taste. Not at all. I only peek in his direction two or three or seven times.

"You like K-pop?" blurts out Yoo, who is seated next to Chae-young.

"Yes, why not? It's very popular in the West, isn't it?"

It takes me a half minute to realize Chaeyoung's addressing me. Is she thawing again? "Yes. Super popular. Everyone listens to it." That's a complete lie, but if Chaeyoung had proclaimed that she saw two dragons flying over Hangang, I'd back her up.

"I'm not listening to this," proclaims Soyou from the other side of the room. "This is offensive."

"Rap is not offensive," Yoo replies.

"I didn't say rap was offensive, but these particular lyrics about how men are on top and women are below them? That's misogynistic."

"You women are so sensitive." He mutters something in Korean that I can't make out, but both women grow furious.

This innocent idea is quickly devolving into a giant mess. Beside me, the quiet one, Bong, drops his head into his hand. I need to salvage this and prevent a massacre of Yoo.

I reach over and pull *Bujang-nim*'s notepad toward me and

start balling up paper. "Here." I toss the balls down toward Yoo and Soyou. "Let's get this over with before *Bujang-nim* returns."

Bong nods in swift agreement. "Yes. Basketball." He scoops a paper ball in his hand and tosses it with a light touch and a good arc. It drops neatly into the bottom of the can. Chaeyoung goes next and everyone else joins in, even Yoo and Soyou, who glare at each other the whole time. I sag into my chair with relief. We're going to make it out of this terrible idea of mine in one piece.

Five minutes later, I eat my words. What started out as a simple, friendly paper toss turns into a full-fledged office-chair derby. Even Bong's competitive spirit awakens. The sound of metal and plastic colliding is punctuated by curses and shouts. A wheel from one of the chairs falls off. Someone loses a shoe. The trash can gets knocked over. The team-building exercises have turned into team-building Olympics. Chaeyoung and I are the only ones not in the fray.

"This is going well," I deadpan.

"Are you making a joke?" she asks.

"Yes. It's not going well at all."

"Yes. It is not going well," she agrees.

"We should do something before *Bujang-nim* arrives with the coffee."

"We should."

Neither of us moves.

"This reminds me of one time during middle school. A girl brought in a *seongnim manhwa*. That's like . . . an over-nineteen comic book. We crowded around her desk and read it with her. Suddenly, we hear footsteps running in the hall, and running is not allowed. We know our teacher is coming and we all try to help the girl hide her cartoon, but too many of us try at one time and it slips out of our hands and lands between two desks as *Seonsaeng-nim* walks in. To avoid getting caught, my friend pretends to twist her ankle and falls on the floor. She manages to shove the cartoon up her sweater and then pass it off to me before she is sent to the principal's office."

This is the most that Chaeyoung has ever spoken to me. "What happened to the *manhwa*?"

She covers her mouth but I can see the corners of her eyes tilt up. "I still have it."

We dissolve into a quiet, shared laugh. The game finishes shortly after, with Bong the winner. Only one chair broke during office basketball, and it's Yoo's, so no one is really unhappy. We also let him win the house of cards, and everything is back to normal by the time *Bujang-nim* appears with our coffees.

"Done already?" He's shocked. It's been barely an hour.

"It went well," I chirp.

"Good. Good. *Jal haesseo*." He hands out the coffees.

You did good. He's saying it to everyone, but I wrap that compliment around me like a cashmere blanket, and I stay warm for the rest of the day. Not even Soyou's sneers or Chaeyoung's retreat pierces my shield. At six, *Bujang-nim* has us shut down our computers for the day and go to dinner. As promised, he hands over his company card. We troop off to a *hanwoo* restaurant on the edge of Mapo-gu. It's one of those down-the-alley-without-a-lot-of-obvious-signage places that looks tiny from the outside but is massive inside. There are dozens of tables. A server motions to the corner where three tables are unoccupied. We push them together and take a seat on the floor. All the phones are turned off and dumped in the center of the table. No texting, no checking your socials, no searching the web during the *hweshik*. It's no surprise that everyone drinks heavily during these events.

The soju hits the table almost before the *banchan*. Soyou orders three sets, but Yoo always has to have the last say and holds up two fingers and shouts for more. I go around and pour everyone a drink without being asked, and I swear I see a look of approval in Bong's eyes. Soyou doesn't even glare at me. I pour her another right away. Yoo demands that I do a *poktanju*, or soju bomb. Of course I oblige, even though I don't have much in my system—the tuna *gimbap* I ate for lunch long forgotten.

The platters of beef arrive and Yoo and Bong place long strips of aged beef onto the cast-iron grill. The smell of the sizzling meat makes me dizzy with hunger. Around me, the buzz of conversation fills the air.

"You are terrible at basketball. Did they only have soccer at your school?"

"Better than you. Those shots you made were all luck, no skill."

"Did you see *Penthouse* last night?"

"It's too over-the-top. I don't watch that."

"Don't look at me. I don't watch it either."

"Are you going to say you don't watch it either, Bong? Because one of you is lying. Half the metro watches it."

"I never said I didn't watch it," Bong replies.

"You didn't say you did."

In lower tones, Soyou says to Chaeyoung, "She's suggested more ideas than she's done work."

"At least *Bujang-nim* was happy," Chaeyoung replies. She fidgets with her diamond necklace.

"In my next life, I want to be a *chaebol*. Not related to one. Not married to one, but I want to be . . . Suh Minjung."

"The Amore Pacific heir? If you're wishing for better in your next life, why not wish for Jun Jihyun? Beauty and money."

"Also married to money."

"Isn't that always the case? Money marrying money?" I interject and then hiccup.

Two heads turn toward me. I squint and count again. Maybe it's three heads, or is Soyou swaying? They're looking at me oddly. Something's wrong here and it's not my blurred vision. Something that I can't quite put my—*oh my fucking god*. They're speaking in Korean and I'm understanding them. I jerk upright and knock my glass over onto Bong's lap. He curses and pushes my hands away as I try to dab his shirt with my napkin.

"She's hopeless," Soyou declares.

"I can hear you." The entire table stops talking, and maybe that should've been my cue to shut up, but I've had too much booze and too little food to catch the hint. "I can hear you. No. That's wrong." I shake my head until the right word falls to my tongue. "I can understand you." A grin stretches across my face. "I can understand what you're saying." I point to Yoo. "You were talking about Bong's lack of basketball skills." My finger moves left. "And you, Kim Soomin-nim, you are a fan of the show *Penthouse*. And you"—my finger stops at Soyou—"say I'm hopeless."

Soyou knocks my finger away. "It's rude to point."

I fold my finger inside my fist. "Sorry." But I'm too pleased with my language breakthrough to care about Soyou's scolds. Half the team looks mildly horrified as they try to recall all the snide remarks they must've said about me, believing I didn't understand them. I hadn't before, but I might now. I gaze with bright, challenging eyes at everyone at the table, and most of them drop their gazes to their laps. Oh, it feels good to be a dragon, clawing my way up the mountain. I pop a piece of *hanwoo* into my mouth and chew, savoring both the meat and the achievement.

The conversation at the table falls into a lull, which may have bothered me some other night, but not this one. Tonight, nothing is making me unhappy.

CHAPTER EIGHTEEN

DESPITE A MASSIVE HANGOVER, I TAKE MY NEWFOUND CONFI-
dence to work with me the next day, and as soon as *Bujang-nim*
appears, at precisely nine, I pounce and demand more work. I make
my request in Korean and enjoy the mild shock that fills his face.
He replies in Korean, but whatever magic took place last night has
dissipated. When I don't respond, his shock morphs into resigna-
tion. A week ago, I would've slunk away to my desk in embarrassment, but I'm not moving until he gives me work. After what seems
like an endless standoff, during which all of my department and
half of the sales department next to us watches, he gives in. He
types out three emails with attachments and shoos me away. I skip
back to my desk.

While I'm happy, the rest of my coworkers appear tense. There's
very little chatter. No one is grouping together at the coffee station
making their insta-coffees or downing a tiny bottle of ginseng.

Even Chaeyoung and Soyou aren't making their usual bathroom bonding runs. It's as if my understanding of Korean has actually driven a wedge between us instead of pulling us closer together.

It's a process, I tell myself. Rome wasn't built in a day, et cetera, et cetera. Keep your chin up. I recite a half dozen clichéd platitudes and get to work.

Around midmorning, Sangki texts me.

SANGKI: Now that Yujun is back I never see you it's like he is more important than me

ME: Never

SANGKI: He can't continue to monopolize your time like this you're eating with me tonight

ME: He texted you and said he feels bad about abandoning me and begged you to take me out

SANGKI: Are you reading his phone messages right now?

ME: No but thank you for confirming my guess

SANGKI: . . .

ME: 😄

ME: You looked good on tv last night

SANGKI: Did you watch? I think my face looked puffy. No more fried food. Let's eat at this vegan place that serves temple food

ME: You did not look puffy faced. I did watch and you sounded amazing and were very funny

SANGKI: I am very funny and I do sound amazing

SANGKI: temple food?

ME: Yes. Who would turn down the right to have dinner with someone very funny who sings like an angel and was once in the running for world's most handsome man

SANGKI: I got beat out by the British actor Tom

ME: No one in his right mind thinks Tom is more attractive than you

SANGKI: You're so right. Results were rigged

ME: Biased against Asians

SANGKI: The poll had David Kim in the top ten and we know anything that includes him is sus

ME: Exactly. Let me go downvote his image

SANGKI: Better not. If they catch you, I'll be accused of sending haters after him

ME: Damn and I just finished making ten different accounts

SANGKI: See you tonight

ME: Can I bring Bomi?

SANGKI: A threesome? How kinky. Yes

ME: You're paying

SANGKI: I see how it is

ME: 🙃

I tuck my phone away, and when I look up, I see Chaeyoung staring at me.

"I made plans to eat dinner with Ahn Sangki. He's taking me to a special place that serves temple food. Very exclusive."

"Sawon in Insadong?" Her eyes widen with envy.

I nod even though I have no idea where we are going. She mutters, "*Jonna jogyetda*," under her breath, which I presume is something like "fucking lucky." I make the thumbs-up sign to make it seem like I know what she's talking about. Envy turns to fear and she doesn't even look in my direction for the rest of the day.

I'm about to pack up for the night and meet Sangki when Yujun appears by my desk. There are only a handful of us still working, including Chaeyoung and the quiet guy, Bong. They both jump up from their chairs and bow to him. He waves his hand to stop them. He doesn't need that kind of deference.

"I'm here to take you to Sawon," he says with a huge grin.

"Really?"

"Yeah. I got everything done and was going to text you to see if you wanted to have dinner, but Sangki told me he had already made plans, so I'm third wheeling on your date."

I'm so happy I could float. "It's fourth wheeling. Bomi got invited before you, but that works out because you can talk to her while Sangki and I flirt with each other."

Yujun mock growls. "Flirt with Sangki and he won't be able to show his face on national television for a month."

"He would still go and say that he battled a mugger while helping an old lady across the street, and everyone would clap and a dozen articles would be written about him being the best boy in the world." I sling my purse over my shoulder.

Yujun puts his hand on my waist and guides me to the elevator.

"As long as I am the best boy in the world according to Hara, everyone else is free to say whatever they like about Sangki."

In the elevator, I notice that there are dark smudges under his eyes. Yujun has been really busy.

"You're working too hard." I run a finger lightly over his cheekbone.

He chases my hand with his mouth, and when he catches it, he presses a kiss against my wrist. "Are you saying I look terrible?"

"Terribly exhausted."

His lips turn down. The dimples are in hiding. "Should we go home or to my apartment and have *ramyeon*?"

"If you want to."

"Don't tempt me." He pulls away from me. "Not only have I been a terrible boyfriend, but also a very bad friend. I have not seen Sangki since the pool party, so let's have this dinner and then we can go to my apartment."

I shiver inwardly with delight.

When we arrive at the restaurant, Sangki is already at the table with Bomi.

"I have to sit next to Hara," Sangki insists. "My *sasaengs* think I'm dating her."

"Isn't that bad for your reputation?" Bomi asks. Like Yujun's, her face looks pale and drawn, but I don't know if Bomi is tired from work or she's missing Jules.

"No. She's pretty and rich and somewhat notorious, so it simultaneously makes them proud and also superior over her. Sorry, Hara."

"I'll take it as a compliment." I do not care what crazy stalkers think of me. "Let's discuss why everyone looks so tired. What's going on up on the fourteenth floor?"

"What about me?" Sangki taps his chest. "Shouldn't I be the topic of conversation?"

"We just talked about your *sasaengs*."

"For all of two seconds."

"We'll get to you, but Bomi first."

"Me?" She physically recoils. "I don't want to be the topic of conversation."

"It's LA." Yujun collapses into the chair across from me. "We're going to expand our business to the Americas as the Hallyu is spreading. More Korean companies are venturing into activities in the West, which means they need bilingual service providers to handle things like equipment rentals, shipping merchandise and supplies from Korea to the States, finding local vendors, providing temporary or long-term housing, addressing safety issues. It's non-stop. Not to mention completely different regulatory rules that we have to comply with."

Bomi rubs her temples. "This is why I didn't want to be the topic of conversation. I'm getting a headache listening to you, *Sunbae-nim*."

"Same." Maybe Wansu isn't intentionally trying to keep Yujun and me apart.

Yujun cocks an eyebrow in my direction. "Haven't you seen any of this? International Marketing should be working on this project. It's an important one. Your English skills and editing background are invaluable."

"No. I haven't seen anything. Maybe we haven't received the materials yet?"

"That's odd. You should have been working on it weeks ago." He turns to Bomi. "Is your team still working on the protocol guidelines?"

She shakes her head. "No. That's been out of our department since last month."

An uneasy sensation bubbles in my stomach because it feels like I've outed a secret that shouldn't have been told. The waiter comes with the menus and I nearly fall over in my haste to change the subject.

Yujun is not done. "You order for us, Sangki-ya." He turns to me. "What are you working on?"

"Are you my supervisor?" I pore over the menu, pretending deep interest, but a long-fingered hand slides the linen paper away.

"Hara."

"You should tell him," Sangki says. "He's, how do you say it, the dog with the collar? No. Bone. The dog with the bone."

"You know what this is about?" Yujun looks wounded. He eyes Bomi, who is avoiding his gaze. "You, too?"

I scrunch my nose. "I will tell you, but you have to promise you will not do anything."

"I can't promise anything."

"Gosh, the weather has been really cool lately. Is it always like this in September?" I say, pretending to ignore him.

"Very cool. Unseasonably so." Sangki willingly plays along.

"I can't believe you're picking her side over mine," Yujun complains.

"You've never sent me texts saying I sing like an angel." Sangki delivers our order and then gathers the menus and hands them to the waiter.

Yujun clears his throat. He's reaching the end of his patience.

I give in and spill. "I'm having a hard time at work, but it's my fault because I don't speak Korean, and if you do anything to anyone in my department, you will make it worse and I will feel terri-

ble, so please promise me you will only listen and take no action." I
reach for his hand. "It's a compromise. I'll talk; you'll listen. Only
listen."

Yujun's jaw works overtime as he struggles between wanting to
know what's going on and conceding to my conditions, which he
does not like.

"*Aigoo*, he agrees. He agrees," Sangki bursts out. "Don't you, Yujun? Don't torture her like this."

Yujun makes an unhappy noise at the back of his throat. He
does not like this compromise. "Yes. I'll promise."

I hesitate and he caves completely. "I really, really promise."

Before I can spill the details, the food arrives. Yujun impatiently watches as the waitstaff delivers the bowls of fried mushroom fritters, Korean thistle rice, root chips, salted bellflower root,
and cold soybean noodles. There is a moment when I think he will
stand up and distribute the bowls himself. Finally, the food is set
and the waitstaff is gone and I'm at center stage. I don't like it.

"*Bujang-nim* does not give me much work. My coworkers are
understandably resentful that I'm there, especially when I don't
know the language and all of the customs. I suggested we do some
team-building exercises and everyone got supercompetitive. Yes, I
know. You race across a sidewalk and so it's normal to push your
coworker's chair over in order to prevent him from scoring a fake
point in a trash can basketball game. We ended the day at a *hweshik*
and the alcohol unlocked some gate in my brain. Suddenly, I could
understand everyone. That didn't go over well and now I'm getting
frozen out again. I'm sure things will eventually get better as time
goes on, and I received three more projects today, so the logistics
one is probably next."

"Hmm." Yujun is unconvinced.

"Hmm nothing. It's fine, and even if it wasn't fine, you coming down from the fourteenth floor isn't going to solve any problems. My connection with you and Wansu is why they are unhappy in the first place. I'm a big girl and I can handle it. Do you trust me?"

Yujun clenches his jaw once more but nods brusquely. I ignore his lack of enthusiasm and finish. "*Bujang-nim* is not going to jeopardize this obviously very big project."

And that actually might be the problem. He doesn't trust me to do the work, so he's not going to send anything my way, but I do have a better command of the English language than any of them and they should use me at least in that capacity. Tomorrow I'll finish those three projects and then press my boss for more work, specifically the LA project. I'm not sure how I will do this without appearing like I'm relying on my mother or Yujun, but I'll cross that bridge when I come to it. "Trust me," I say with a lot more confidence than I feel.

"What team-building exercises did you do?" Sangki is intrigued and so is Yujun by the way he leans forward.

"Don't get any ideas," Bomi warns.

"You're not on my team, Kim Bomi-nim. Don't worry. Tell me the activities you did," Yujun half demands, half encourages.

"Don't tell him, Hara. If he does them, all of the team managers, including mine, will believe that this is a good idea."

"Sorry. Siding with Bomi here. No one should be forced to do team building. We already have the *hweshik*." I drink my soju. Bomi reaches across and pours me another glass, her way of thanking me, I guess.

"I didn't realize our *hweshiks* were so reviled." Poor Yujun looks slightly peeved. Out of all of us, he has the highest position and has treated people to the most meals.

"Everyone wants to have *hweshik* with you, baby." I pat his hand.

Bomi and Sangki both roll their eyes. Bomi knocks her fist on the wood tabletop.

"We cannot have meals together if you are making love to each other at the table."

"I patted his hand," I protest.

"You called him baby," Bomi points out.

"You don't have terms of endearment in Korea?" I glance around the table. Yujun called me *aegiya* at times in the sweetest tones.

"Yes. Of course." Yujun flashes a dimple in my direction. "Call me whatever you like."

Bomi groans. "We need more soju if this is how the night is going to go."

"More? I don't think there's enough." Sangki waves down the waiter.

By the end of the dinner, there are more empty green glass bottles on the table than there are people left in the restaurant. Yujun and I make it to his apartment, but we're both too far gone to do anything but collapse on the bed in a drunken stupor.

CHAPTER NINETEEN

MY PLAN TO GET THE LA WORK FROM *BUJANG-NIM* **TAKES A** small detour later that week. I finish the projects, but my manager is gone so I can't pester him for more work. The atmosphere in the office is still chilly. No one is getting over my sudden comprehension of Korean anytime soon. I try to explain to Chaeyoung and Soyou that it was a onetime fluke thing where the barrier in my brain came down for a brief—very brief—moment, but they don't believe me so I give up. I'll rock this LA project and my hard work will win them over. Otherwise, maybe I'll ask for a transfer to the mail room, where I'll sort packages or run coffee errands.

At lunch, I take myself to the fried-pork food truck because that's my comfort food. It takes me back to Iowa, where cheese and pork and corn all exist in perfect harmony. Even before I order, I sense something is wrong.

"*Imo-nim*, are you feeling well?"

Sweat lines her forehead and her usually smiling expression is strained and weary. "*Ne*. Yes." She wipes the back of her hand across her forehead. The hand trembles.

"You're sick. Could you close early and go home?" I don't know if she can afford to.

She shakes her head, but even that's too much for her and she stumbles, catching herself against the stainless steel counter. There are three other people behind me who are straining to see what the holdup is.

"I'm taking you up on your offer to teach me to cook." I walk around to the back of the food truck and open the door. Yang Il-hwa watches silently as I swipe a plastic face shield from a shelf and fit it over my face. "Do you have hairnets?"

She points to a tackle box. Inside, I find hairnets and food-safe gloves. I gear up and push her aside. "How many?" I ask the next customer.

At first, he's a little confused by my appearance, but his stomach reminds him why he's at a food truck and he reels off an order. I don't catch it all, but Yang Ilwha does.

"Two orders pork balls. A corn cup. One Milkis. Put pork balls in batter, then eggs, then crumbs. Fry. I tell you when to take out."

I follow her lead. There are thin patties of meat separated by plastic. She palms one and then flips her hand over, stuffing a square of mozzarella inside. In another two moves, the meat is wrapped around the cheese and pinched into a circle. She repeats this move two more times. The finished balls are dipped in an egg wash and then rolled through a seasoned crumb mixture. From there, the breaded pork is fried, left to drain, and then fried again.

After the second frying, three are speared onto a bamboo stick. She motions for me to pour the sauce into the small paper cup she uses as a serving container.

I squirt some in. She nudges me to add more. I continue filling the paper cup until she is satisfied.

"Good," she announces. "More pork."

I burn the first few batches, and a couple of the customers are ready to curse me out. We give them free food and drinks to pacify them. By the fourth customer, I have the hang of it, which is good because Yang looks like she's going to die.

And for the next four hours, almost without a rest, I pound bread, stuff thin pork fillets with cubes of mozzarella, drench vegetables in tempura batter, and dump them all into different vats of hot oil. Despite being ill, the older woman serves and takes orders and processes cash in a whirlwind of efficiency.

During a lull, I text *Bujang-nim* and tell him that I'm sick. He doesn't respond right away, so I call Bomi.

"Have you gone to the hospital?" she asks with worry when I explain that I need to take a sick day.

"I'm not actually sick. Yang Ilwha is and she needs my help."

"Yang . . . Il . . . wha?"

"The pork food truck lady."

"You're . . . helping her?"

"Yeah. She needs it. I think she needs to go to the hospital, actually. I have to run, but will you make sure that human resources or whoever needs to know that I'm not coming back this afternoon?"

"Your text to your manager is fine."

"Great. I have to go now. There's a customer." I work hard

through the lunch hour, and around two, the steady stream of lunchgoers has ended. I sit down next to Yang Ilhwa with a Milkis.

She pats me weakly on the back. "Good job. Good job."

"Thanks." I stretch out my legs. "This is tiring. I need better shoes." My little flats weren't meant to be stood in for four hours straight. Yang is wearing sneakers with thick soles. I eye them with envy.

"You a good worker. What you do?"

"I work for IF Group." I point off in the direction of the building.

She shakes her head. It's not a company with which she's familiar.

"You have boyfriend?"

"Y-ye—" I start to say and then stop. Yang Ilhwa is the perfect person to ask about Yujun and me. She's an impartial party who doesn't know who I am, what my place in the world is. She doesn't know Yujun or Wansu and will give me an honest cultural perspective. "*Imo-nim*, do you remember earlier in the summer, in June, the young couple that made an extreme choice because they were from the same clan and their families refused to allow them to marry?"

She clucks her tongue. "*Aigoo*, yes. Very bad."

"As in tragic?" I gnaw on the side of my lip.

"Yes, but also bad. Law allows, but still bad. Should find someone new, different. Many people out there."

I swallow a frustrated sigh. "What about stepsiblings? *Euiboot nammae?*"

Yang Ilhwa's expression turns green. She grimaces and shudders. "Those two should not eat rice for a month. Sooooo selfish."

She shakes a spoon at me. "Their family would be bloodied and heartbroken. You know the Chun brother goblins story?"

"No." And I don't think I want to, but Yang Ilhwa tells it anyway.

There were two Chun *hyungjaes*—brothers. The older Chun was lazy and spoiled, but the younger brother worked hard as a woodcutter and gave all his earnings to support his family. One day, the young brother was in the forest gathering acorns for himself and his family. He found a house and entered, believing no one to be home. Inside he heard voices, and so he quickly hid in a closet. Through a crack in the door, he saw a gang of goblins form a circle, bang their clubs on the floor, and chant, "Make gold, make gold, make gold." Soon a pile of gold appeared. The goblins repeated this chant, but with new forms of riches, until there were giant piles of silver, rubies, and diamonds all in the middle of the floor.

While the goblins were staring at their treasure, Chun's stomach grumbled. Chun froze with fear, reckoning he was going to be discovered. Instead the goblins assumed a storm had arisen and thunder raged outside. Chun's hunger remained, and, to stifle any noise, he stuffed an acorn in his mouth, but when he bit down, a tremendous noise echoed in the room.

The goblins were terrified and believed the roof was about to collapse, so they fled the house, leaving Chun behind. The younger brother worried the goblins might return and remained hidden until dawn.

When the first ray of light broke through the dark sky, Chun gathered up as much of the treasure as he could carry, along with the club that one goblin had left behind, and returned home. With his stolen riches, he built a mansion, furnished it with the finest of goods, and showered wealth upon his family. When his treasure was depleted, he took out his stolen club and repeated the chants until jewels and gold filled his floor.

The elder brother grew jealous of his younger brother's status in the family. He demanded to know his brother's magic. The younger Chun immediately shared the details of his forest adventure, but the older brother's ears were closed. He only heard what he wanted. He picked up an acorn, went to the house, and hid in the closet. When the goblins appeared, he bit down on the acorn. Thunder filled the room and Chun rushed out to gather up the treasure, only to find the goblins waiting for him. "Thief," they cried out and beat him with their clubs.

Some say he died. Other tellings have him returning home in shame.

She taps my shoulder with the spoon and points toward the counter with her chin. "Customers."

I get to my feet and resume cooking. Yang Ilhwa isn't familiar with my circumstances so she could not have known the folktale she chose to share closely mirrored my life. The parallels are eerie. Wansu took a rich man's wealth. To want more is to end in tragedy. Yang Ilhwa's message is that I should not bang a stolen club against the ground and ask for more lest I be beaten, shamed, or worse. We end the afternoon quietly. I can't stop thinking about the goblin brothers and Yang Ilhwa is exhausted.

After the last customer leaves, I give Yang Ilhwa my number. "Call me if you need anything. Anything."

When I get home that evening, smelling of grease and meat and eggs and bread, I hide inside my suite of rooms, texting Yujun and Wansu that I'm not feeling well. I manage to get a shower in before Yujun knocks on my door.

"Should I call a doctor?"

"No. I'm tired. I think all the alcohol I've been downing is catching up with me. I don't have the tolerance that you all have." I open the door and let him in.

He has a tray of clear broth and rice porridge. He sets it aside and places his hand against my forehead. "You do feel warm."

Wansu appears in the doorway. "I'll call the doctor," she says.

"No." I wave my hand. "I'm tired is all. I had a tiring day."

"Oh, more work, then?" Yujun perks up.

"Yeah, something like that." I feel bad about lying to him. I'll explain tomorrow when Wansu isn't here.

"Get some rest, then. Come along, Yujun."

Wansu has to drag him out. I receive a text a minute later.

YUJUN: I'm staying here tonight. Txt me if you need anything.

I eat my soup and rice and climb into bed. I'm physically tired from the work and emotionally tired from the goblin story. If I never hear another Korean folktale again, I'll be happy. I need to pick a new book to read to Choi Yusuk. These stories suck. I close my eyes, and the next thing I know my phone is beeping. The number is unknown but I rarely get phone calls.

"Hello?"

A thin, strained voice says, "*Son-nim*, perhaps you can help me today as well?"

I jump to my feet. "Yes. Tell me where I should go. To Yongsan?"

"No. I text you."

She sends me her address. I hurry and wash up in under five minutes and head out. It's barely four in the morning, so I end up walking quite a distance to find a cab. When I arrive at Yang's

apartment building, I'm a sweaty mess. She's too ill to care. I make
her a cup of citron honey tea from the jar of marmalade in the refrigerator and force her onto the sofa. Ten minutes later, the
woman is passed out. Quietly, I finish the prep work, rolling hundreds of pork and cheese balls, cutting the vegetables, and mixing
up the batter. She barely stirs as I move in and out of the apartment, carrying the food down to her truck. Yang Ilwha's food has
been a comfort to me for almost two months, so despite my lack of
a license and my fear that I will screw this up, I drive the truck to
Yongsan.

While I know how to do everything, I'm not as proficient as
Yang Ilwha. I am going to need help. I text Jules.

ME: Please say that you're in Seoul and not in Hong Kong or
Singapore or Bali

JULES: I'm not in HK, SP, Bali

I ignore the part where she doesn't admit to being in Seoul.

ME: Come to this address. Wear sneakers. Prepare to work

JULES: U must have the wrong number

ME: This is your KakaoTalk ID!

JULES: Fine. But you owe me.

ME: Hanwoo again?

JULES: No. One of your Chanel bags

ME: Those aren't mine. Those are Wansu's

JULES: She gave them to you and you haven't even taken them out of the shopping bags. It's a crime. You're committing a crime

ME: What're the charges

JULES: Too many for me to type but just know you should be locked up

ME: I don't doubt it

I'm lifting the window away from the stainless steel counter when a taxi deposits Jules across the street.

"I'm afraid to ask what is going on here." She sticks her hands into her back pockets and rocks back on her heels.

I grab the chalk to letter the signboard for the day and bark out orders. "There's a prep sink to the side and some antibacterial soap. Wash up, use a good helping of sanitizer, and pull on some plastic gloves. Maybe wear one to handle the food and use the other hand to handle the money. There are a lot of cash customers, surprisingly."

"Is this yours? Did Yujun buy this for you? Are you on some variety show with Ahn Sangki and I'm on a hidden camera?" She spins around and then starts finger combing her hair. "You could have at least given me some warning," she hisses behind a fake smile she points in different directions where she thinks the cameras might be.

"Yang Ilhwa, the owner, is sick, and she called me for help today."

"She called you for help?" Jules eyes me incredulously.

"It's a long story, but basically I helped her yesterday and today she was too sick to even finish a cup of tea before she passed out. The food is prepped and it will go to waste if it's not used, so let's sell until I run out. We're usually done at two. You don't have to stick around to clean up. I can do all of that. I'll pay you . . ." I'm not earning anything here, but if Jules wants a Chanel purse, then she should have one. "Your pick from my closet."

"Where did you say the prep sink was?"

The great thing about Jules is that her real-life job is flight attendant so she knows how to handle customers. It's as natural to her as breathing. She never stops smiling, no matter how much people complain, knows exactly which customer needs an extra serving for free and which needs friendly banter. Her Korean is excellent, and while she might have a slight foreign accent, every Korean who comes to the counter is completely charmed by her fluency. I swear the crowd picks up. Around noon, our supplies are dangerously low.

"I think we might have to close up soon. I'm running out of pork balls." I swipe my sleeve across my forehead. Working all the fryers has turned me into a giant ball of grease. I don't remember a time I've felt more gross. Once I get home, I plan to take an hour-long shower. Hell, I might even go to a sauna and soak in one of their special tubs.

"Hope you have enough for a group of four because there's some businessmen headed our way. I'll tell them that they're getting a special and charge them more."

"I honestly believe you could get away with that."

"Watch and learn, baby." Jules turns to the customers. "*Annyeonghaseyo . . .*"

The last part of her hello trails off oddly.

"Jules? What are you doing?" asks a familiar voice in sharp, formal Korean.

I freeze and beside me so does Jules.

"Ch-choi Yujun," she stammers, shoving me slightly to the side so I'm farther away from the opening and out of Yujun's gaze, but it's too late. He recognizes me.

"Hara?"

I pretend I don't hear him and hide in the far back of the truck. Not only do I feel gross, but I know I look terrible with my grease-splattered apron, bread crumb– and batter-covered hands, the hairnet; the plastic face shield; the sweat.

"I'm sorry but we're all out of everything. Closed. We're closed."

There's some Korean chatter beyond the counter. Jules replies, "We don't speak Korean. No speak *Hanguk*!" Under her breath she hisses, "How do you close the damn window?"

"From outside."

"Seriously?"

"Yes."

She curses and I want to curl up into a small ball in the corner. There's a knock at the back door of the truck and I know it's Yujun. I'm not answering it.

"Hara, Yujun is coming—" Jules's warning dies in her throat as the door is pulled open and a very confused Yujun, dressed in dark slacks and a crisp white shirt, appears in the frame. The tail of his green tie is tucked inside his shirt and his sleeves are rolled up to expose his fine veiny forearms. His head is covered with a black baseball cap to block out the sun. He looks scrumptious. I look like a raggedy dishcloth—one with holes and stains.

"When you weren't home this morning, I assumed you went to work early, and I see you are working but not where I expected you to be."

"I'm going to the store to get a lemonade. Want one? No? Okay, bye." Jules slips away while Yujun and I engage in a staring contest.

"It's a long story," I repeat.

"I'm all ears."

Someone says something in Korean. "I have customers." I start to close the door on him. He slaps his hand against the steel.

"I'm coming home early."

"That feels like a warning."

"Consider it prior notice. Don't run off. I'll find you." He reaches out and tugs on my red silk cord, which had escaped from inside my T-shirt. "I'll find you," he repeats. He steps back and lets the door swing shut.

My cheeks are hot when I serve him and his coworkers, and not from the heat of the deep fryer. Jules returns and allows me to retreat to the back of the truck.

"What did he say?" she hisses between customers.

"That he's coming home early and not to run off."

"Or what? He'll spank you?" She waggles her eyebrows. "Didn't know Yujun was that type of guy. Although . . . he does seem like he enjoys being in charge."

I'm 100 percent certain that there's no redder color on this earth than my face at this moment.

"You didn't answer me," Jules teases. At least, I think she's teasing.

"I can't hear you over the noise of this deep fryer." I make a loud buzzing noise.

She says something else so I increase the volume of my own sound. I vaguely hear laughter and then chicken sounds.

"You're happy. You get back together with Bomi?"

Jules's giggles cut off. "How did you know?" She sounds annoyed. "Did Bomi tell you?"

"No, but a giddy Jules either means you're high, which is illegal here, or in love."

"Which is also illegal here."

"But you don't care."

"No. Not really. Bomi says that we'll not officially come out, but there's no reason I can't be around her. It's normal to see girls and even women holding hands. We won't share a registry, and medical issues will suck, but that's a long way off and a lot can change. Even if it doesn't, we can still be together." She grins. "We'll be like those fossilized remains that are wrapped together and the historians interpret as good friends."

"I'm really happy for you." Jules and Bomi are not afraid of the goblins. Be a dragon, Hara.

CHAPTER TWENTY

YUJUN: I'm working late. There's no one here. I'm scared.
please come and hold my hand.

YUJUN SENT THAT TO ME A HALF HOUR AGO. DESPITE HIS EAR-
lier threat, he did not get off early, but I didn't run away either. I
want to see him. I haven't done anything wrong other than not
come to work at IF Group. I explained in an earlier text that Yang
Ilhwa had been sick and I helped her out. He was confused about
how I knew the food truck owner well enough to fill in for her, but
accepted it in the end.

I clean up in record time, throw on the first blouse and pants I
can find, and nearly get hit running down the street to hail a taxi.
"IF Group," I say. "Yongsan-gu, *gamshamnida*."

The driver takes off and I slump in the seat, texting Yujun a
reply.

ME: am in cab. on my way.

YUJUN: Excellent

The lobby of IF Group is empty but for two security guards sitting behind the reception desk. I wave my badge in their general direction and then swipe it over the security sensor. When the elevator doors slide open on the fourteenth floor, he's waiting, looking deliciously rumpled with his shirt collar open and the tie nowhere to be seen.

"I thought you were scared," I tease, slightly breathless at the sight of him. When was the last time we made love? The other night, we sloppily kissed each other and then passed out. It was in his apartment, a week ago. Maybe longer. Time's a construct, and right now it feels like it has been an eternity since I've felt his weight pressing me into the sheets.

"I am. That's why I'm waiting under all these lights." He points upward to the LED panels in the ceiling.

I don't look. I'm too busy staring at his body and the way his toned figure is still obvious beneath the white work shirt and the slim-fit pants. He has the perfect shape for a man, all wide shoulders and slim hips. His arm falls to his side.

"Hara?" he husks out.

My eyes jerk upward to see his dark brown eyes turn black. Heat skates up my spine. I don't know if I fall into him or he pulls me close, but before my heart beats once more, I am flush against him. His erection presses into my stomach; his mouth slams against mine.

"Bathroom. Closet. Desk," I gasp against his lips.

He laughs and it fills me with so much joy. He backs me down the hall, pausing only to swipe his badge against the security panel. We fall into the bathroom and tear at each other's clothes. I hear a button ping against the tile, but I don't know if it comes from his shirt or my pants and neither do I care. My hands are on his chest, sliding over his shoulders. His palms cup my ass and boost me onto the sink. The cold steel should have sent a shiver up my spine, but I only feel his hands stroking my back and his lips kissing their way down my neck. There's only the heat of his mouth, the way his fingers tug on my blouse, the scrape of evening stubble against my sensitive skin.

I run my hands up his bare chest, skimming over the hard slabs of muscle, reaching his neck and pulling him back to my lips for a deeper, longer, sexier kiss. While our tongues are busy, our hands are busier. Shirts come off, pants are unzipped, underwear is pushed away, or—in my case—torn at the side. I hated this pair anyway.

He dips lower, tracing a warm trail down the column of my neck, pausing to pay sweet attention to my breasts, and then leaving me breathless as he pushes my thighs apart. I close my eyes and lean back against the mirror. Blood pounds in my ears and in other, sensitive places. My toes curl and my body shakes as the sensations roar over me. He rises to his full height and surges inside. Every node of my being is electrified. I'm on fire, on the edge of an explosion. I grip him fiercely, clutching him to me as if I don't hold him tight enough I'll lose him. I am greedy, like the oldest brother, but I will not let the goblins win.

With a harsh groan and thrust, he spends his last bit of energy and slumps his heavy body into mine. I wrap my arms around him and run my hands over his sweat-slicked shoulder blades, over the bumps of his spine. I am not with Yujun because he's the first man to pay attention to me, the first one to say he loves me. I'm with him because the sun is brighter when he's in its rays, the food is tastier when he's at the table, the laughter is richer when he's telling the joke. Being with him makes me happy. That's why I am with him.

He plants a tender kiss on the side of my neck before straightening. "You okay?"

His fingers brush a lump of hair away from my face. I am a mess, but I don't care.

"Yes. Wonderful."

A smug smile stretches across his face, but I'm not irritated. He helped me achieve a spectacular orgasm, so he's entitled. I wriggle off the counter and start looking for my clothes. Yujun scoops up my pants and shirt and helps me dress. It's an odd but weirdly thrilling experience having him button me up. I return the favor. It feels wifely.

"You're missing one." I point to the empty space where the fourth button from the top used to be. Only a stub of threads remains.

He clasps my finger and kisses the tip of it. "I have more at home."

"Shirts or buttons?"

"Shirts with buttons."

He tucks my hand into his and leads me down to his office. He doesn't have a big office like Wansu's even though he's part of management. His space is much like *Bujang-nim*'s, where a wide desk is positioned perpendicular to smaller ones. It's rather messy. There are papers in disordered piles. A cup of old coffee rests on the edge.

One good nudge and it will fall onto the floor. He swipes it up and tosses it in the trash.

"I have a system," he says and there's a hint of pink on his cheekbones, as if he's a little embarrassed that his workspace isn't picture perfect, but I like it. It humanizes him.

"Sure you do," I tease.

He cocks his head. "I don't know if you are agreeing or disagreeing. Your tone says you don't believe me."

Yujun's nearly accentless English makes me forget that he is not a native English speaker and it makes me wish I spoke better Korean so when we teased each other, there was complete understanding.

"I was teasing you so I was saying that I don't really believe you but in a joking way. Who are these two?" I point to a photo of two adorable children sitting on swings. Their hands are clasped and their windblown cheeks look like peaches.

"Nephew and niece," he says proudly.

My eyes grow huge. "You have a sibling?"

"*Ani. Ani.* No. Cousin. My father's sister's children's children."

"Ah, okay." My heart resettles in my chest.

"I am an only child like you. I'll introduce you to them. We can go to PIM. It's a kid's café on the Han River. We'll take *insaeng shot*."

"Life photos?"

He beams. "You have learned more words. I'm proud of you. *Insaeng* does mean 'life' but in this case it is 'shot of life' or 'best shot of my life.' There's a ball pit that overlooks the Han but the balls are all translucent so they look more like bubbles. It's very Instagram-worthy."

"Am I allowed in that?"

"With children. I borrow Choi Juwon's children all the time for things that I enjoy doing but I am too old to do, such as go on rides at Everland or play laser tag at Lotte."

"It's a date." We smile at each other in harmony until my stomach growls.

"You did not have dinner?" He checks the time. "It is so late. We should eat. Shall I order something? Or do you want to go out?"

"Let's order. I'm too tired to sit at a restaurant." I smother a huge yawn. A wry grin quirks up the corner of my mouth. "I am usually not this physically active."

Yujun coughs into his shoulder, hiding a bit of smugness. "What do you want?"

"Anything. I don't want to think. Surprise me."

I sit down in his chair. He perches a hip on his desk and lifts my feet into his lap. I let my eyes flutter shut as he taps away on his phone.

"Tell me about the food truck. Please," he adds.

With my eyes still closed, I answer. "Sangki first took me there about a week or two after you left. The food isn't the greatest. The fried pork-cheese balls are the highlight, but the *yachae twigim* can be soggy and undercooked. The corn cups have too much sauce in them and the corn is sometimes dry. I think she should serve a cold dessert in the summer."

"And *hotteok* in the winter. There are never enough *hotteok* sellers in the winter."

"I'll tell her. Anyway, the food reminds me of Iowa. Corn, cheese, pork. I started going there regularly, sometimes two or three times a week. She'd always call me *son-nim* and I'd call her *Imo-nim*. One day she joked she would teach me how to cook."

"And so yesterday you decided you had to learn immediately?"

"No. Yesterday when I went there for lunch, she was sick. I helped her out and then left my number for her. She called me this morning"—I yawn again—"and said she needed my help. She was half passed out when I arrived. A lot of the food was already prepared and it would've gone to waste, so I loaded her truck up and drove it to Yongsan. Jules came and helped me. You know the rest."

"You're something else, Hara."

The admiration in his voice fills me with warmth.

"I'm tired."

"Did you drive the truck back?"

"Yes. She met me at the door and said she'd been to the doctor and had an IV and that she should be better tomorrow, but"—I yawn yet again—"who knows."

"It's late. I'm taking you to my place."

"Wansu won't be happy." But I don't protest when he pulls me to my feet.

He tucks me close to his side and leads me to the elevators. We don't encounter anyone on our way to the basement garage and he keeps me next to him the whole way. My eyes are heavy, but my heart is light and my soul is full. This night is perfect even without a bed for the lovemaking. My job may suck, my family situation is a mess, but at least I have Yujun, and I wouldn't trade him for a perfect life. If Wansu could come around, then maybe all would be okay.

"What are we going to do, Yujun?"

"Be patient. It will work out." He's confident and he knows Wansu best, so I'm going to trust him.

CHAPTER TWENTY-ONE

THE SECURITY GUARD AT THE ELEVATOR BANK DOES A DOU-
ble take when I reach him.

"Choi Hara-nim?"

"Yes?"

There's a slight smirk. *"Aniyaeyo."* And he turns back to his
desk.

Never mind? And with that look? That is so odd. I've been
coming here for almost eight weeks. He should know my face and
my identity by now. I give myself a quick once-over and see nothing
out of place that would cause him to check me at the entrance. My
outfit of navy blue pants, yellow-and-white-striped shirt, and navy
coat is unremarkable unless yellow is an offensive color, which
would not be likely as people here aren't called yellow-skinned like
back home. I'm stain-free, since I have eaten only a buttered bagel

this morning that Yujun bought me at the bakery next door to his apartment building.

I dismiss it, telling myself I have an overactive imagination. When I log in, there are new projects in my inbox. I almost clap in excitement. See, everything improves given time. It's not the LA deal, but it's work. Someone else must be working on the LA deal. Like Bomi said, I only need to keep walking. No need to worry about the security guard downstairs. I'm on my way to becoming a functioning member of this team. Not even fifteen minutes into my work, *Bujang-nim* materializes at my side, his dark-wool-clad thigh right in my line of sight. I have to tilt my head to meet his concerned gaze.

"Your mo— Choi Hywejang-nim would like to see you." His voice, never quiet on a good day, feels extra loud. I wish he had sent me an email.

As I get to my feet, I can feel the eyes of all my coworkers following me. This is like getting sent to the principal's office. I throw on my suit coat, awkwardly struggling with the sleeves as I make my way to the elevator bank. Outside Wansu's office, Yujun is idling with one hand propped on the receptionist's desk and the other holding his phone.

"Hara?" he says in surprise.

My shoulders slump to my knees. If Yujun is here at the same time I am, a lecture is incoming. "Do you know what this is about?"

He shakes his head, but we both know it's not good. I knew she wouldn't be happy I didn't come home last night. Wansu was hoping we'd lose interest and we haven't, so now she has to increase the pressure. I clench my teeth, remind myself that I am a lizard with scales or possibly a turtle with hardened skin. No matter what she says, as long as Yujun and I stick together, we will make it through this. What is she going to do? Disown us both?

"You can go in," directs Wansu's admin.

Wansu is standing in the middle of her office. Behind me the assistant quietly closes the door. Without a word, Wansu points her hand toward the wall. A light flickers on and a translucent screen display situated in front of one of the bookcases flickers to life. The lights dim and a grainy image appears. There are two people in front of a bank of elevators and they are— *Oh hell no*. No wonder Wansu is silent. The video speaks for itself. Even Yujun is stunned into speechlessness as we watch the two of us stumble toward the glass doors of the office. There's a cut and we reappear in the hall, just outside the bathroom. I'm pawing at Yujun's clothes and he's fumbling with the door handle behind him because I will not let go of him for even a second.

The time stamp skips ahead thirty minutes and we emerge with hair mussed and clothes untucked, and even from this distance, with the low resolution, the smug, satisfied expression on both our faces is clearly visible. Yujun presses me back against the wall and kisses me hard, his hand disappearing up my shirt. Wansu shudders. That scene snaps Yujun out of his paralysis, and he crosses to his mother, swipes the remote I didn't even know she was holding out of her hand, and switches the video off.

I'm numb from embarrassment. I hadn't realized that was an actual state you could achieve, as I've only experienced hot flashes of embarrassment, where it burns, but there's a point where a situation is so humiliating that you shut down as a defense mechanism. Sound is muffled, as if there's cotton in my ears. My vision is blurry. My limbs feel like stones. My head is full of nonsense noise. That's how full of shame I am right now.

"How dare you." Her voice is quiet, but she is literally vibrating with anger or distress or both. "How dare you come into this place of work, engage in these activities, display yourself to all in violation of every known principle. It is not *right*." Wansu is serious. "The thought of you two together"—she shudders again—"it is *bulmyeong-ye*." I'm not sure what that word is, but I can guess because it sounds like she's vomiting. "You cannot do this." She is not saying this because it could cause a scandal and jeopardize the people here in this building but because the thought of the two of us together well and truly revolts her.

"*Eomma*, we were not raised together," Yujun pleads. He's not paralyzed by the throes of embarrassment like me. "It is not the same thing, and her name is not Choi anyway."

"It will be."

"Have you discussed that with Hara? Perhaps she wants to remain a Wilson."

Wansu isn't listening. She slashes her hand down. "Do not speak of it again. This has been deleted and the security staff have been told if they leak the footage, we will bring criminal charges against them, so none will act, but how could you?" There is genuine revulsion in her voice that I've never heard before. "It is not right, what the two of you are doing. You are my children. This is wrong. It is immoral and you must not ever again touch each other."

This is why I got the weird look from the security guard. She might have paid them off, but it's spread among some of the staff. It won't be long until it migrates to the seventh floor, where Soyou and Chaeyoung will watch it. I want to sink into the floor.

I can't even look at Yujun.

"*Eomma*," Yujun attempts.

"Wansu," I say at the same time.

She shakes her head sharply. "I do not want to hear it. Your excuses and explanations do not matter. It does not matter what happened before you knew you were siblings. It is now that matters. You will not see each other. Do you hear me?"

She's not yelling, but she could be. She points a finger at her son. "You are going to be sent on another business trip. This time it will be to Los Angeles and it will be much, much longer than four weeks. And you." She turns to me. "You will go home. You are done for the day. I will clean up your mess here."

That's it. We're dismissed. She turns her back and rifles through papers on her desk, and the rejection is sharp. Yujun opens his mouth to argue, but I don't have the stomach for it. I grab his elbow, and when he looks at me, I shake my head as well. *No more, please.*

He gives in and follows me out. The assistant is so well-mannered, she doesn't even look up from her computer monitor when we pass by her desk, but she has to be curious. Or maybe she isn't curious. Maybe she's watching the video. I want to drop to the tile and army crawl out of the building and all the way back to Wansu's house. All the warm feelings from last night are eradicated, and what had been a fun, sexy memory is now tainted. The whole thing has gone from quirky hijinks to sordid hookup.

"I'm sorry," Yujun says quietly as I wait for the elevator.

"It's not your fault. You couldn't have peeled me away with a razor."

"I should have protected you. I knew there were cameras."

"Forget it." There's no point in recriminations.

"Go home and try to put this out of your mind the best that you can. I'm going to talk with *Eomma*. We'll work this out."

"Sure." I don't believe him and he knows it. This is the river-park date all over again, but this time it isn't some random girl who I will never see again. This is the woman who gave birth to me. This is my mother, and isn't that the damned problem? How do we work this out as Yujun says?

The prospect of going back to my desk to get my purse and phone is daunting, but I manage. Wansu has conveyed some message to *Bujang-nim*, because as soon as I appear in our division, he jumps to his feet.

"Choi Hywejang-nim says the car is waiting. It is nothing serious?"

"No, nothing serious," I echo.

My coworkers watch me with varying degrees of envy for getting off work early or suspicion that I might've ratted them all out. I do nothing to clear up misconceptions because the truth is worse than anything they can think of. *I'm being sent home like a child because I was caught boinking my mother's stepson in the bathroom. There's security footage. You might get to see it!* I slink out as quietly as possible. Downstairs, Park, the Chois' regular driver, is waiting. Does he know? Does he think I'm disgusting?

I hide in the back seat, sinking out of the line of sight of the rearview mirror. Mrs. Ji isn't at the door to greet me, so at least I don't think she knows. She does come out of the kitchen, however, as I stumble down the hall to my bedroom.

"You need anything?" she asks.

A redo maybe, but what point in the past do I want to go back to? Yesterday, before I mauled Yujun in the hallway? Or to the minute I spotted him at the airport? Or to Pat's funeral? Or to the moment that Wansu met Lee Jonghyung? I run my knuckles down the center of my forehead and order myself to stop feeling sorry for myself. My mind is racing, going in circles until I burst out of my room, unable to be alone one second longer.

Nurse Park startles when I open the door.

"I'm going to sit with *Sae Appa*," I tell her. "I'll call you if he needs anything."

She gives me a brief bow and slides out of the room. I collapse in the chair next to his bed.

"I'm sorry to bother you, but I need the distraction. I'm going to pretend nothing happened this morning and that this is a normal workday. What should I read today?" I pick up the folktale book. It falls open to the story of the two brothers and the goblins in the forest. I swallow a scream and throw the book to the side. "Let's watch television." I search for the remote, finding it tucked next to *Sae Appa*'s leg. "Yujun says Wansu watches dramas with you. There aren't any subtitles so I have problems understanding everything they're saying but who cares." A slightly hysterical laugh escapes. "Do you know what I'm saying? You speak pretty good English, though. You would hate that Yujun and I are together, wouldn't you? Do you know the story of the two brothers and the goblins? The oldest brother got greedy and was nearly beaten to death. That's me. I'm the eldest brother. I want all of it. Ellen, Wansu, Yujun . . ." I pause. "You, too. I want to live here in Seoul and speak like a native. I want to be able to go back to Iowa and not feel like I don't belong. I want my boat of life to always sail calm waters. How do you stop yourself from wanting more? Wanting too much?"

I bend over and scrape my fingers through my hair. The answer to my problems is right in front of me. Give Yujun up. I can have all of it—or most of it—if I give him up.

CHAPTER TWENTY-TWO

"NO." YUJUN SLAPS THE BLUE PADFOLIO AGAINST HIS THIGH.
"I'm not going on any blind dates and neither is Hara."

The two came home a half hour ago. Yujun's jaw was tight and
Wansu's mouth was flattened into a straight, unhappy line. She
asked for me to come into the living room, and when I arrived,
there were four of those cursed blue folders on the table.

"Don't you think Hara should make her own decisions?" Wansu
cocks her head. "I've spoken to Ellen about this. She thinks it is a
good idea."

"You're talking to Hara's American mother?"

There's something halfway gratifying about the fact that Yujun
is as taken aback by this nugget of information as I was when I
learned of it. "They talk all the time," I supply.

Yujun arches an eyebrow. *Really?* He silently questions.

Really. I nod back.

"What parent who cares for their children does not do this?" Wansu spreads her hands innocently in front of her.

"Many, *Eomma*."

"As I told you previously, when I first shared Kim Seonpyung's profile with you, he is not your only option. Only one of several who I think would be a good match for you."

"She is not interested," Yujun repeats.

"It is understandable if you do not find a lawyer appealing." Wansu pretends Yujun didn't speak. "I have heard they can be difficult partners. Perhaps you might like this one." She pushes two blue folders aside and selects a third. "Chang Doyun is an assistant producer at CBC, one of our terrestrial broadcasting channels. You and Ahn Sangki-nim get along well and so someone in entertainment might be better suited."

"*Eomma*, enough!" Yujun explodes. "Hara does not need this."

"You mean you do not want this," she snaps. "You wish to carry on an illicit affair that will result in your social ostracization and the disapprobation of your family. Your grandmother would not allow you into her home. Your cousins would close their doors to you. No Chuseok. No Seollal. No *jesas*."

Yujun clamps his mouth shut. A muscle jumps in his jaw.

Don't be greedy, Hara. Don't be greedy. "What does this blind date entail?" I ask.

"Hara!" exclaims Yujun. "This is unnecessary. What goes on between you and me is our business and no one else's."

"And how would you enter her in our family registry when the law officially recognizes her as your sister. It cannot be done, Yujun. It is best that you two move on now before you hurt yourselves more." Wansu turns to me. "Meet him for coffee. There is no commitment being made here. It is like trying on a new dress or a pair of shoes to see if they fit."

"She already fits with someone," Yujun interjects.

"Do you want Hara to be accepted by your friends? To not be shunned here in her mother country? Or do you want her to be the subject of hateful gossip, a trending topic on the internet forums for being a *nappeun gijibae*?"

Yujun fumes but he has no response. I do not want to be the subject of hateful gossip or a *nappeun gijibae*. I don't know what that is, but I'm certain it's bad. Neither do I want to be separated from Yujun. I don't have a solution right now, so I need time. We both do.

"I'll meet him." I take my folder. "Set it up."

When I walk out, I keep my eyes in front of me so I don't see Yujun's hurt expression.

CHAPTER TWENTY-THREE

MY PHONE PINGS WHEN I REACH MY ROOM. I KNOW IT'S YUJUN.

YUJUN: I heard Kim Seonpyung hates animals.

I burst out laughing, a little wildly, on the verge of hysteria, but it's a laugh. That wasn't in my report

YUJUN: You can't go on a blind date with someone who hates animals

ME: I'm not! I'm pacifying your mother

YUJUN: She's your mother too

ME: Which is the problem

YUJUN: Right

The three ellipses show up and then disappear and then reappear. And then disappear. He doesn't know what to say and neither do I.

> YUJUN: She's kicking me out of the house. She gave me
> containers of banchan and told me to go to my apartment.
> I'm retreating for now. We can talk at work tomorrow.
> Don't go on that blind date. I love you.

I rub the red silk cord between my fingers and then type back. I love you, too.

After a moment of hesitation, I pull out the blue portfolios. The top one is the animal hater. The second one, ironically, is a dog trainer, and Bomi has written in the margin *Kind! Patient!*

I toss them aside and face the ugly truth. I've been a people pleaser all my life. Ellen was right. Because I was abandoned, I have two modes: avoidance or capitulation. Either I reject you before you can reject me or I do everything I can to make you like me. Since the latter is a sad and humiliating way to live, I opted for the former most of the time.

Here, surrounded by Yujun and friends, having found my birth mother, ensconced in this beautiful modern palace, I have let my guard down and allowed people inside. I find myself wanting desperately to be liked by my coworkers because they are the ideal version of me—smart, chic, *Korean*. If I was accepted by these two women, then I would belong here. Until then I would be the perpetual outsider in this country in which I was born. Everyone looked like me on the outside, but there was something infinitely American about me on the inside, and that part was on display like a billboard in Times Square. Look here, in flashing letters, a *gyopo*—an overseas Korean who hasn't bothered to learn the language and is pretending she fits in.

I don't.

I will always be a girl raised in Iowa, and yet, in Iowa, I will always be the one who doesn't look like anyone else. At least here, if I never open my mouth, I will be *one of them*.

What misery. I don't need anyone's approval. Not those girls at work and not Wansu here. I've been going around proclaiming I have two mothers, but I only have one, and that is Ellen. She didn't give birth to me, but she raised me. She sat by my bedside when I had nightmares, sang songs to chase the monsters away, commiserated when I failed but pushed me back on my feet. We have laughed together and fought each other, and I know that if I don't see her or talk to her for six months, she'll still open her arms upon seeing me and press smacking kisses on my forehead all the while sobbing about how much she missed me.

I stomp into the dressing room and dig around for my old suitcase. I swing it up onto the center island of cabinets and begin packing. My old jeans, the one polka-dotted dress I brought, my cardigan, all get tossed into the case. I'm leaving everything else here. Wansu can live in this marble tomb of a place by herself. I am going to be with Yujun. I'm going to—a sob catches in my throat.

Sometimes Wansu will talk about her job and her love life. . . . She's lonely.

I clasp my hands on the edge of the suitcase and sink to my knees. The metal edging bites into my hand. Wansu is my mother, too. She carried me for nine months. She tried to keep me, but she couldn't. Her family didn't support her. There was no government aid that could feed me. She made the ultimate sacrifice. She gave me up so that I could have a better life, and now I want to take everything away from her.

What would Bomi put in the margins of my dating profile. *Demanding! Confused! Irrational!*

Selfish.

I will not be the older brother that comes to ruin. There has to be a way. There has to be a way to make this work. Yujun believes there is. We can't see it clearly right now, but if we give it time . . .

I push to my feet and walk through the sitting room and into the bathroom to splash cold water on my face. What we need is time, I decide. Time for Wansu to get used to the idea of Yujun and me as a couple. We will go through Chuseok and *jesas* and whatever else she said Yujun would not be invited to, and she will see how her worries are for naught.

Dinnertime rolls around. Completely composed, I join her at the dining room table. If she's surprised by my appearance, she doesn't show it. Dinner is hand-packed spinach ravioli with a mixed green salad, cherry tomatoes, cucumbers, and feta cheese. Red wine is the drink of choice. I have two glasses.

Wansu speaks of the weather—the cool weather is nice; the pollution—I'll need to carry a mask with me in case the air quality grows bad as it does in the late autumn months; and even the drama she's watching—it's outrageous.

It's the most verbose she's ever been. At the end of the meal, having eaten everything on my plate and tasted nothing, I let her know that tomorrow night I will not be home for dinner.

Her mouth tightens, but maybe because she doesn't want to know the answer, she doesn't ask why. She wouldn't like my response.

CHAPTER TWENTY-FOUR

THERE'S A SMALL SUSHI BAR NEAR YUJUN'S APARTMENT. AC-
cording to the Naver profile, it only seats ten. I reserve one table
and send a text for Yujun to meet me there after work. I take a leaf
out of Bomi's book and arrive fifteen minutes in advance. As I wait
for him to arrive, I am assailed by second thoughts. What if I'm
being too impulsive? What if we end up arguing? There are other
places that are less public. Maybe we should go to the river. That's
where we first kissed. Where I first cried in his arms. Where we
had our first breakup. I stare at my phone screen.

Then he walks through the door.

I remember the first time I saw him at the Incheon Airport. He
was standing to the side of the kiosk where I was leasing my internet modem. Dressed in a blue suit with one hand scrolling through
his phone and the other stuck into his pocket, he looked more like

a model for some expensive clothing brand than a traveler who had disembarked from an international flight. I had to fix my tongue against the roof of my mouth so it wouldn't fall out. Tonight, I'm struck speechless again at his male beauty.

There are only two other people in this small restaurant—a couple, but they both turn and stare at him for longer than is polite. He's *that* attractive. But Yujun has eyes for no one else. He never has, not since I've been with him. His face lights up when he spots me.

"Hara, have you been waiting long?"

"No. I just arrived."

"You should've had the cab drop you off at my place. We could have walked over together." He pulls out his chair and settles in.

"I wanted to make sure there was a table available." I wonder if I should've brought a gift. Do people do that for breakups? And what is an appropriate breakup gift? A tie? A book? A journal? Before I decided to live in Seoul, I bought him hand-painted notecards to write to me. Conversely, what is the right present for a "stay with me even if I ruin your life" request?

"Should we order Set 1? It's light but that leaves enough room for AeMangBing at the Shilla Hotel and a walk up along the fortress wall. It's prettiest at night."

He knows my weak spots. The Jeju Apple Mango Bingsu Shilla serves during the summer is one of my favorites, and since the fall is here, it will be out of season soon. And the view of the city from the old fortress wall is pretty at night. My gut clenches at the thought of Yujun hiking those trails with another girl's hand in his.

"Set 1 is fine, although maybe we should go to the Shake

Shack. It's around the corner. We can order and take the food somewhere."

"The Shake Shack? If that's what you want, we can do that." He studies the menu. "If you're here to break up with me, then I will want my necklace back."

"What?" My hand flies to my chest to cover the jade duck nestled under my sweater.

Without looking at me, he extends his hand, palm up, and repeats his demand. "The necklace. I gave it to you with the belief that we would be forever, but if you're quitting on me now, you need to return it. Give it back."

"I am not quitting on you."

"Better not." He sets the menu down. "I've been thinking."

"Wait. Let me go first."

He drums his fingers against the table. "I'm afraid to let you go first. You almost broke up with me."

"I did not." A moment of madness in my closet doesn't count. "But, listen, we can't abandon Wansu. She's lonely, you know."

Yujun's face softens. He stretches out his hand and clasps mine. "This is why I love you. Or one of the reasons, Hara. You aren't consumed with thoughts only of yourself."

Gosh, if he only knew the truth of how selfish my thoughts have been.

"I know she is lonely," he continues. "Father is . . . not in a good condition, and she should let him go, but I don't have the heart to tell her. She will need to come to her own decision on that."

So that's why he's not been broken up about his father or why he doesn't visit often. He's said his goodbyes to his father some time ago.

"I've been thinking that we should go to LA. We can live openly as a couple there with no one to question us. *Eomma* will not have to face awkward questions or suffer any loss of face with her friends." He doesn't see my growing horror. "We'd be helping IF Group expand and grow larger. You would have no problems, obviously, with the language." He smiles, two dimples winking at me. "It's really a perfect solution." I shake my head in slow but real dismay. His smile fades. "How is it not perfect?"

"You don't belong in LA, at least not to live. I don't want you to go through what I go through with the constant low-grade insults about what you look like or how you speak or how your food smells funny or how your customs are weird until you turn out like your aunt Sue, who refuses to speak Korean and pretends she's white so that she doesn't feel like she's a constant interloper in a country she's lived in for over thirty years! You developed a stutter, for God's sakes!" I slam my hands on the table before remembering we are not alone. I should've said to meet at the river. The other couple is staring at us and this time not because Yujun is gorgeous.

I don't mean to make a scene but stepsiblings cannot marry legally, and even if it were legal, it would be a social death for Yujun. He would not be able to see his cousins. His friends would turn on him. I suspect that his business dealings would suffer. Going to America is not the answer, because doesn't that mean he could never come home? He is not his aunt Sue, who prefers to live in Malibu pretending she's white, never speaking Korean, never eating the food of her motherland, disassociating herself from all things Asian so as not to be tainted by otherness. I know Aunt Sue. I was her in Iowa and I don't want that to happen to Yujun. Not my Yujun from Seoul.

"Thank you for reminding me as if I have forgotten," he shoots back. "But I am not a child anymore, Hara, and the careless words of a few will not diminish me."

"You don't know that. You don't. And it's never a few words. It's a thousand cuts, piled on top of you, until the wound is so deep it doesn't heal. Instead, you contort into whatever box someone has defined for you and are utterly miserable, and you will hate me for it and that's the last thing I want." If Yujun thinks the only place we can be together happily is outside South Korea, that makes all his platitudes about things being fine into a lie.

We sit there in silence as the roads in the map of our future are slowly erased. Finally, Yujun speaks. "Hara, do you still feel like a striped dress in a polka-dotted country?"

"You remember that?" I'd told him once that being adopted in America felt like I was the only polka-dot-wearing person in a place where everyone wore stripes and that I'd foolishly thought if I came here, I'd fit in, but there's something distinctively American about me—in my halting, accented Korean, in the makeup I wear, in the way I walk, smile, laugh, and so here I still feel other.

"Of course I do. Have you forgotten everything I said to you?" he teases gently.

No. I remember everything. I remember his first words were, "You're American," and the first sight of his dimples almost put me on the floor. I remember the way he carried my suitcase up the mini mountain over by Cheonggyecheong-gu. I remember when he first brought me to the river, fed me *gimbap* and beer, and kissed me so thoroughly I had stars in my eyes for days. I remember peering through the Namsan Tower camera to the cute couple in Busan and Yujun telling me that distance is a construct. I remember the last time we went to the river after Wansu said she'd acknowledge me as a Choi but that meant that Yujun would be my stepbrother and we could not be together.

He stretches his arm across the table and fishes out the red cord of my necklace, on which the jade carved duck hangs. I remember when he gave this to me and said ducks mate for life.

"We will find a way, Hara. Trust me."

CHAPTER TWENTY-FIVE

THE FIRST TRUST TEST COMES IN THE FORM OF A COUSIN OR,
more specifically, Yujun's cousin's family. Choi Juwon is the eldest
son of Yujun's aunt, an older sister of Choi Yusuk. He has two
children—a girl and boy under the age of five. These are the kids
that Yujun borrows when he wants to play laser tag or ride the
roller coasters at Everland. Today, we're taking the two children on
a playdate while the parents have some adult time. We will then all
have dinner together as a pre-Chuseok event. Tomorrow, the entire
extended Choi family will descend upon Wansu's house, and Yujun thought it would be nice for me to meet some of them before.
That his cousin agreed to this knowing that I was Wansu's biological daughter cheered me considerably. It meant not everyone was
going to react negatively to our pairing.

We pull into the parking lot of the Hello Flour café and grab
the gifts from the back seat. One bag has a large blue koala with a

purple nose and the other is some indeterminable animal with yellow plushie fur and big black floppy ears. Yujun said it's a dog, but I'm not sure I believe that. He has a few smaller items as well—jelly bracelets, paper craft airplanes, and sweets. It's obvious that one never arrives at a Korean event empty-handed, not even a breakup.

"These feel like a bribe," I joke as I heft a bag into my arms.

"It is a bribe."

I stop short. "Seriously?"

He laughs at my naïveté. "Of course. Why else do we say, 'Please take care of me in the future,' whenever we give a gift? We want them to look at the present and remember us with warm feelings. And for little children, the bigger the gift, the warmer the feelings. Trust me. My cousins love me."

"For your gifts?"

"And my great personality." He grabs my hand and pulls me toward a short flight of stairs leading into the café. Before we can even place a foot on the granite stairs, two kids burst out the doors and launch themselves at Yujun. He drops his bags and catches the tiny tots and spins them around.

The air is filled with shouts of laughter, and my knees grow weak at the appearance of his deep dimples. The little girl in his arms, Choi Nayeon, loves them, too. She pokes her finger into the right one and then presses a kiss in the same spot. The boy, Choi Nara, is already wriggling free. He wants to go inside. *"Milgaru! Milgaru!"* he chants.

"He wants to play in the flour," Yujun explains, his face creased with the biggest smile. He loves these two little ones.

"You don't say." I can't help but grin back.

What's the saying? Happiness looks good on you? Yujun is at

his sexiest when his dimples are deep wells of joy and his eyes are crinkled tight. I love how the eye smile is celebrated here. Plushies' expressions are stitched with upside-down crescents, cartoons are purposely drawn like that to portray extreme pleasure, people pose like that for their life shots. There's not enough appreciation for the eye smile in the West.

Inside, there's a bustle of people obtaining locker keys and suiting up their children in tan-colored jumpsuits that will protect their clothes while they frolic in the flour.

Yujun introduces me as his "*Yeoja chingu*, or girlfriend, Hara-nim," and something else in Korean that sounds a little like "as I told you before." He explained earlier the children don't speak much English, but as my vocabulary level is around that of a kindergartener, I feel like I'll be a good companion.

I hand out the gifts and am rewarded with squeals and baby hugs, which I find are the best hugs second only to the Yujun hug. There's something endearingly sweet about being embraced by small arms that are barely long enough to wend around your neck. The parents bow and smile and wave goodbye, taking the bags of gifts with them, although two bracelets get left behind—one for each of the children.

Yujun helps the kids off with their shoes and their jackets, which I stuff into the lockers. Once the kids are in their protective clothing, bigger aprons are produced for us. We are then shown to a small room filled with flour, a slide no higher than my chest, and a plastic kitchen stowed against the wall. The two kids dive in—literally—and Yujun isn't far behind.

He takes a shovel and dumps flour over both kids' heads. They get their revenge by attacking him from both sides and taking him down. I help by filling small containers with flour that the kids use to fling all over Yujun. It's not long before we're coated like a set of vegetables ready for our tempura bath.

Our time in the flour sandbox speeds by fast, and soon the clock above the door says we have to go.

"*Aaaani*," cry the children, or maybe it was Yujun. No one wants to leave.

"*Beiking.*" I pretend to hold a bowl and stir. The English loan words in the Korean vocab are helping me communicate with these adorable babies.

"Mmm, cookies." Yujun rubs his stomach, and that's enough to convince the other two to move on. We meet in the corner and take turns blowing the flour off with the pneumatic air hose. Yujun sticks the air blower up the sleeve of Nayeon's shirt and then pushes her arm at the elbow so it looks like she's flexing. I pull out my phone and take several photos, smearing flour all over the screen and not caring one iota.

The afternoon with the kids might be one of the best ones I have had here in Seoul. We spend the next hour mixing, baking, and then decorating cookies. While they cool, the kids eat a kid tart, which consists of white bread, cream cheese, and assorted fruits. They each make their own. Nara offers me a bite and I take a small one although he's poked holes in the bread with his sweaty fingers. He could've smothered the sandwich in spit and I would've gladly eaten it. These two children are precious, and I can see why Yujun is so attached.

I would also never want to separate him from them. Fingers crossed, though, everything is working out well.

"Where should we go from here?" Yujun says as we are grabbing the things from the locker.

"Lotte World!"

"Everland!"

"Hmm. A tie. What is your vote, Hara?" Yujun asks.

I glance from one expectant face to the other. "Why not do rock paper scissors?" I improvise. I am not going to be the one to disappoint either child.

"Good idea."

The three play that complicated game of rock paper scissors that all Koreans must learn in the womb. Lotte World, aka Nayeon, wins, but her brother doesn't look too disappointed.

Nayeon whispers something in Yujun's ear and then looks at me shyly.

"I don't think you're old enough for the uniforms, but I'm sure Hara will ride the carousel, won't you?"

"Of course. *Ne!*" I nod vigorously. "What's this about the uniforms?" I ask as we follow the kids outside to Yujun's car.

"Near the carousel, there's a uniform rental shop where you can dress up as a student and take photos in their fake classroom like you're in a drama."

"Oh, that sounds adorable."

"Nayeon is too young. You have to be twelve."

"That sounds like a crime against children. We should protest."

Yujun relays this to Nayeon, who gives me a look of frank approval, which is the best compliment I've received in months.

Our progress comes to a halt when we see Yujun's cousin and his wife step out of their car. Their somber faces send a chill down my spine. They aren't supposed to be here. We're meeting for dinner and there's still a whole afternoon left.

Yujun leaves the kids with me and walks over to hear what must be bad news. Is it *Sae Appa*? Even little Nayeon senses something is wrong and slips her small starfish fingers inside mine.

But as the three talk, Yujun's expression darkens in anger rather than grief. His dimples disappear and his lush lips thin into a tight line. My hand tightens around Nayeon's. Over Yujun's shoulder, the mother catches sight of her daughter's hand tucked in mine and rushes over to tug her children away, as if holding my hand for another second might infect her daughter with something unsavory. In the frown on her face, I read the words my ears can't understand. They've discovered something about me that is distasteful, so much so that leaving their children with Yujun and me for another hour is repugnant.

"Yujun and you. No belong," she says. "Wrong. Wrong."

"*Ya*, Kim Jinae." Yujun steps to my side. "*Hajima*."

Kim Jinae is not cowed. "You hurt him." She points to Yujun. "Family not accept. Stop or hurt."

I want to shrink down into a small ball and roll into the patch of grass a few feet away. Kim Jinae might not know much English, but it's enough to get her point across.

"She's wrong," Yujun tells me. His hands come up to cover my ears. "Don't listen to her. What is going on here, *hyung-nim*? I told you who Hara was on the phone when we agreed to this."

Choi Juwon, or *hyung-nim* as Yujun called him, shrugs almost helplessly. "I told her but she must not have understood."

Yujun glares at the older man. "You fucking liar. You never told her because you knew if you did, she would not have agreed. You wanted a free afternoon to have sex with your wife and lied about it."

The man looks at his feet. Yujun swings and I catch him just in time. "The babies!" I cry. "Not in front of the children."

Yujun vibrates with anger under my hands.

Choi Juwon backs up. "I'm sorry, Yujun-ah, but Jinae is right. I shouldn't have agreed to this. I said you were bringing your girlfriend. She didn't realize it was Choi Wansu's daughter until my mom called." He pushes a hand through his hair. "Don't bring her to Chuseok. No one will approve. You push your father to his death, but maybe it is good he cannot see or hear so that he does not witness what his son has become."

Gasp. Yujun flinches as the blow from his cousin lands hard and solid. Yujun slander? Not on my watch. It's one thing to insult me. I'm used to it, but Yujun is the kindest, sweetest person alive, and insulting him is low-class and terrible.

"You should not come. You aren't worthy of breathing the same air as Yujun," I snap. I don't know if the two understand me, but we're done here. I'm not going to allow them to hurt Yujun, of all people. "I want to leave," I demand, knowing it's the only way to get Yujun away from here. He's always put me first, unfortunately, and this time is no different. Face tight, he unlocks the door to his car and wrenches the door open. I slide inside. Once he's behind the steering wheel, he hesitates, and for a minute I wonder if he's fantasizing about ramming his cousin's car into the next province. The cousins watch us as he pulls out, perhaps having the same fearful thoughts. I hope so. I hope they don't sleep tonight and they step on their kids' LEGO bricks every morning until Nayeon and Nara get to middle school.

The car ride back to Wansu's is silent. Yujun is pissed. His fingers are tight around the steering wheel, and anger roils off of him like a magnetic wave, crashing against me. I know he's not mad at me, but I can still feel it and it sets my teeth on edge. I clamp them together so that they don't shatter, so that I don't start crying, so that I don't make this situation worse than it is.

I'd somehow convinced myself that this would work out. The afternoon was so fun until the parents showed up and sucked the joy out of us like a high-powered vacuum.

I'm mad for Yujun as well. That asshole had the audacity to suggest Yujun put his father in the grave. *How dare he?* I know that cousin is jealous. His car was a domestic one, while Yujun's is foreign. The cousin's handbag is a name brand, but not one of the luxury brands that Wansu piles in my dressing room. Those hurtful words were full of bitterness at what Yujun has and the cousin does not. I hope Yujun sees this.

"He's jealous."

"They're jealous."

We both say it at the same time. Yujun huffs out a small, disbelieving laugh before reaching over to grab my hand.

"Good. I thought you might be hurt."

"Me? You're the one—" I can't even bring myself to repeat that vile comment.

"It's nothing I haven't heard before."

"From your cousin?" I'm astonished.

"No. Not from him, but I've heard it from others."

And he believes it. It's become a part of the truth in his life regardless of the actual medical diagnosis. In some ways, Yujun has been as alone as I. He lost his mother young and was shipped to America, where his aunt refused to speak any Korean and where the kids were so cruel that he developed a stutter. His father finally collected him and brought him a new mother in the form of Wansu, who for all her strengths is not an incredibly warm person, whereas Yujun is the physical incarnation of the sun. He radiates strength, brightness, and warmth.

As his fingers twine through mine, I realize that this is what love is. It's when their pain is your pain and their loss is your tragedy as well, and you would do anything to absorb that hurt inside yourself so that the other knows nothing but a flower path.

CHAPTER TWENTY-SIX

"DINNER IS READY." MRS. JI GREETS US AT THE DOOR.

I toe off my flats, but before I can put them away, a hand appears and picks them up for me. My gaze travels up a pair of crisply pressed heather gray slacks and a matching cashmere sweater.

"We'll be making *songpyeon* tonight," Wansu informs us. "For Chuseok."

"About Chuseok," Yujun begins.

"You do not need to tell me what happened with Choi Juwon's family. His mother already called me." Wansu opens the closet door and stows my shoes inside. "Nothing that has happened will change our plans. We will introduce Hara to our family, honor our ancestors, eat our meal together. Afterward, the children will play *yut nori*. Tomorrow, we will visit the grave site, and the day after we will rest. Nothing is changing."

The last sentence is said with such certainty that I think an earthquake would not move her. I don't know if it's a good thing or not. I'm even more puzzled when I arrive at the table to see chopsticks, the matching long-handled spoon, a large shallow cast-iron pot on a burner, and six different dishes of *banchan*: lotus root, pickled radish, marinated cucumbers, kimchi, candied potatoes, and roasted sesame seed spinach. It's a Korean spread.

"Tonight we are having *mandu jeongol*. Have you had it before?"

The smell wafting from the soup pot makes my stomach clench in delight. "No, but I watched a video on it."

The chef used prepackaged *mandu*, or dumplings, as the seasoning for a soup made out of leftover ingredients from the refrigerator. Basically any vegetable that you liked in soup could be added along with a handful of *mandu*. The spices and seasoning in the dumplings flavored the water to create a broth. With a little garlic, ginger, and soup soy sauce, you had a complete meal. It looked delicious and so does this.

"Mrs. Ji made the dumplings last night for our soup. It is very good. Sit."

I can't move fast enough. Yujun is slower, but he, too, pulls out a chair.

"What did Choi Juwon's mother say?"

"That Hara should not attend Chuseok."

I stop reaching for the chopsticks.

"What did you tell her?"

"That she was welcome to hold her own *charye*." Wansu eats a piece of radish *banchan* as if she hasn't had an afternoon of fighting with her in-laws.

Yujun nods his approval. "Mrs. Ji, the soup smells delicious."

"I put extra *samgyeopsal* in for you," she says from behind the kitchen counter.

"Thank you. Did you know, Hara, that most Koreans don't eat anything but *samgyeopsal*? Your food truck is unusual."

Is this what we're doing? Talking about pork eating habits? We're going to ignore what happened in the parking lot of Hello Flour and that at least some part of the family is threatening to boycott this important holiday dinner because of my presence? I'm not okay with that.

"Is it because I'm adopted? Or because Yujun and I are seeing each other?"

"It is not you. It is me." Wansu reaches over and places a piece of *samgyeopsal*, or pork belly, on my rice. "I am not a Choi and these are not my ancestors and therefore not your ancestors either. What is the purpose of you honoring them when they do not know you? That sort of thing."

"Oh."

"Not all families celebrate Chuseok like this anymore," Yujun supplies. "No one cooks all the dishes for the *charye*. They buy their *banchan* at the *banchan* markets. There are more Christians, and they believe the honoring of the ancestors is like worshipping false idols, so they go on vacations to Jeju."

"Or Hawaii." Wansu sounds almost wistful.

I've always hated the holidays. I never felt particularly close to Pat's or Ellen's parents. Pat's mother always seemed to wear a perpetual frown of disapproval. Maybe that's why he turned out the way he did. She never expected him to amount to much and would frequently say so, and so he lived up to her low expectations. She had a sharp tongue and never spared anyone—not her son; certainly not her daughter-in-law, who never managed to get pregnant; and not me, the foreign-born adopted child. Ellen would never admit it, but the best part of divorcing Pat was never seeing his mother again. When Pat's mother died, we went to the funeral, but Ellen didn't shed one tear. For my mother, that was essentially the same as ringing bells and singing the refrain from "Ding-Dong! The Witch Is Dead" from *The Wizard of Oz*.

Sounds like Wansu wouldn't mind humming the same melody.

"I don't have to attend tomorrow." Hiding in my room or even going to stay in a hotel and enjoying the spa services sounds pretty grand to me right now.

"No. You're my daughter and you have every right to attend a celebration of family in this, my own home." That's the end of the discussion for Wansu.

"Next year we should go to Jeju," suggests Yujun. "These traditions are old-fashioned. Send the money in the mail and no one will complain."

"Money?"

"Every year, *Eomma* hands out the red envelopes of money to every person. Most families do it for solely the kids, but *Appa*"—he points upstairs—"started it ever since IF Group went public as sort of a thank-you for their support. *Eomma* has carried the tradition on."

"I'm sure they come for other reasons." Wansu is mildly reproving.

Yujun pops a piece of pork belly into his mouth and considers this possibility. He swallows and shakes his head. "No. I don't think so. These are miserable affairs, which is why when you said that I wouldn't be able to attend these in the future if I stayed with Hara, I didn't mind much. Hara and I can honor the ancestors by ourselves. Our offerings aren't less valuable because we make them together instead of with spiteful relatives."

"I mind," Wansu replies. "I do not approve of the two of you together."

I tense up, not wanting to get into an argument at dinner, especially after the day we've had.

"We know. About that pork, did you watch that series on pork with Chef Baek, Hara? He talks about how a lot of the pork is going to waste because there's low demand. In the early days of the Gor-yeo dynasty, only the royals ate the pork belly and the rest of the pig was given to the poor villagers. They ate everything from the head to the hoof, but now we've reverted to eating only a certain cut. In America, you eat other parts, right?"

I appreciate Yujun's attempt to change the subject, but I don't think I can eat without making it clear to Wansu where I stand. "I want to be part of this family with you, Wansu, but when I met Yujun, I didn't know he was your son. He was a boy from Seoul who opened his heart to me. I can't change my feelings for him. Or, even if I could, I don't want to. Where do we go from here?"

A muscle in Wansu's jaw flexes. "Perhaps this is a conversation we can have after dinner."

"Besides, I heard Kim Seonpyung hates animals," I add.

Yujun muffles a cough. I know he's laughing behind his hand.

Surprise flares in Wansu's face. Her eyebrows arch slightly. "Well, we can disregard him."

"All of them," Yujun presses.

"Have you had intestines, Hara?" Wansu lays another piece of pork belly on my rice. "It's supposed to be good for your skin. It has a lot of collagen in it."

"We can go to one of those *pojang machas* and have intestines and soju this week," proposes Yujun.

"Is that one of those blue soju tents with the temporary tables?" I allow myself to be led away from the topic of Yujun and me. It's not a fight worth having now. At least we all know one another's positions. It's a question of who is going to bend first.

AFTER DINNER AND the plates and dishes are cleared, Mrs. Ji brings out three platters full of a number of small bowls. "Mrs. Ji has made everything else, but we have to make the *songpyeon* ourselves or the ancestors might smite us." Yujun lays out strips of wax paper. "Here is the dough." He points to five bowls of purple, deep green, pink, yellow, and white rice-flour dough. "Chuseok is called *hangawi* and it is held on the day of the harvest full moon. The rice-cake dough is made of ground rice and it's used to make the *tteok* in *tteokbokki* and the *tteok* in our soups. The dough is dyed only by natural means. The purple comes from blueberries and the yellow from pumpkin powder and so on. Mung bean, honey-roasted sesame, and chestnuts in syrup are the fillings. *Song* is for 'pine tree.' After we make the half-moon cakes, Mrs. Ji will steam them on a bed of pine needles."

"You make pretty. Pretty *songpyeon*, pretty children," Mrs. Ji declares.

Yujun winks at me, his dimple popping out. "The saying goes if your *songpyeon* is beautiful, then you will have beautiful children."

"Wow. I'm sweating. No pressure here." The late Mrs. Choi must have made award-winning *songpyeon* in order to have conceived Yujun. "How do I do this?"

He hands me a pair of gloves. "You take a small bit of dough about the size of a golf ball and press it into a disc." His fingers spin the small circle of dough in his palm until it's flattened into a circle. He folds his fingers slightly together so that the dough forms a cup.

A spoonful of the filling is placed in the middle, and then he closes it, pinching the edges together. Some of the filling is spilling out and there's a tear developing in the center, but the end result is a *mandu*-shaped delicacy that looks like a stuffed half-moon.

In the time that Yujun has shown me how to make one, Wansu has set five perfectly shaped *songpyeons* on a sheet of wax paper.

"*Eomma* makes pretty *songpyeons*, doesn't she?" Yujun winks at me.

"What are some of your Thanksgiving traditions, Hara?" Wansu invites.

"Mom—Ellen—and I would go to her parents' until they passed. For the last few years, we've experimented with cooking turkey different ways. We've done the deep fry, where you dunk a turkey into a vat of hot oil. It didn't work out. The outside was crispy and delicious but the turkey meat was raw and we were both afraid to eat it, so that was a disaster. Last year, we cooked one with a mayonnaise mixture and it was really good. Other than that, I guess the only tradition is Ellen spending a few weeks ahead of the holiday decorating the house with fall leaves and a variety of stuffed, ceramic, and clay turkeys and then taking all the decorations down the day after."

"We should invite her here for Thanksgiving. She can stay with us until after Christmas. I know you Americans spend that holiday with family as well, yes?" Wansu wipes her gloved hands on a wet towel and moves on to the purple dough.

"That's right." It'd be nice to have Ellen here, but it might also mean that Wansu is calling in reinforcements. I cast a worried look in Yujun's direction, but he's bent over his *songpyeon*. While Wansu has made nearly a dozen and I've somehow managed to put out half that, he's still on his first one.

"I'm worried about your children, Yujun," I tease.

He sets one mangled *songpyeon* onto the table. "Beauty is in the eye of the beholder, Hara. It's still the same inside. What does it matter that it's a little"—he pauses to pat another piece of dough onto a crack that's appeared in his dessert—"imperfect here or there?"

He's right. Mrs. Ji delivers the first batch of steamed *songpyeon*. The steaming process has brought out the colors of the natural dyes and made the small pouches of dough and sweets glossy and vibrant. They're almost too pretty to eat; even Yujun's malformed ones somehow came out well, although some of the cracks in his overstuffed pockets are covered with flower petals made from excess dough.

As he said, they all taste the same whether he made them or Wansu did or even I did. A sense of peace settles over me, and heat pricks behind my eyes as I savor the chewy sweet. I'm sitting here with my love and my biological mother eating a traditional Korean dessert, about to celebrate one of the most Korean of holidays. This is my home. I can come here whenever I like. Mrs. Ji knows me. I have a bedroom here. I have family here. I'm only an outsider if I make it so.

"Do you like it?" Yujun asks. Wansu waits for my response as well.

I nod because I can't speak with my mouth full of *songpyeon* and my heart full of love.

CHAPTER TWENTY-SEVEN

"HOW MANY PEOPLE ARE COMING?" I SQUEAK. THERE'S A LIT-eral army of staff here.

"Thirty-four." Wansu directs a man wearing black pants and a vest to move a flower arrangement she doesn't like.

"Thirty-four?" No wonder we made so many *songpyeon* last night.

"Two brothers, two wives, a grandmother, a great-grandmother, four sons, three daughters, twelve grandchildren, assorted other relatives."

"That's nearly forty people."

She doesn't spare me a glance at that inane comment. If Ellen were here, she'd be running around, leaving half-finished projects in her wake—a flower arrangement here, canapés half-done there, the back part of her hair still in Velcro rollers. Wansu is directing this production like a general, and not a single glossy strand of hair is out of place. Dressed in a navy *hanbok* with elaborate silver embroidery of birds sweeping across her bodice, she consults with florists, caterers, and hospitality staff and has even approved the wine selections.

It's not quite dawn and everyone is working hard. The ancestral rights occur in the early morning hours.

My *hanbok* is possibly one of the most beautiful creations I've ever seen. Mrs. Ji helped me dress. It consists of a diaphanous ombre silk top called a *jeogori* in deep blue at the top bleeding to light pink almost white at the bottom.

The overskirt, or *chima*, is that same sheer cream over a multi-colored tiered ruffled underskirt that makes the most delicious swishing sound when I walk. On my feet are a pair of cream Miu Miu kitten heels that are so cute it is a crime they're hidden under the voluminous fabric. My black hair is pulled back into a neat ponytail and secured with a white jade clip. Matching jade earrings dangle from my lobes.

Yujun is dressed in a severe navy *hanbok* with elaborate navy embroidery outlined in silver. He looks like a historical prince and I feel like I should be kneeling at his feet and waving a palm frond in front of him. His eyes shine when they land on me. "*Ippeusi neyo,*" he murmurs. You're beautiful.

When every piece of fruit and rice cake is set on the table and the flowers are positioned precisely and the incense sticks are readied, the staff disappears. Wansu leads me to the entry, and Mrs. Ji opens the door. A line of black cars appears in the driveway and out spills relative after relative.

Wansu and I stand at the doorway, like some kind of reception line. She introduces me. We accept gifts, some wine, some gift sets, some fruit, some envelopes. I tense when Juwon arrives with his wife, Kim Jinae, and their two tots. The girl waves her small hand at me. "*Gomo*, you're here," she says in perfect English, as if she's been practicing.

"Yes." I crouch down so we are at eye level. "Are these new earrings?" I playfully touch her earlobe, which sports a small pink plastic flower.

She nods vigorously and reaches out to pat my earrings. "I like yours, too, *gomo*," she whispers in quiet Korean.

A hand descends on the little girl's shoulder and Kim Jinae says something quietly. It must not have been very kind, because Yujun's head whips around like it was jerked on a string. Wansu puts her hand up to stop him. "Kim Jinae, do your children need more care and attention than normal? In your preoccupation, I believe that you forgot to greet my daughter."

"You're looking very pretty today," I tell Nayeon in Korean before straightening. I give Kim Jinae a cool, brief bow of my head and welcome her to my home.

The other woman's cheeks are slightly flushed, but she returns the slight bow and moves on to Yujun, who barely dips his head. He unthaws to ruffle Nayeon's hair.

"*Samchon*, do you like my *hanbok*? It's new." She holds her pink skirt in her hands and twirls.

"You look beautiful." She beams.

One of the last to arrive is an older woman. Beside me, Wansu stiffens.

"*Eomeo-nim*, thank you for coming today." Wansu gives a deep bow. This must be Choi Yusuk's mother, Park Kyungsook. "This is my daughter, Hara Wilson." I fold in half, bowing so far I think she can see the bumps on my spine.

Park Kyungsook flicks her eyes up and down my figure, and she does not like what she sees. She makes a slight movement of her chin, which could be acknowledgment or more likely dismissal, gives Wansu the same cursory treatment, and stops in front of Yujun. He takes one of her hands in his and bows deeply as well.

"Yujun-ah, I have heard that you are moving to Los Angeles. You should rethink this. I don't think more time in America is good for you. You are forgetting all our customs and traditions," she accuses loudly.

He straightens, and there's a tightness to his smile. She's not getting even a hint of dimple. "Not all traditions are good, *Halmeoni*. We used to disapprove of single mothers, but that's outdated thinking, isn't it? All family structures are good if they provide a good home for the children."

"Hmmph. As I said, your time away from Korea and your family is making you think strange things. After Chuseok, you will come and spend time with me." After delivering that command, she moves on before Yujun can argue further with her.

My jaw is tense and my back is tight. The sun has barely risen and I already feel as brittle as a potato chip.

Once the rest of the family arrives, Yujun carries over the food to the low wooden table in front of a large screen and carefully places each dish. The first row—nearest to the screen—is for the chopsticks and spoons, cups and rice cake soup. The second row contains noodles, meat pancakes, fish—with the head pointed toward the east—and rice cakes. The third row is meat, beef, and fish soup. The fourth contains dried meat, vegetables, soy sauce, kimchi, and a sweet rice drink. The last row—or the one closest to us—is the dessert, with the white-colored fruits, the pears and melon, on the east side of the table and the jujubes, apples, and persimmons on the west.

"The apples should be in the center," orders Park Kyungsook. Yujun obliges.

"The fish head isn't pointed in the right direction. It is not straight," she complains.

Yujun adjusts the fish head a scant centimeter.

"The melon isn't white enough. Where did you buy it?" she asks, not really addressing Wansu but the room at large. She wants to exert her dominance in Wansu's own home, put the interloper in her place. "At the *banchan* market?"

"All of the food is made by Mrs. Ji or Lotte catering," Wansu replies.

"Made nothing yourself, did you?" Park Kyungsook delivers the insult with a sniff.

"We made *songpyeon*, *Halmeoni*, with extra candied walnuts, as you like." Yujun comes to Wansu's rescue. "Let me light the candles and you can eat some and see for yourself."

She might have had more to say, but Yujun starts the ceremony and Park Kyungsook snaps her mouth shut. After the two candles at the uppermost corner are lit, Yujun places a shallow brass bowl next to an incense burner. He kneels before the altar and Kyungsook hands him a cup of rice wine, which he pours in three equal measures into the sand of the incense burner. Kyungsook takes the empty cup and places it on the table before stepping back. Yujun pushes to his feet and then returns to the floor, and behind him, the men line up from oldest to youngest. They all bow to the altar in remembrance of the ancestors. This is not a slight nod or even the ninety-degrees-at-the-waist bow. It's a full on-your-knees, forehead-to-the-floor bow. It doesn't escape my notice that Choi Juwon is quite far back from the table. None of the women are bowing either. We are all standing with the girl children in the dining room observing this ritual.

Once the men are done bowing, Kyungsook leads the women. All of them flock into place, but when I step forward Wansu stops me with a hand on my wrist. Her fingers slide down and clasp mine tight. Her fingers are cold and she pulls me down to the floor, in the dining room, not even in the same room as the others, as if the ancestral spirits will rage if we cross some invisible line. Has she done this by herself all these years? Knelt in solitude away from the rest of the family? Anger swells in my chest. She's run the company for nearly a decade, expanded it, brought wealth to this family, and she doesn't even get to kneel in the same damned room?

When we're all done bowing, Yujun kneels again and pours more wine for the ancestors. After doing this three times, he distributes the chopsticks to various dishes, the fish, the soup, the *hanwoo*, and then a final set into the center of a bowl of rice and bows one more time before rising.

Kyungsook marches out the door, leaving Yujun inside. We all file out behind her. The men stand facing the west and the women the east. Again, Wansu and I are last. Wind blows our skirts against our legs and the dark sky threatens to rain. She hasn't released my hand. I wouldn't allow her to.

"The ancestors are coming to eat," she tells me. "Yujun will appear and cough three times to let us know that it is time to return."

It doesn't take long. I guess the ancestors were hungry. We return to the house and Yujun spoons rice and soup from the bowls to mimic the ancestors eating. We bow twice more, with the men going first, the women following, and Wansu and I last, outside the main room. This whole process is followed ten more times.

I'm exhausted by the time they burn the pieces of paper, on which are written the names of the dead we are honoring. All this rising and bowing is hard on my body but also my heart. Each time we leave and enter the house with Wansu at the very end, I think of all the times she did not have anyone by her side. *Wansu is lonely*, I hear Ellen saying.

Ellen has no idea. Or maybe she does. Maybe everyone knows how awful it is to be Wansu except for me. The kids are ushered into a different room, where they can take off their *hanboks* and eat their meal.

Yujun brings me a small plate of glass noodles and mixed vegetables—*japchae*—and a glass of wine for Wansu. She finally releases my hand. I finally allow it.

"You did well," he tells me. He also looks worn-out.

"You did well, too." I want to hug him. I want to hug Wansu, too, even though we have never embraced. I've always thought she didn't want that kind of contact, but maybe she doesn't know how to ask for it; maybe she doesn't think she deserves to ask for it.

"What would you like from the table? I'll fetch you a plate," he offers.

"No." The sharp negative rings out in the large space. Park Kyungsook glares at me from her position at the head of the table. She's sitting in the chair Wansu usually occupies. "She should not eat the food of the ancestors." She waves her hand at Mrs. Ji. "Surely you have food in that kitchen of yours that you will be eating. Staff food. That's what this girl should be served. Yujun, come and attend to me."

Yujun doesn't move.

"Your father would not approve," Kyungsook declares.

"He would. He did, in fact. He knew of Hara's existence before we married and he gave me money to find her. He would approve of her if he knew," Wansu replies, her tone cold and hard.

"He would not approve," Kyungsook insists. "I do not approve. She should not be in this house while my son lies upstairs in his sickbed. And, you, Yujun, I hear that you have been sullying yourself with her."

"Hara has a name," Yujun says.

Choi Juwon laughs cruelly. "Yujun-ah, you have done nothing but spit on your father's legacy. The changes you've instituted at IF Group will result in disaster, and now you bring that girl into the house? Choi Yusuk would definitely not approve. She's a *doenjang* girl."

I have no idea what that means other than it's an insult.

"You can leave right now." Yujun points to the door.

Choi Juwon tilts his chin up in defiance. "I'll leave when the owner of this house tells me to leave."

Wansu gasps. It takes a moment for the full cruelty of Juwon's statement to sink in. The owner of this house has been in a coma for the last three years. He is not getting out of his bed to say anything and we all know that. *You push your father to his death, but maybe it is good he cannot see or hear so that he does not witness what his son has become.*

This time, when Yujun's fist comes up, I don't stop him. It only takes the one punch and Juwon drops to the floor. Kim Jinae screams.

Kyungsook gets to her feet. "I always knew you weren't good enough for this family." She spits on the table and walks out, the skirt of her *hanbok* billowing behind her. No one else moves. At the doorway, Kyungsook opens her mouth again. "What are you all waiting for?"

"Our envelopes . . ." murmurs a small female voice.

Yujun snorts in disgust.

"We are leaving. Now!" Kyungsook's voice tolerates no objections, and one by one the family members gather up their belongings and their children until the house is completely empty but for a few staff members and Mrs. Ji.

Wansu stands stick straight, her shoulders not slumping even a half degree. The steel she has in her spine is industrial-strength. I would've folded. Tears would've been in my eyes. My hands would be shaking.

"I trust that you will oversee the cleaning up and the distribution of the food," she says to Mrs. Ji.

Mrs. Ji gets to work immediately.

"I'm going to sit with your father," she says. She makes her way across the house, past the main room where the bowls and dishes of food still sit, barely touched. Her gait is steady and her head is high. She plants her foot on the first step, and that's when it happens. She falters. Her hand shoots out to grasp the railing. Yujun starts forward, but I pull him back. She doesn't want his help. I know this because even though Wansu has not raised me, we are alike in many respects. I'm not one to be loud or cry easily. I don't like others seeing me weak. I'm not always comfortable with physical contact even with friends. Whether this came from Wansu, whether this is in my blood, it is hard to say, but I won't deny these similarities.

He tenses in my grip, and for a worrying moment, I wonder if we are going to struggle, but he gives in. It's the right call, because a second later, Wansu pulls herself upright and climbs the stairs as if the hesitation never occurred.

How long has she lived under the disapproval of her mother-in-law? How many Chuseoks and Seollals has she suffered through? Her disapproval of Yujun's and my relationship makes perfect sense in this context. She was trying to protect us—both Yujun and me, but mostly me. She did not want me to spend the rest of my life on the outside, kneeling by myself.

"I'm sorry," Yujun says. His long-fingered elegant hand comes up to cover his face, to hide his shame.

I pull his hand away and sweep his bangs off his forehead. "What are you sorry for? You are not your grandmother. You have no control over her, over Wansu, over me. There's nothing to be sorry for."

His eyes darken. "No. I put you in this position. I should've—"

"What?" I interrupt. "Gone back in time and never met me?"

"No."

"That's the only answer to the 'should've' intentions. I'm not sorry we met. I'm not sorry I love you. And I'm not going to leave you because your grandmother doesn't like me or your cousin doesn't think I'm fit to play with their kids or the friend at the river park finds our relationship offensive. None of that matters to me." I'm not on the outside and I am not alone. I have Yujun. I have Ellen. I have Wansu. I have so many people who love me and care for me. I only have to open myself up and accept them.

Yujun shudders and collapses into the dining room chair. His shoulders drop to his knees as he drags in breath after breath of relief, of sorrow. I lay a hand across his broad back, the one I've leaned against so many times in the past.

"Hara," he says on a gruff, raspy breath. "I've been afraid."

"Me, too." I release a watery laugh. "But haven't you told me that we belong together? Our hearts are one. We shouldn't anger the gods who have pulled so many strings to get us together. They even arranged for Wansu to fall in love with your father. Isn't it our destiny to be together? I am not going to be the one to thumb my nose at the heavens. Whether it is here in this house or in your apartment or in LA or Des Moines, wherever it is, we will be together."

His back muscles tense and then relax as he takes in my words. He brings my hand to his mouth and presses a warm kiss on it.

"Go sit with your mother," I urge. "She needs your warmth. I'm going to go watch YouTube ASMR cooking videos."

"What?" He jerks upright.

I grin, my first true smile of the day. "Yeah, I watched a ton of them while you were gone. They were very soothing. Go!" I push his shoulders. "I'll be here, waiting for you."

"You promise?"

"Yes." Forever. I'll wait for him forever.

CHAPTER TWENTY-EIGHT

I DO NOT GO AND WATCH YOUTUBE VIDEOS. INSTEAD, I HELP Mrs. Ji clear away the *charye* table. The food is handed out to the staff members because I know that Wansu and Yujun will not be able to eat this. I divide up most of the *songpyeon* as well.

"You make pretty *songpyeon*," Mrs. Ji tells me as she leaves, basically declaring that I will have pretty children.

"Thank you. Have a good night, Mrs. Ji."

"Take care of them." She walks toward her car.

I wave to her. "I will."

After Mrs. Ji departs, I tie on an apron and inspect the refrigerators. There are hanks of *hanwoo* and pork, fresh vegetables, *banchan* that Mrs. Ji made earlier this week, and even broth. I pull out ingredients and start prepping.

I'd read once that in Korean, the word for "butcher" is *baekjeong*. The word itself has no literal English translation because it's not related to the word "meat" or the act of cutting. Instead it comes from a class of people.

In the Joseon period, there were distinct classes. First, of course, was the crown, the *wangjok*. After them was the *yangban*, or nobility. They collected the taxes, made the laws, meted out the punishment, served as advisors to the *wangjok*. Below the *yangban* were the commoners. These were the workers, laborers, farmers. The *doers*.

Even the commoners, or *sangmin*, had those they looked down upon. If you weren't a commoner, then you were a lower class still, a *cheon-min*. *Kisaengs*, or pleasure women, were part of the *cheon-min*, but even they had status greater than the *baekjeong* because they were recognized by the government. The *baekjeong* were essentially ghosts. They had no status, no rights, and no protection. For some reason, butchers fell into this category, and that's how the word *baekjeong* came to stand for "butcher."

A person without status or rights or protection—unrecognized by the state. This is why Wansu agreed to acknowledge me, so that in this, her country, I would not be unrecognized. Being unregistered means you don't exist. You have no status. You cannot get a job. You cannot obtain medical care. You cannot be educated. I suppose it is no different at home. Without a social security number, you are a *baekjeong*. Here, though, there is cultural meaning attached to being registered. Some families can trace their roots back ten generations or more through the local *gu* books.

These are the things she wanted to protect me from. But recognizing me meant separating me from Yujun. Siblings could not marry even if they were not blood related. The answer, then, is to not be recognized. Does it matter that my name is never entered into the registry? Isn't that the greedy part? She still acknowledges me as her daughter. I am the daughter of her flesh if not her heart.

Jules and Bomi are prepared to live together without special status for as long as is necessary. They are prepared to be dragons and fight for their love. I will do the same for Yujun but also for Wansu. I have a tough outer shell; scales protect me. Those scales are made up of the love of all of those in my life.

As the pork browns in the oven, I finish brushing egg white on the pastry pockets stuffed with apples and then move on to making honey rice cakes. Mrs. Ji has a whole fresh honeycomb in the pantry, so I cut that up into little bits and stuff them inside the rice dough.

The pastries are done quicker than the meat. I make a plate of the small apple pastries I shaped like *mandu* and the honey rice cakes and pour myself a glass of hot water from the dispenser.

The pastry is flaky and the apples are tart. It's the perfect combination. I pop another one in my mouth. *Makgeolli* ice cream would be a perfect topping. In fact, these small apple desserts are an ideal food truck item.

A crazy idea pops into my head and I shove it aside but I can't keep it out. The idea returns. The one with four wheels, a stainless steel service counter, and deep fryers with automatic drains and filters. I look down at the apple pastry *mandu* and wonder what they would taste like fried instead of baked, served with *makgeolli* ice cream, and topped with powdered sugar. I wonder how long it would take to prep enough for one day of sales and how many I would go through. I glance at the refrigerator, where the leftover shredded pork sits alongside the small compotes of relish.

It's not something I could do by myself, but if I had someone who would partner with me . . . My eyes climb up the stairs but I shake my head. He makes a decent cheese *ramyeon* but his skills are in numbers and making deals. There's another person I know who is in the service industry. I pull out my phone and text her even though it's a holiday and she's probably doing something with Bomi, but there's a thrum of excitement coursing through me. My whole body is buzzing.

The reply from Jules is, Are you crazy, to which I type in return, That's not a no.

There's motion on the stairs, so I shelve my idea and go to greet my family. It's a relief to see that some of the tension has eroded. Wansu's face isn't so tight, and there's even a hint of dimple creasing Yujun's cheek.

"I could smell the food from the bedroom."

I scrunch my nose. "I should've cooked in the back kitchen."

"No. It's good."

Wansu looks at the relatively clean countertops, which are cleared of everything but my dishes. "Where is the *charye* food?"

"I sent it home with Mrs. Ji and the staff. They were very grateful. In the meantime, I made us a meal. Sit and I'll serve you."

The pork loin is marinated with honey, *gochujang*, soy sauce, garlic, and ginger. I slice it thinly and coil a few pieces on top of a bed of fresh rice. The remainder goes on a rectangular white china platter. Yujun helps me serve Mrs. Ji's *banchan* but I add my own version of potatoes—mashed with cream and butter, topped with scallions and a spicy yogurt dressing. For dessert, I present my apple pie.

"You don't have pie tins, so I used these stone bowls instead. I also made apple pie *hotteok* for you, Yujun." I lift the edge of a dish towel to reveal the golden fritters.

"Can I start with dessert?" He stares wide-eyed at the spread.

"No," Wansu answers for me. She straightens her chopsticks and dives in. None of us have eaten since last night, and so we lapse into silence as we attack the food. It might be because I'm hungry, but the food is some of the best I've tasted. I give myself an internal pat on the back.

"This is very good, Hara. I didn't realize you were such an accomplished chef." Wansu pats the side of her mouth with a napkin.

"I don't know if I'm much of a chef." I love the compliment, though. I'm sure I'm glowing.

"Hara worked on a food truck," offers Yujun between bites. He snags more sliced pork loin from the platter in the center of the table.

Wansu's eyebrows slide up.

"For two whole days only, but it was fun. Hard, but fun."

"What about IF Group?"

That's a good question. Yujun shoots me a silent apology for not having thought through his comment. It's too bad the table is so wide or maybe I could've kicked him in the shin.

"I took a sick day to help. The *Seonsaeng-nim* who runs the food truck was very ill and I worried that she might suffer an economic hardship if she had to close down." Wansu doesn't appear to love the idea that I took a day off to work on a food truck, and I'm not sure if it's because of the work or because I left IF Group.

I test the waters. "Is working in a food truck bad?"

"No. All work is honorable; however, sick days are to be used if you are truly ill and not to avoid your place of employment."

"No. I wouldn't want to do that," I lie.

We talk about nothing important for the rest of the meal. It's as if the events earlier in the day never happened, and if it weren't for the reddened knuckles on Yujun's right hand, maybe I could convince myself it was all a nightmare.

After dinner, Yujun helps me clean up and Wansu returns to Choi Yusuk's room.

"How is your father?" I broach the subject as Yujun has his fourth apple pie *hotteok*.

"Same as always." He taps his fork against the ceramic plate. "I think it is time for *Eomma* to let go."

As this is the first time Yujun has spoken about his father in really any context, I keep my mouth shut and practice my listening skills.

"She has hoped for a different result for a long time, but there's no medical opinion that warrants keeping him on these machines." He blows out a deep breath and sends me a sad, rueful smile. "That's a perfectly depressing topic upon which to end our very eventful day, isn't it?"

"I have one of your Hermès ties in my closet if you need something to wipe your tears with," I offer.

"Kept that, did you?" The smile turns more genuine.

"I think I have almost everything you gave me including the paper that wrapped this." I tap the necklace under my blouse.

"I have something else for you. Let me get it. I'll meet you in your room."

My eyes fly upstairs to Wansu.

"It's okay." He shoos me off.

I don't waste my breath arguing because, frankly, I don't want to. I run to my bedroom, pushing aside the beautiful *hanbok* I wore earlier, and find the gift I bought for Yujun. It was a splurge for me, but Chuseok and Seollal are the major gift exchange holidays. I didn't want to screw up so I spent more than I ordinarily would.

I'm glad because while I'm putting money aside, my money situation will be tight if I go through with my wild idea and I might not be able to buy much for Seollal.

He knocks before opening, a small red package with a gold bow in his hand. "Is that for me?" His eyes light up.

"No. It's for me. I bought presents for myself and I plan to open them while you watch me." I grin.

"Perfect, as I have bought this for myself as well." He shakes the box. "Shall we?"

I snatch the box out of his hands and run over to the sofa. "Yes."

As I carefully untie the gift, wrapped ingeniously with no tape so that the paper falls aside with a few tugs, Yujun sits next to me, rubbing a hand over my head and kissing my crown.

"I love you, Hara. Thank you for staying with me."

I abandon the small blue velvet box to cup his cheek. "Thank you for being my Yujun from Seoul."

He dips his head to kiss me but draws back at the last moment. "Gift exchange first." He taps the box. "Open up."

Inside the small box is a pair of red enamel ducks with white jade bellies. The tails and necks of the ducks are adorned with dozens of tiny diamonds, and the eyes are brilliant rubies.

"When I saw you today, I wished I had given them to you last night after we made *songpyeon*. You could have worn them with your outfit."

"I'm glad I didn't." They won't have any bad memories attached to them, which I can't say for the *hanbok*. Even looking at it makes my stomach clench.

"Now me." He holds out his hands.

I lay the package on his palms. "I wrapped it myself." I feel like I have to explain away the tape and the hand-tied bow.

"It's perfect." It doesn't matter because he rips the paper off and lets it flutter to the ground while he opens the box. Inside is a navy leather portfolio with his initials embossed in silver on the front.

"This is gorgeous." He smooths his hand over the luxe leather. "Feels super soft."

"Open it up."

Obligingly, he unzips the case.

"It's for your electronics while you travel. You can put your tablet here." I point to the large expandable pocket on the right. "And this lower pocket is for a battery charger and cords. You can put your passport in this outside flap. And obviously these loops in the center are for a pen or an electronic pencil."

"And this?" He pulls out a surprise I had hidden in one of the pockets. It's a light blue silk Hermès tie with white and blue ducks. A whimsical accessory that cost me two paychecks, but when I saw it online, I knew it was perfect for Yujun. He wears blue a lot—blue suits, blue jeans, blue sweaters, blue long-sleeve casual shirts.

"It's to replace the one I took from you."

"Mmm." He drapes it around my neck and pulls me close. "It's perfect."

Our kiss is openmouthed but tender. There's so much love in him and I feel it in the way he touches me, handles me. I don't feel so much possessed by him but rather cherished. I lean into him, bracing my palms against his hard thighs. His hand sweeps under my hair to angle my head for a deeper, hungrier kiss.

The bed is ten feet away, but we don't make it there. He makes love to me, with me, on the sofa. My needy hands pull at his clothes and his deft fingers undress me.

He moves slowly, each movement deliberate, as if he is trying to make a statement, trying to imprint himself on my flesh, on my

soul. I take him inside me, welcoming each thrust as an affirma-
tion of his promise that he will be with me, and I return the same
vow, worshipping him with my own body, my mouth, my heart.

He lifts me and carries me to the bed. As we lie there, sweat
soaked and replete, the rain beats against the window of the bedroom. Mom once told me that the sky cries to clean the earth. I
clasp Yujun's hands to my chest and drift off on a cloud of con-
tentment.

No. I will not thumb my nose at the heavens. I will not reject
this gift I've been given. I will hold fast to Yujun, to Wansu, to
Sangki, to Bomi, to Jules, to Seoul, to Ellen, and to Iowa, because
these people and these places are where I belong.

CHAPTER TWENTY-NINE

ON THE WEDNESDAY AFTER THE CHUSEOK HOLIDAY ENDS, WE
all return to work, but *Bujang-nim* is late. Since I could set my
watch by him, this is worrisome. Yoo noses around *Bujang-nim*'s
desk and, finding nothing, moves on to the elevator. Chaeyoung
nibbles on her Chanel necklace and watches Soyou work—she's
the only one who appears unbothered by the lateness of our boss.

At half past, he finally appears wearing a large smile on his face
and calls us all to the conference room.

"Today, we are having another team-building exercise. It's a
company-wide program that was adopted on my suggestion during
this morning's meeting." His chest is puffed out with so much
pride he might float away. "It is a city-wide scavenger hunt. You
will be divided into teams." He starts to hand out cards randomly,
or so I think until Chaeyoung, Soyou, and I all receive green cards.
"As a team, you must figure out the clues and bring back something

SEOULMATES   233

from a store nearby the location that identifies it. It can be a coffee sleeve or a receipt from a convenience store. The amount you spend at each location can be no more than five thousand won. All the locations are within walking distance of a subway stop. The team with the most items who returns the earliest will win a *hanwoo* dinner set and five hundred thousand won."

I don't know if it's the money or the meat that lights a fire under my coworkers, but their mild expressions of horror turn into anticipation.

"The cards have the clues. You have until the end of the day. *Hana. Dul. Set. Go!*" He barely has the last word out before people are exploding out of their seats.

Soyou and Chaeyoung speed off and grab their purses. I'm a step behind. We jockey for space on the elevator but are shoved aside by the men.

The three of us look at one another and decide immediately to take the stairs. It's only seven floors. We're sweaty and panting by the time we reach the bottom.

"That was a dumb idea," Chaeyoung complains as we tumble out of the stairwell.

Soyou glares. "Keep up."

I'm not sure whether that's an admonition for me or Chaeyoung. "What's the first clue?" Soyou asks, flipping over the card. There are five of them. The first one asks for the breath of fire.

"Breath of what?" Chaeyoung's forehead wrinkles.

"It's Yongsan," I say. "*Yong* means 'dragon.'"

"I know what *yong* means," Chaeyoung snaps, irritated that I guessed right. "I'll go buy coffee. Cross it off the list."

"I think we should split up," Soyou suggests.

"*Bujang-nim* said to stay together," I remind them, feeling like the student in class that reminds the teacher they didn't hand out homework.

"If another team sees us separated, they will report the rule violation," Chaeyoung agrees.

Soyou relents, but she's not happy about it.

"What's the next one?" Soyou asks after we buy gum, not coffee, at the mart next to the subway exit. She wants to look ahead, which is a good idea. We can plan our attack and choose the shortest route.

"A crystal-clear stream full of wisdom," Chaeyoung reads, swinging her pendant along its chain.

I snap my fingers. "Seongsu."

Chaeyoung rolls her eyes. "It's obviously the Starfield Library at the COEX Mall. The aquarium is attached to it. Crystal-clear stream full of wisdom."

"Seongsu is named after Seongdukjeong, where scholars would hang out and drink the water from the nearby stream." I know this. I had a whole lesson in subway name etymology.

"Starfield is right. Let's go." Soyou, in her scuffed black heels, starts down the stairs into the subway station.

"But—" I protest and then give up. These two are not listening to me. We take the train to Starfield and buy three drinks at the café.

"The needle in the haystack," Chaeyoung reads.

"That's Namsan Tower," I offer, although I don't know why since they have no interest in my input.

"It's Lotte Tower." Soyou sips on her coffee as she looks over Chaeyoung's shoulder.

"Lotte is a tweezer. It has two ends. Namsan is a needle. It's what the Space Needle in Seattle looks like."

"We aren't in Seattle. We're in Seoul. It's Lotte." Soyou will not be swayed.

"I'm telling you it's not."

The two have an exchange in rapid Korean. Soyou turns to me. "Go to Namsan, then. We are going to Lotte."

"We have to stick together as a team," I remind them.

"The team is going to Lotte." And we do. At Lotte, the skies open, and since none of us remembered to bring an umbrella, we get drenched. Chaeyoung's expensive Dior blouse grows completely see-through. A few men who walk by make some remarks that turn her cheeks scarlet.

"I need to go and buy a new shirt," she tells us.

"We don't have time." Soyou wants to move on to the next clue.

"The department store is right here." Chaeyoung points down the metro tunnel toward a swarm of people near an entrance of a shopping complex.

"Just buy one here." Soyou gestures toward a nearby vendor who is selling a selection of cheap mall clothes.

Chaeyoung visibly shudders. The thought of putting something on her body that is not designer is obviously one of the more horrible concepts in her life. "No. I can't."

"We don't have time," Soyou repeats. "Bong is good at these games. He's going to win if we don't move."

"Chaeyoung needs to change so she isn't being catcalled for the next hour," I point out.

"Of course you support her. All you rich girls stay together. Five hundred thousand won is a joke to you. You get envelopes during Chuseok worth twice that, but I don't. I buy my shoes down here in these mall shops." She kicks out her black pump, the one with the scratched heels that she colors in with marker.

"We know you do, but I'm not wearing a ten-thousand-won shirt. It will have mixed content and I don't wear anything but natural fibers. You know this." Chaeyoung is adamant, and in a rare, but maybe displaced, display of spine, she starts walking toward the department store.

Soyou refuses to budge. I bury my face in my hands. If I support Soyou in this useless endeavor, Chaeyoung will be forced to walk around looking nearly nude on top. If I support Chaeyoung, Soyou will feel like she's being ganged up on by two spoiled rich girls. In the end, I decide Chaeyoung's modesty is more important. We got the Lotte Tower and the Starfield clues wrong; we aren't going to win anyway.

"Come on, Chaeyoung. What do you want to buy? Is there a Dior boutique inside the Lotte department store?"

"Yes." Gratitude shines in her eyes.

I can only return a tight smile because Soyou is feeling like an outsider right now, which I know sucks. There's not much traffic in the Dior boutique and a helpful saleslady quickly finds a replacement blouse for Chaeyoung. Along with the shirt, Chaeyoung selects three umbrellas and offers one to Soyou.

Soyou's nose flares. She's offended. "I can afford my own. Even I have that kind of money."

Before Chaeyoung or I can stop her, Soyou whips out her wallet. Her face pales when the clerk rings up the umbrellas, which are twice the amount of the gift certificate that *Bujang-nim* is offering. Her pride prevents her from backing down and I watch in dismay as Soyou's credit card is declined.

Chaeyoung silently puts her credit card on the counter, and the saleslady takes it, but before the transaction can be completed, Soyou curses. "Keep the damned umbrella. I don't want it."

She whirls on her heel and nearly runs out of the store.

"I was trying to be kind." Chaeyoung's lower lip trembles.

"Yeah, I know." What a fucked-up situation.

We have two more clues, and while I know the answers thanks to Yujun's impromptu lesson, which he gave me weeks ago, I keep my mouth shut. Soyou is in a dark mood; Chaeyoung is pouting. No one feels like talking. Chaeyoun's lower lip is starting to get rubbed raw by the chain of her necklace, which she keeps chewing on, while Soyou's face is so hard it rivals a rock. We make two more stops and return to *Bujang-nim*, but Bong's team is there before us, full of smiles.

"You won," Soyou says flatly. Her straight, shiny hair lies in wet clumps around her neck. Her blouse is sticking to her arms and stomach. Some of the black marker on the toes of her shoes has been worn away by the rain. There are dirt stains on the cuffs of her black slacks.

She crumples the card in her fist and whips it at her screen. It bounces off harmlessly, which seems to enrage her even more. She turns to Bong and interrogates him in swift Korean. I hear "Lotte," and then she turns and glares at me.

"It was Namsan, wasn't it." Soyou could be speaking French and I'd still understand this exchange. Her anger is writ large all over her body.

Bong glances down at Soyou's fisted hands and nods slowly.

Soyou's jaw works, as if she's swallowing screams of frustration. Chaeyoung senses a pending eruption. "Let's go to the bathroom," she suggests quietly.

When Soyou doesn't move, Chaeyoung grabs the other girl's arm and drags her away. I know I'm supposed to sit here and wait for them to come out, but I'm tired of being left out. I'm tired of them gossiping about me. At least have the decency not to be so obvious.

I march after them and slam the door open. The two women jump about a foot in the air.

"Why hide in here to talk about me behind my back? Speak in Korean."

"You understood us fine at the restaurant," Soyou shoots back.

"Then you shouldn't talk about me at all."

"Or you'll run to tell your mama, just like you told her about this stupid team-building idea?"

"That did not come from me."

"Don't lie."

I can continue to deny it, but she's never going to believe me. "Believe what you want."

There's a knock at the door. "We're leaving. Are you ready?" It's time for our *hweshik*. This sounds as fun as getting my wisdom teeth pulled. I wonder if I will get fired if I don't go. That might be the best possible outcome.

None of us want to go, but Soyou, ever ambitious, swallows her anger and her pride and leads us out of the bathroom. Downstairs, a row of taxis awaits. They fill up one by one. When it's my turn, I climb inside, sliding over to make room for the other two. Chaeyoung bends down but her phone rings. Soyou's text alert pings as well. I check my phone but there's nothing. Chaeyoung leans over. "We will meet you there." She says something to the cabdriver and then slams the door shut. I blink in surprise as the car begins to move, leaving Soyou and Chaeyoung at the curb.

Ten minutes later, the driver drops me off in front of a barbecue place. I don't see anyone familiar, but maybe it's because I'm early. Since it's a seat-yourself type of place, I plant myself at one of the long tables and wait. And wait and wait and wait. After thirty minutes, I pull out my phone and wonder whom I should text. It strikes me as odd that the name of the restaurant wasn't sent to the group chat when all the others have been posted there.

ME: I must have gotten lost. Where is the dinner?

But there's no response. Not in the first five minutes after and not in the next fifteen. Of course there's no response, because there's no texting during the *hweshiks*.

The server comes over and says something sharp in Korean, which I guess is "get out." I put money on the table even though there's no tipping in Korea because I've occupied this space for nearly an hour. If Soyou and Chaeyoung wanted me to feel humiliated, they have succeeded. I slink out of the restaurant and stand in the street. It's dark now and it's beginning to mist. The umbrella I bought at the Dior boutique is leaning against my desk at work.

The mist turns to a sprinkle, which turns into a downpour. As the water causes the silk fabric of my shirt to stick to my skin, I make up my mind. IF Group is not for me.

CHAPTER THIRTY

THE BUILDING I WORKED IN BACK HOME IN IOWA WAS FOUR
stories and had its own private garden, where the garden staff
would grow various plants, set up photo shoots, host company
events. The staff was small, in part because of increasing budget
cuts, but also because it was once a family-owned company, which
sold out to a national conglomerate a few years before I started
working there. Yujun calls IF Group a family, and maybe it is—if
the family is full of dysfunctional backbiters. It's unfair of me to
characterize the whole of the company because of one section of
the marketing department, but I really don't care. These are my
feelings and they aren't going away.

The seventh floor is empty when I step out of the elevator car.
The chairs are all pushed in against the desks. My work space is full
of binders and extra supplies. The clock on the screensaver of Chaeyoung's computer bounces from one side of the monitor screen to

the other. A low hum of noise from the air purifier mixes with the fans of the hard drives, but there aren't any sounds of actual life. I won't miss this place.

Footsteps and then a gasp startle me. I spin and nearly knock over the stack of binders. Soyou is at the door of the department, one hand clutching the frame and the other clapped over her mouth. Her hair is a mess and her shirt is only half tucked in. Even in the dim light, I can see the flush on her cheekbones. Another head appears behind her, and this time I'm too shocked to keep my own sharp inhale quiet.

"*Bujang-nim?*"

"What are you doing here?" he snaps in full Korean.

"I forgot my umbrella." I lift the white nylon up in the air. My slow brain is putting two and two together, and I do not like the sum. The love bite on Soyou's collarbone a few weeks ago, her mussed hair now, the empty office, the two of them together, create a picture that I don't want in my head. It's none of my business, really. I straighten the binders and move toward the elevators. "Nice to see you."

The two move aside as one, and no one utters a word. The elevator takes a year to arrive and I don't actually take my first breath until it starts its descent. Soyou needs this job. You can tell by her modest clothing, the wear on her shoes, her near-desperate work ethic. And while I don't like *Bujang-nim*, he has two kids. Losing his job could really screw up their lives.

I have no idea what to do. If Soyou is being sexually harassed, then family or no family, *Bujang-nim* needs to go. If she's having an affair with him because she likes him, is it my business? Would she even tell me the truth if I ask?

I can't talk this over with Yujun because he'll immediately want to investigate the matter. If I tell Jules, Miss Open Lines of Communication Are Good for a Relationship, she will tell Bomi, who will immediately want to investigate the matter.

I need to talk to Soyou, which means tomorrow I have to come to work. Damn it all anyway.

I ARRIVE EARLY at Yongsan the next day, not just to catch Soyou but to say goodbye to Yang Ilwha. Since this will be my last day, I want to let her know I won't be seeing much of her in the future, but when I arrive in the alley where the food truck has been parked for the last three months, the space is empty.

I rub my eyes to make sure I'm not missing something, that I'm in the right alley, in front of the right convenience store with the auto-body repair shop next door. My view remains the same.

Inside the convenience store, the clerk informs me that Yang has not been here for several days. Panic blooms in my chest. What if she didn't have the flu? What if she's *sick* sick? I send an anxious text to her.

ME: Seonsaeng-nim, are you doing well?

I tap my fingers impatiently against the back of my phone, waiting for a response. One doesn't come. I call a cab and give the driver the address to Yang's apartment. It takes way too long to arrive, and when I finally do, there's no food truck in the parking lot. Has she gone to another location? Why wouldn't she have texted me? Then again, why would she? I'm a customer.

But I'm a customer who manned her food truck for almost two days, which is why I stopped referring to her as *Imo-nim* and

switched to *Seongsaeng-nim*. Doesn't that deserve some consider-
ation? Yang's apartment isn't an enclosed unit. Instead there are outdoor hallways, like in the older motels back in the US, with concrete
walls that come up to your chest. I read that many of these were
built shortly after the war, which explains all the drab gray stone.

I knock on her apartment door, but there's no response. The windows of the apartments on this row all have iron bars, and none look
very inviting. The neighbors aren't going to appreciate me knocking
on doors and asking in my inexpert Korean if Yang is okay.

I hate bothering Yujun because he's so busy, but if I was in his
shoes, I'd want me to call.

He answers immediately with concern in his voice. "Hara?"

"Nothing's wrong," I quickly reassure him. "Well, nothing is
wrong with me. I'm at Yang Ilwha's apartment but she's not answering the door. Is there an apartment manager I can talk to?
Where would I find him?"

"Yang Ilwha is the *ahjumma* who owns the food truck, yes?"

"Yes."

"Didn't you say you helped her before because she was sick?
Maybe she is at the hospital?"

"The hospital?" I exclaim. "She only had the flu!" Maybe it was
something more serious.

"To get an IV," he reassures. "It is not like in America where
you have to be dying to go to the hospital. Here, we go and get an
IV if we have a cold or flu. State health care, remember?"

I do now. "What hospital would she go to?"

"Can you text me your location?"

I send him a pin. "Did you get it?"

"Yes. There's a clinic close by. Let me call. Stay where you are
and I will come get you."

Yujun arrives twenty minutes later, looking deliciously disheveled in a pair of dark blue slacks, loafers, and a white shirt with a familiar-looking tie. On his head is a navy snapback with a leather bill so worn that it almost looks coppery.

"Nice tie." I flick the tip of it up. He dips down and places a kiss on the side of my mouth.

"Thank you. Someone lovely gave it to me."

"She has great taste."

"Yes." His left dimple makes an appearance. "Very good taste. Now, for your friend, I found her. She's at the hospital and has pneumonia."

My hand drops away from his tie. "Oh my God."

"She's okay. I talked to her son. He was confused as to why a stranger was calling. I explained it was his mother's helper, to which he replied he was unaware his mother had an employee." Yujun rubs a hand down the back of my head and I know what he's going to say before he even finishes the rest of the conversation.

"I'm fired, aren't I?" I joke.

"Not exactly, although the son wasn't happy about the possible tax implications of hiring a foreign worker without a proper visa."

I guess it was one thing to work for my mother and another to work for a stranger.

"If it makes you feel better, the sons do not want her to continue to work. They believe it is bad for her health, so I don't think you're fired but rather the company has gone out of business."

He presses another kiss to the top of my crown and ushers me into the car. We drive over to the hospital. The eldest son is there, and he is, as Yujun warned, on the chilly side. After some Korean conversation, none of which I understand, the son steps aside and allows me into the hospital room.

Yang Ilwha struggles to sit up.

"No. Please stay, *Seonsaeng-nim*!" I rush over to the bed. "I didn't realize you were so ill. I could've run the food truck for you again."

"*Aigoo*, always so polite." She pats my cheek and then peers over my shoulder. "Who is with you?"

Yujun steps forward and dips his head. "Choi Yujun. I am Hara's boyfriend."

"So nice-looking. What do you do?" She runs her eyes over him, cataloging how much his clothes cost.

"He's rich, *Seonsaeng-nim*," I assure her.

Yujun smothers a laugh, but it was the right thing to say. Yang settles back onto her pillows. "I did not ask for help because I'm selling the food truck. It is too much for me and my sons want me to quit."

I rub my lips together as the idea that sparked in my head a few days ago starts to burn a little brighter. "What will you do with your truck?"

"Sell. Food trucks very popular these days."

"Do you have a buyer in mind?"

"No. I will put with a broker. Maybe lose some money but"—she shrugs—"will be easy—easier."

Yujun's hand comes down on my shoulder, and I know he thinks this is the wrong time to broach the subject, and he probably wasn't aware until right this moment that I had thoughts in this direction.

"*Seonsaeng-nim*, this is not the right time for me to ask you, but would you call or text me before you list the truck with the broker?"

She tilts her head up to stare at Yujun again. "He's rich, did you say?"

I nod.

"Then I will call you after I am out and we can meet. I know you kids like coffee these days. We will have a coffee and talk about the truck. In the meantime, you go to Majang Meat Market and buy meat. Cook at home and bring me something. I will see your seriousness."

Yujun waits until we are in his car before asking, "Are we buying a food truck?"

"Maybe? Do we have enough money for that?"

"We do. May I ask why we are buying it since both of us work at IF Group?"

"Right." I rub my nose, then my forehead, until I blurt out, "I quit."

There's a long silence during which I presume Yujun sorts through a number of responses to arrive at, "I'm glad I didn't put the car in gear."

"Yes. It's good you aren't driving." I peek through my hands to see how upset he is, but the only emotion I can see on his face is confusion.

"Is it the people you work with or the work itself?"

"It's all of it." I give him a very brief summary of yesterday's events, the clues, and how the day ended with me getting sent off to the wrong address for the *hweshik*. "It could have been a mistake, but I don't want to go back there. It's not good for my mental health." I smile sadly. "I don't know how to run a food truck, but Yang Ilwha does. She can teach me about the business. I can spend the winter preparing dishes, researching, running the numbers. It's a lot to ask from you, to buy the food truck for me, but I'll pay you back. I have some savings . . ." I trail off, realizing that my savings is likely Wansu's money funneled through Ellen.

"It's not the money. We both know I could buy ten food trucks and not even notice that my bank balance had dipped. If that's what you want to do, I know you will be great at it. The real problem here is if the International Marketing Department is so dysfunctional that they drove the CEO's daughter away, it's going to result in greater harm to our business if we don't do something. An investigation will have to be launched."

I hang my head. "I figured. I don't want anyone to be fired because they were mean to me. It should only be because they're terrible at their job or they did something wrong."

"Agreed." He starts the car. "Do you want to break it to *Eomma* or should I?"

"Oh, I want you to do it."

"Okay."

I laugh. "But it is my responsibility, so I will tell her."

Wansu takes it much better than I expected. The hated see-through technology screen of death doesn't pop up to show me how many food trucks fail within six months of their opening. She doesn't glare me into submission.

"Do you have projects to be finished?"

"No. None."

She rolls a fountain pen between her fingers. "Is the department not very busy?"

"It's busy. There are some good workers there. Bong Hyoseob. Kim Soyou." I mention her specifically because I'm afraid for the security of her job.

"Will you be going home or do you have plans?"

"I'm going to go to the Majang Meat Market. It's where Yang Ilwha buys her product."

"You are serious about this food truck, then?"

"Yes. It might sound like foolishness, but feeding people is really rewarding."

"I'll see you at home, then, for dinner."

In the bathroom on the fourteenth floor, I call Ellen.

"Darling! Aren't you working?"

"I quit today."

"Oh my goodness! What did Wansu say? Is she okay?"

I release a confused laugh. "Wansu? What about me?"

"Of course I'm concerned about you, but didn't you take the job and stay in Korea because if you didn't Wansu's company would fall apart? I hope that's not happening."

"I told her and she didn't appear to be worried."

"Honey, she is not going to admit that the company is going to be a wreck if you quit because that's not what mothers do."

"You really like Wansu, don't you?" I lean against the wood-paneled wall and take a moment for this to sink in.

"I told you! We have a lot in common. By the way, did she let you know I'm coming out to celebrate Christmas with you? Wansu wants me to decorate a tree and make Christmas cookies and a ham and everything. I'm already starting to think about gifts. Do you have any ideas? Not only for Wansu, but her son, too. Text me any thoughts you have. I want to get her things she can't buy in Korea."

A woman walks in and arches an inquiring eyebrow in my direction.

"Mom, I have to go. Someone's here to use the bathroom."

"Okay! I love you. Bye-bye!"

I give a nod of acknowledgment and slip out of the bathroom. Next stop, seventh floor.

Everyone is at their desks when I arrive. *Bujang-nim*'s face turns an ugly shade of red, while Soyou grows pale.

"I'm leaving for a new job," I announce. "You have all been very kind to me"—someone coughs in the distance—"but there are new challenges on the horizon. Soyou, you and I have an appointment to go to."

"You do?" Chaeyong's brows crash together. She can't envision a gathering with just me and her angry friend.

"Yes, don't we?" I stare challengingly at Soyou who silently retrieves her purse and rises. I start to walk off when she calls me back. My umbrella, the Dior one, is in her hand.

"Here."

"Thank you." I take it and gesture for her to walk ahead of me. The eyes of the entire department follow us but I'm used to it. From Soyou's stiff neck, she's not.

"Where are we going?" she asks as we wait for the elevator.

"Majang Meat Market."

"Are you serious?" She examines my unsmiling face.

"As a heart attack."

By her confused expression, it's apparent she doesn't understand the colloquialism. Too bad. I don't feel like explaining it to her.

We take the subway to the Majang station. The entrance to the market is adorned with a large, plastic, unsmiling bull's head. Peeking out from behind the cattle is the head of a happy pig. The English phrase "Welcome to Meat Market" with the misspelling sits on top of the original Hangul "Majang Chuksanmul Sijang." They could've used my services.

The main corridor of the meat market is covered in red-domed acrylic with a line of faded translucent yellow tiles marching down the center. The sides of the narrow cement roadway are lined with glass display cases full of beef and pork. There aren't as many people here as I thought there might be. Motorcycles with coolers strapped on the back speed away, while a flatbed truck rumbles down the road.

Every cut of meat imaginable is available, from entire slabs of ribs to wafer-thin sirloin that they serve with *shabu-shabu*, the hot pot soups you can order at counters in food halls in the basement of the Lotte department stores. Vendors advertise the use of an upstairs grill for only five thousand won per person. I bypass what feels like a hundred beef butchers and finally land on a pork one. While Soyou watches silently, I ineptly haggle with the butcher until my poor Korean frustrates her so much that she shoulders me to the side and arrives at a price well below the advertised one. The butcher even throws in free bones. She shoves the bag in my face.

"Are we done?"

"Not yet." I walk down the entire alleyway, cataloging the various merchants, documenting prices, getting ideas. Soyou follows. At the end, I buy two Milkis and a paper boat full of beef bites wrapped in perilla leaves. "I hope you're with him because he's awesome and he really cranks your engine and not because he's promising you a promotion."

"Cranks my engine?" she says in a small voice, nothing like the Soyou who always looked at me with narrow eyes and spoke to me with a sharp tongue.

"Hot. He makes you hot. Turns you on." God, this discussion about my former boss is the worst. I try again. "Be with him because you want to be with him, not because of some fucked-up work dynamic."

"Oh."

"I want better for you, Soyou. You're gorgeous and smart and you deserve more than a middle-aged middle manager with two kids."

Her head comes up defiantly. "You don't know how hard it is. There are thousands of women who are smarter or better credentialed. If I ever got let go from IF Group, who would take me? I am not Samsung or Kakao material. I do not have a family like Chaeyoung who will find me another job. I need job security. I cannot become a *baeksu*."

She means a person with white hands, one who isn't working, or, in more base terms, a loser. I pass her the paper tray with the beef bites. "Here. You'll miss lunch."

She takes it with a grimace. "When I first came to Seoul, I felt out of place. I wore the wrong clothes, my accent was too strong. There are many different dialects in the country, but Seoul dialect is the standard. If you speak *satoori*, people will look down on you. I still remember my first days, and so when we were told we always had to speak English around you, I hated it. My English isn't good, and if you're not good, someone will think you're ignorant, someone will judge you."

"Meaning me?"

She nods. Her lips tighten and she blinks rapidly, as if she's trying to stave off tears. Soyou is not the type to cry for sympathy. She'd much rather curse you out, so her show of emotion convinces me of her sincerity. Or I could be a sucker.

"I would not have ever judged you for that. I was embarrassed to speak Korean."

"But you tried. We all admired it. Then when you spoke it so well that night at the dinner, it scared us. We could not remember all that we had said in Korean believing you could not understand us. I am sorry. Very sorry." She bows, one hand holding the paper tray of food and one hand pressed into her stomach, deep enough that I can see her spine.

My first instinct is to say she doesn't have to be sorry, but she did make my life difficult and I don't need to dismiss that. The times that I felt left out, put down, and criticized by her and Chae-young in the last few months are too numerous to count. I could let it go and say that it doesn't bother me, but that would be a lie. I can let it fester or I can drain the wound and allow it to heal.

"You weren't great to me, Soyou, and sending me to the wrong place for the *hweshik* was really terrible, but I'm not going to hold a grudge. I've got some good things in my life and I'm going to focus on those. I suggest you do the same."

I hand her the drink and the umbrella. "Take this. Sometimes you need to not let your insecurity drive all your decision-making. I haven't told my mother or Yujun about what I saw. You should come clean about that. If he's harassing you, he should be fired. If you're sleeping with him to get ahead, that's not going to end well for you. If you're with him because you love him, you might remember he has two kids who would be devastated by their family breaking up. You're a good worker, Soyou, but I don't think you're proud of yourself."

CHAPTER THIRTY-ONE

"ARE YOU A CHRISTIAN, HARA? YOU AND ELLEN?" WANSU ASKS
as we sit in the living room with a pot of tea steeping between us.
She'd invited me to tell her more about my food truck adventures,
which aren't many. I explained to her about Ahn Sangki's and my
trips to various outdoor eateries around Seoul and my affection for
Yang Ilwha. I mentioned that the food reminded me of August
in Iowa and fair food, which somehow made her ask about my
religion.

"Yes, I suppose we are, but we don't go to church. I believe
in God."

"In Korea, there are many Christians, but most people would
say that they are agnostic or Buddhists. Many believe in reincarna-
tion. There's a famous saying when something good happens that
you must have saved a country in your past life." She hands me a
cup of tea.

I curl my hands around the heated porcelain. "I've heard it before."

"When you returned to me, that is how I felt. That I must've saved a country in my past life. I am sorry for what I said about Yujun-ah and you. The images were a shock to me and I spoke imprudently. It will take some time for me to adjust, but please accept this apology with my sincere heart." She bows her head deeply.

My breath catches as cautious joy seeps into my veins. She'd been silent on the topic of Yujun and I since Chuseok but this is the first overt acceptance. I try not to smile too happily when I respond. "Thank you and please accept my own apology for not treating the workplace appropriately."

"I accept. We do not need to speak of this again." She looks relieved and so am I. She takes a sip of her tea before speaking again. "Your father had a food truck of sorts. It wasn't a mobile unit like yours, but more like the stalls you see at the markets. He made fish cakes. They were very good. He also sold banana milk. We should see him, you and I."

"He's . . . dead, though?" I am not following, although I get the intention.

"Yes. I mean his resting place in Seoul Choomo Gongwon. It is a columbarium where I brought him after the funeral." She stirs a spoon in her tea even though she hasn't added any sweetener or milk. "It is very nice there, Hara. Your father would like it. The building is set at the foot of Woomyunsan. The ceilings are tall and there is good light."

"Seoul park?" I know *gongwon* is "park" but am unsure about *choomo*.

"You are doing so well, Hara. *Choomo* is 'honor the deceased,' so *choomogongwon* literally means 'public park where you can cher-

ish the memories of a deceased,' but in English it is called Seoul
Memorial Park."

I have no memories of Lee Jonghyung to cherish. The only
thing I've experienced with him is his funeral. I knelt for more
than twenty-four hours next to two women I didn't know, and neither of them was Wansu. She'd paid for it. She'd come and bowed
and said things to my dad's landlady and his girlfriend or lover or
random hookup at the time of his death. She hadn't stayed. I wonder what memories she cherishes. If there are memories she cherishes.

"You do not have to do this for me."

"It is not for solely you, Hara. It is for me as well."

Once again, Ellen's words ping-pong in my head. Wansu is
lonely. Her husband has been nonresponsive for three years and in
bad health the previous two. The man she made a child with, who
either rejected her or, as he said in the email he sent me, hadn't believed he was the father, died as well. I had lost two fathers but
Wansu had effectively lost two husbands. *It is for me as well.*

"Yes. I'll go."

Wansu reacts as if I've agreed to carry an umbrella on a rainy
day. In other words, no big deal, but it is important enough for her
to have come home early on a workday, important enough that we
head straight out to the car. It takes us forty minutes to arrive at
the columbarium.

We talk a little about the economics of a food truck. Wansu
brings up all sorts of hidden expenses and legalities that I will need
to navigate. She instructs me to use the family lawyer to obtain the
proper licenses. I will have to get a commercial driver's license,
given the size of the food truck. She thinks it is a good idea that I
will be preparing for a spring opening. I have a lot of preparatory

work to do. The advice is good and the conversation makes the trip pass quickly.

The Seoul Memorial Park is situated in the basin at the foot of the mountain. Dug into the ground, the massive structure is surrounded by huge evergreens on nearly all sides. The building is four wings centered around a large reflecting pool with a giant metal lotus-flower sculpture in the middle. The walls facing the courtyard are all glass. Inside, the building is divided into smaller well-lit bereavement rooms with niches from floor to ceiling.

Wansu guides me to a unit at the end. Lee Jonghyung's resting place is spacious, two niches wide, and set at eye level. Behind the protective glass is a white porcelain urn that takes on a light green hue at certain angles, and two white flowers, which I presume are fake, lie at the base. The only other item in the niche is a small picture of young Lee Jonghyung in a simple wooden frame. He's leaning against the counter of his food stall with a pair of sunglasses dangling between his fingers, and everything about him, from his relaxed pose to his jeans and white T-shirt tucked in tight, shouts effortless cool. I can see why he attracted so many girls and so easily.

"Even though Lee Jonghyung did not raise you, he is still connected to you by blood. I could not doom your future by not honoring his death. That is why I paid for his funeral and placed him here in this place of peace. In the next life, we will pray that he will have a better life so that he does not wrong another you. I have brought my family here as well." She points to the rectangular niche next to Lee Jonghyung. "These are my parents. They died before I married Choi Yujun's father. We were dating at the time and he paid for their funeral, sat three days with me, and after asked me to marry him. He said I had lived with the burden of being alone for so long and would I allow him to take care of me."

He sounds like Yujun. That's something he would say. *Would you allow me to do this small thing for you, Hara?*

"And I said yes. I did love him—do love him—" she corrects herself. "Before I said yes, I told him about you, about my past. I did not want those secrets to unravel later. He said we should look for you and he would place his entire fortune in my hands to do so."

I suck in a breath at this. Wansu had mentioned this at Chuseok, but I never asked her about it further. I wanted to put that whole awful memory behind me.

Wansu hardly notices my response. She is lost in her past. "I accepted both the offer of marriage and the offer of aid. We found you after a long search. It is only because the police recorded your discovery. We traced you from the police to the agency that took you in. If I had left you anywhere else, you would have been lost to me forever." Wansu doesn't cry, but her voice is thick with emotion. "The investigators sent me photos of you and Ellen, and you were happy, Hara. You were very happy, and I did not believe I had a right to that happiness. I did not believe I had the right to hurt another woman by taking her child. What you are going through now is because of my decisions, and they have not been good. If it is Yujun you want, I will not stand in your way, but the path for the two of you will not be easy. "

Yujun said that his mother would come around with time, and maybe that's true or maybe in this, the valley of remembrance, she is recalling all that she has lost in her life. Her parents, her first love, her only child. She has had gains in her life, but sometimes it is the absence of things that sits heavy in your heart for far too long.

"Why did you not have another child?" I ask, a question that's been weighing on me for some time.

"I could not have another. We tried, but the seed never bore fruit. I think it is because I gave you up. The gods decided that I did not deserve another child, but I did receive Yujun and I am content. It did not matter to Choi Yusuk that I could not bear more children."

"He had Yujun."

She nods. "I am not the best mother or best wife. If Choi Yusuk were sitting at the chairman's desk, the company would not be the same, but there are women out there who cannot get jobs because they do not go to the right school or they are single mothers or they have made mistakes in the past. If I can help one of them, then maybe those sins in my past can be forgiven and my next life will be different."

My throat is hot with emotion and the space behind my eyes burns. I used to never cry, and then I came here and it's like the plug in the dam has been popped loose. I will never stop drinking that stupid wheatgrass smoothie, and if she wants to use forks and spoons at her Korean table, that's what we're going to use. Chopsticks can go to hell.

I reach for Wansu's hand, my *eomeo-nim*. "Thank you for bringing me here."

"You should come whenever you feel like it."

CHAPTER THIRTY-TWO

ONE OF ELLEN'S BEST DISHES IS PORK SANDWICHES. SHE'D put the pork in the slow cooker in the morning, and by the time I got home, the meat would be falling apart in a bed of fragrant juices. She'd toast big sesame buns while I forked the tender meat into smaller bits. Ellen liked her sandwich with relish and would spoon a giant portion from a store-bought jar. I'm in Korea and the best kind of relish here has to be made with *gochujang*, the ubiquitous red pepper paste with its twin pleasures of sweet and hot.

Mrs. Ji watches with interest as I set a heavy steel pot on the gas stove in the back kitchen. I go through the routine of double washing my hands before gloving up. I've two cuts of meat: the shoulder and the loin. Pulled pork, the kind that Ellen made, comes from the shoulder. I don't have a slow cooker, so I put water in the base of the pot and make a bed of crumpled foil for the shoulder to rest on. Along with the garlic, I add Korean apple pears, a handful of black peppercorns, brown sugar, cloves, *gochujang*, and thyme. It already smells good and it's not even begun to cook.

The loin gets a different treatment. It needs to be crispy on the outside. I do a simple salt-and-pepper rub, sear all four sides, and then wrap it in foil and bake in the oven at a low heat.

Now I need the toppings. The kimchi fridge has four different kinds of kimchi: cubed radish, white radish, cabbage, and perilla leaves. I take all of it out. Mrs. Ji helps me and then adds a small bowl of chive kimchi she had in a different part of the refrigerator. I finely chop all of them, putting them in different bowls, and then I start to add other ingredients, like tiny bits of apple pear, vinegar, and salt-soaked cucumbers, lemon zest, caramelized onions, mustard, ketchup, peppers. Some of it is terrible. Mrs. Ji ends up spitting the one with lemon, onion, and vinegary cucumbers into the sink, but she gives me a thumbs-up for the apple pear and cubed radish version with hot peppers and *gochujang* paste.

As I cook, Mrs. Ji tidies up, putting things away, washing dishes. I try to stop her but she insists. The clutter was getting to her. "What will you do with all this food?" she asks.

"Have a party."

I send out a group text. Ahn Sangki sends a happy dancing bear emoji, Jules a thumbs-up, but Bomi wants an engraved invitation.

BOMI: to Sajang-nim's home? Is this okay with her?

I text Wansu.

ME: Im making dinner and invited friends. One of them is Bomi but she wont come unless you say that its okay. Please tell her its okay.

I then text Yujun.

ME: Im making dinner. I invited Bomi Jules Sangki

YUJUN: Sangki beat you by five seconds

ME: He lives on his phone. Im elbow deep in kimchi relish

YUJUN: Kimchi relish?

ME: Trust me

YUJUN: I do

Those two words settle around my shoulders like a warm blanket. I toast a baguette, slice off some of the pork tenderloin, and pair it with provolone cheese and the napa cabbage kimchi cut finely and mixed with pineapple. Mrs. Ji downs her small portion in about three bites. When the last bit is swallowed, she gives me the thumbs-up. "*Jal meokkesseumnida.*"

She ate well. Pleasure and pride fill me. This woman who cooks for us every night said that my food is good. It's a huge compliment.

Mrs. Ji puts out the Western china along with forks and spoons, even though this is a finger-food meal. Almost by habit, she prepares eight different *banchan* dishes while I make french fries. Thank goodness every Korean kitchen has a mandoline or I would have still been cutting the potatoes when everyone spills into the house. The back kitchen smells like roast meat and fried potatoes, which makes me think of Ellen and Iowa. When I was young, I remember Ellen trying to cook Korean food for me. The house smelled funny and my school friends made fun of me for it, so I made her stop. She would cook the occasional Korean dish, but mostly she returned to her staple meals of pork chops, loin, hamburgers, roasted potatoes, corn on the cob. Everyone has their comfort food, and I suppose this is mine. It brings to mind hot days on the back porch, mosquitoes, butter dripping off freshly boiled corn, and Saturday movie nights. All good memories.

There are some things I won't want replaced by bulgogi and seaweed soup. The things I miss can all be brought here, including Ellen, my comfort food, even entertainment, since Wansu is willing to risk internet jail for me to get illegal streams. As we were driving home from the columbarium, she asked if there was anything I missed and I told her subtitles. She brought an IT tech from IF Group to hook my television up to a computer so I can get a feed from the US.

There's a place for me here in this city. I don't know exactly what it looks like or how it's shaped, but I am not a *moomyeong*, a person of no name or no identity.

When everyone arrives, they try to crowd into the kitchen with me, much to Mrs. Ji's and my dismay. Lightly, lovingly, but determinedly, I push them out. "Go sit at the table."

"But I want to see what you're doing," protests Yujun.

"We're washing up."

"There's food over there." He points over my shoulder.

"And it will be on the table quicker if you leave." I manage to shove him out and quickly close the door.

Mrs. Ji delivers the *banchan* while I remove the last of the fries from the oil and give them a tiny sprinkle of sugar and a large dose of salt. She returns and helps me carry out the sandwiches. My three friends look ready to pounce.

"There are three different kinds. One is pulled pork with apple pear chutney spiced with *gochujang*. This one is sliced pork tenderloin with provolone and caramelized onions with kimchi slaw.

This last one is sweet-and-sour pork tenderloin with chive kimchi and fried onion bits. Finally, we have french fries."

"And *banchan* from Mrs. Ji," adds Wansu, looking serene and pleased at the head of the table.

"Definitely. The kimchi is Mrs. Ji's, too." She told me that she made all of it herself every winter. I clap for her, and after a surprised pause, everyone joins in. Mrs. Ji blushes and beams before disappearing into the back kitchen. The attention might be too much for her, or her scrub brush is calling.

Sangki has half of one of the pork melts already devoured by the time I sit down. "Ah, this is so good. *Masitda*."

"Did you make these, too?" Wansu asks, a french fry speared on the end of a fork.

"I did."

"These are better than Shake Shack," Bomi declares.

"This doesn't taste like *samgyeopsal*." Yujun holds up a sandwich and peers at the thin slices of pork layered inside the crunchy baguette.

"No. It's loin and shoulder. Yang Ilwha used these pieces in her pork balls because they were cheaper."

"This is true. Seoulites either eat *samgyeopsal* or *gopchang*. Nothing else." Yujun opts for the pulled pork.

"Loin is leaner," I point out.

"But usually so dry." Bomi makes a face. "Like cardboard."

"The pork balls weren't." This attack on Yang Ilwha's food seems personal.

"Everything that's fried tastes good," Sangki chirps.

"Et tu, Brute?"

Yujun intercedes before Sangki and I argue more. "This is great, Hara. The best meal I've had."

My gaze flies to Wansu. "He means recently."

"He means it is the best meal he's had. I do not cook, Hara. Do not be worried about my feelings, but thank you."

This is the best meal that I've ever had, too, not because the food is good but because everyone sitting at this table is a person I care about and they are enjoying food that I made. There's something immensely satisfying about this. There are some things in life that cross borders and boundaries, that are not limited by language. Music is one, but food—food is another.

CHAPTER THIRTY-THREE

WINTER HAS FALLEN ON SEOUL. THE POLLUTION HAS BEEN
driven away and cold winds are keeping many people inside. The
food truck is closed, and most days I'm in the back kitchen, experi-
menting with different pork dishes. I'm contemplating making ba-
cony things. Yujun is down in Busan today and the snow is keeping
him there until morning.

Wansu is with *Sae Appa*, as she always is this time of the night,
so it is a surprise to me when I see her at the doorway of the kitchen.

"Is everything all right?"

"Would you come out and sit with me? I made some tea."

Immediately, I turn off the stove and dump the syrup I was
making into the trash. Something is wrong. Wansu doesn't make
tea. Mrs. Ji makes the tea. "Is Yujun okay?"

I reach for the phone to see if there's trending news. Wansu's
hand covers mine. "Yes. He's upstairs with his father."

"He's upstairs? I thought he was in Busan and couldn't leave because of the weather."

"He came home because I asked him to. Please."

I don't make her repeat herself. When I'm seated, she pours steaming tea into a celadon-colored cup, a traditional color and style with no handle. It reminds me of the tea rites they performed at Chuseok when Yujun poured the soju into the brazier. I make no move to drink mine and Wansu leaves hers untouched as well.

"Yujun's father has not been well for many years, and Yujun and I believe it is time we let him go."

"Oh, I'm so sorry."

She takes a deep shaky breath. "Before we cease all life-support activities, I am divorcing him and taking back my family name of Na. I will also be leaving IF Group."

"What?" I nearly shout I'm so shocked.

"I have been offered the opportunity to head a new association for the development of women-owned small businesses. It is a place where I can do good work. Yujun will be promoted to vice president of operations to be groomed to take over my old role."

"Why? What?" I can't even put a whole sentence together.

"I saw our family at Chuseok and how they looked at you. They made you feel like an outsider and you are not. You are my blood, my daughter that I birthed, and while I gave you up, I have always held you in my heart."

"I know." I have accepted that, so her proposed plans confuse me.

Suddenly, she reaches out and grasps my hand. "You have never asked me for more, but you deserve it. As long as I am a Choi, you and Yujun cannot be together and that is not right. I would like you to be part of my family, Hara. To have you be legally recognized as my daughter. I have asked Ellen for permission and she has agreed to this."

Her hand feels hot in my grip. "You're divorcing *Sae Appa*, giving up IF Group, all so that Yujun and I can be together? We are together. We don't have an official document to say that, but I don't need it."

"I do. It's not a sacrifice." Her hold tightens. "My favorite drama heroine has always been Sim Cheong. I loved her selflessness and her resilience. I imagined I was like her, but while I was strong, I was never selfless." A ghost of a smile wisps across her mouth. "We admire in others that which we lack in ourselves. My *hyo*, my filial piety, wasn't to my own parents, but to survival. That was what birthed me, and that was the altar at which I worshipped. I thought I had received the emperor's blessing when Yujun's *appa* asked me to marry him, but the true blessing was when you were returned to me. I was given a second chance despite all I had done in the past. I will not waste that chance and I will not ask more from you than you have already given. This company has always been meant for Yujun. I was only the chatelaine holding the keys until he was ready for them."

It makes some sense as she lays it out, but it feels like the sacrifice is too enormous and that I am not worthy of it. "I don't want you to look back in regret."

"I will not, but neither should you." Wansu releases me and picks up her cup of tea. "You should call Ellen. She will tell you that what I am doing is right. And then, Hara, our Yujun will need you."

My gaze lifts toward the second floor as the realization of what is happening sets in. Yujun is saying goodbye to his father. Wansu has given me only a little window to process things, likely realizing that if I had too much time, I'd turn myself into a pretzel trying to convince Wansu that her solution isn't everything I wanted.

I hurry into my bedroom and make that call.

"Mom, Wansu told me she's divorcing *Sae Appa*."

"Is that what you call him? Yes, darling, I think it's the right thing for her to do. She has clung to him for so long, but it's time for her to move on. Taking back her old name is a power move. I'm so proud of her."

"Proud?"

"Yes. She's reclaiming her past, the one that she didn't like, and transforming it into something she's no longer ashamed of. I hope you support her."

"Of course." I hadn't looked at it that way, not from Wansu's point of view.

"We're going to have a ceremony. Did she tell you that?"

"No." A lot is happening.

"Yes. I'm coming back to Korea and we're having a registry ceremony. Wansu is creating a new registry for her and you. It's exciting, isn't it? You're starting a new clan."

These aren't terms that Ellen would ordinarily use, so it must be from Wansu. She's a good salesperson, I'll give her that. "I'm excited to see you again. I've missed you."

"Darling, I've missed you, too. Having two mothers is really a blessing. You'll always have someone watching over you."

"You mean spying on me?"

"You kids always use such funny terms. Ah, she's calling me. We're going to make plans. I'll chat with you later, okay?"

"Okay." Wansu is ever the mastermind, but in this instance, I'm not irritated. I need to prepare for Yujun.

"He will be down in about fifteen minutes," Wansu informs me as I pass by her on my way to the kitchen. It's enough time for me to prepare *hotteok*, this time with the traditional filling of brown sugar, butter, and walnuts. I wrap them up in paper and place them in a sack along with two bottles of soju.

His eyes are red when he emerges from his father's room. I pick up the sack of food and hold out my hand. "Want to go for a drive?"

Wordlessly, he folds my fingers between his and leads me down to his car. We drive down the mountain past the high brick and stone walls, the treed lots, as the quiet street expands into four lanes and then eight. The cement apartments rise on either side of the road and the north mountains fade as the south peaks start to take shape on the horizon.

He takes us straight to the river park where we first kissed. This time of night, there is no one here save the occasional kid speeding by on a motorized scooter or skateboard.

We sit on the bench on the long stretch of cement while the Han laps quietly against the rocks and the traffic behind us hums low in harmony. The normally talkative Yujun has no words. His hand remains glued to mine. I hear a gasp, an indrawn breath, and then he breaks. Quiet, fierce sobs shake his shoulders. Heat burns the back of my eyes as I scramble to my knees and press his face to my chest. His arms come around me, tight and hard. I can feel his muffled cries reverberate through my frame, drawing out an echo of remembered pain. He and I have suffered the same loss—our parents—and shared trauma, but we also have our love of this city, our longing for something more.

He said we were destined to be together, that our fates were tied by this fabled red cord, no matter where we went, no matter the distance between us, no matter the obstacles. He was right.

"Ah, *gomawo*." Thank you, he says. "I did not think I would lose it."

"My shoulders are small but sturdy." I dab his cheeks with my shirt. He allows me the privilege of caring for him and I am so grateful to be needed.

I came here searching for something, not just my father, Lee Jonghyung, or my mother, Na Wansu. I'd found my mother, Wansu; my love, Yujun from Seoul; but also my sisters, Jules and Bomi; and my brother, Sangki. I found that home is not a city or state or country or even a continent. I don't belong because of the shape of my eyes, the way I pronounce *about* or *gomawo*, or whether I wear stripes or polka dots, but because of the people I belong to. I allowed myself to be vulnerable here, or maybe being here stripped away my defenses. Either way, people found their way into my heart and I can't let them go.

These people are my home. These people make up who I am and will affect who I will be in the future. I love this place. I love this man.

Once I said to Yujun that I did not feel like a Korean and he'd replied that what is a Korean but a person who has suffered and survived? In the bitter and the sweet of this city, I have found my person, my soul.

"*Saranghaeyo*," I whisper against his silky hair. "*Saranghaeyo*." I say it again and again and he says it back, quietly, and then louder. We stay in this moment, breathing the same air, repeating our love in English and in Korean as many times as we can until it takes shape between us. It is too big to become undone. I am a part of this place, this man, this clan. I love you. *Saranghaeyo*. I love you. *Saranghaeyo. Saranghaeyo.*

EPILOGUE

"WHO ARE YOU STARING AT?" I WAVE MY HAND IN FRONT OF
Yujun's nose. His hands are suspended in midair, one with a ball of
hotteok dough and the other holding a spoon full of brown sugar,
cinnamon, and roasted nuts.

He squints. "I think that's Kim Seonpyung over there."

"Who is that?"

"Your blind date," Bomi supplies.

This clarifies nothing. "I've never gone on a blind date."

"The animal hater." Yujun straightens and dumps the filling inside the dough.

"Ah." The light bulb turns on. He was the guy that *Eomeo-nim*
thought would distract me from Yujun.

"Animal hater?" Bomi echoes.

Yujun pinches the dough shut and drops it onto the griddle. "I
heard he was studying at Oxford."

"Nursing a broken heart from being rejected by Hara." Sangki clicks his tongue against the roof of his mouth. He tamps down one side of the dough fritter with a flat metal disc and then flips the dessert over.

"We never dated," I remind them as I slide two pork sandwich boats down to Jules, who serves them to the couple in front of her.

"Which is why he's heartbroken. Makes perfect sense." Yujun nods.

"I didn't know he hated animals. I wouldn't have put him on the list if I'd known that." Bomi sounds distressed.

"He's lying. Hi, can I help you?" I ask Kim Seonpyung as he steps forward.

His mouth opens but no words come out. His jaw is slightly unhinged as he stares at Yujun. "Choi Yujun-nim? Is that you?"

Yujun adjusts his face shield and smiles brightly. "Yes. Can I take your order?"

"Is the IF Group testing out a food-truck franchise?" Kim Seonpyung leans back to read my food-truck sign. "Taste of Ee-hwa?"

"Iowa," Yujun corrects. "And, no, it is my girlfriend's food truck." He pats his wrist against my back so he doesn't contaminate his gloved hands. "I'm helping out because"—he gestures toward the crowd—"it's a busy night."

"We're doing a/b testing. Order two *hotteoks* and then vote with the jelly bean for which one you like better. The traditional brown sugar one or the raspberry jam one," Sangki chirps.

Kim Seonpyung's jaw drops even lower. "DJ Song? You're . . . inside the truck?"

The sight of the heir to a half-billion-dollar international logistics company and one of the most famous singers in the country frying french fries and filling *hotteok* dough is taking Kim Seonpyung out. He can't seem to process what he's seeing. Behind him the line of people is starting to get restless. A few are craning their heads to see what is holding up service.

"Two pulled pork with kimchi slaw and fries coming right up." I decide for him.

"Two?" Yujun asks.

"It's time for you to take a break." I bump my hip against his.

Jules pulls on his apron ties while Bomi knocks his face shield off. I throw two buns onto the griddle and toast them while Sangki works the fryer. He's surprisingly good at it. We work like a well-oiled machine, and soon Yujun is pushed out the back door. It's crowded when all five of us are in here anyway, but I need the extra hands tonight. The end-of-the-summer river festival is huge, which would be reason enough for the lines, but word got out that Ahn Sangki would be here helping, and that always draws a number of people wanting to see him wield a spatula.

He looks cute, though, so I don't blame them.

"*Oppa*, you sounded awesome tonight," cheers a young woman who ordered three of everything. We pile up several paper trays and she passes them out to her two starstruck friends.

"Thank you. Are you a Songbird?" Songbirds is the name of his fandom.

She nods eagerly and lifts up her hand to display his light stick dangling from her arm. The acrylic globe on the end of the plastic handle is still lit.

He grins. "Extra fries for you."

One of her friends lifts up her camera phone to take a photo, but the girl buying the food pushes the device to the side. "You know the rules. No photos of *oppa* outside of official schedules."

The friend grimaces.

"Extra *hotteok*, too." I place another raspberry jam *hotteok* on the paper tray. Good behavior should be rewarded.

The trio waves to us as they carry their food away. "Your fan situation seems to be improving."

"Yeah. I mean, certain parts are never going away"—he nods toward the group of five that seem to follow him everywhere—"but I get Squirtle out of it." He taps the charm dangling from the window that one of his fans sent to the food truck when it opened.

"And you helped launch this place. I'm going to tell you a secret. I think you have so many fans because you're a decent person and people like to be proud of the people they stan."

His ears pinken. "Isn't it my awesome voice?"

"Yes, but David Kim has an awesome voice and his last two singles were flops. Didn't even chart for a day."

Sangki's grin widens. "I know. Isn't it great?"

"Stop yapping and start cooking," Jules interrupts. "Two porks, two fries, and two corns."

I get to work and so does Sangki. When Jules and I first opened, Sangki sent a wreath, which is a Korean tradition. You send wreaths to weddings and funerals and school graduations and new business ventures and maybe even failed ones. Some are basic ones you'd find on a door at Christmas in Iowa, but many are three tiers with large satin banners hanging on either side. Sangki, of course, gave an extravagant one with four tiers instead of three. The banner said he hoped Taste of Iowa became his favorite place and, even if it didn't, at least my blue truck was pretty.

Eomeo-nim and Yujun were slightly put out that their congratulatory wreath was outclassed, but I wrapped myself in Yujun's banner that night and made it up to him.

The soft opening in Yongsan-gu right before Seollal, the New Year celebration, went well. Yujun brought his staff over and Bomi came as well. People who were used to getting food from Yang Ilwha were apprehensive at first, particularly because I wasn't serving the same kind of food, but the good eats won them over. After Seollal, Sangki showed up with a camera crew. He videotaped himself in the tiny kitchen running potatoes through the mandoline, toasting buns for the sandwiches, and serving customers. He said he needed the fan content. I protested that it wasn't fair, but after seeing how much he enjoyed working with us a couple of times a month, I didn't have the heart to turn him away. He said that manning the deep fryer and hanging out after the truck closes down is the most normal thing in his life and he needs that. It is also the only time that all of us see one another because we are all so busy these days. Bomi and Yujun are neck-deep in work for the LA expansion. Sangki put a new album out and has a couple of television variety shows. I'm not sure if he sleeps even two hours a night some weeks.

For Jules and me, the food truck keeps us occupied. We are only open during the week in Yongsan because on the weekends we take the truck on the road to different festivals. There are several going on every weekend. Jules and I have worked seven days a week since February, but we made enough over the summer to take a long winter hiatus. After tonight, we'll close and spend our downtime with our loved ones—Jules plans to fly home to introduce Bomi to the family, and Yujun, *Eomeo-nim*, Ellen, and I are spending Chuseok in Hawaii.

When Jules and I get back to Seoul, we will search out new recipes and perfect them. We don't want to grow stale, and the competition is fierce, with more vendors popping up every day. Yujun and Sangki are ridiculously excited about the winter cooking bonanzas and have been sending us suggestions on the regular for everything from fried ice cream, which sounds intriguing, to matcha pasta, which does not.

The two also got into a big argument about mint chocolate chip, which has become a huge trend—so huge that there are actually vendors here that are selling mint choco pork cutlets and mint choco fried chicken. When Yujun argued that the chicken wasn't bad, Sangki demanded to know whether Yujun had the audacity to kiss me with that mouth. Yujun, like all Koreans, brushes his teeth after every meal and so was mildly offended. I made the mistake of sharing that mole, a Mexican chocolate sauce often paired with chicken, was quite tasty, and Sangki shouted I might as well join David Kim's fan club.

"What are you grinning about?" Sangki asks.

"How offended you were when I said I thought the mint chocolate chicken wasn't bad."

"Don't talk to me," he declares.

"You asked me what I was grinning about."

"You could lie and say my singing."

"Your singing was great."

"I know."

The entire truck bursts out laughing. We're still smiling when Yujun reappears. "What did I miss?" he asks, tying on his apron.

"Everyone was praising me for my performance. Feel free to join in."

"You were great, Sangki-ah," Yujun replies dutifully.

"More enthusiastically, please."

Yujun starts clapping. The line of people outside fall briefly silent, and then they, too, start clapping. Sangki sends a murderous look at my love before bowing to the crowd.

"Kim Seonpyung wants to invest in your franchise," Yujun whispers in my ear.

I roll my eyes. Last winter, Yujun and *Eomeo-nim* surprised me after dinner with a whole PowerPoint presentation about how to transform my unlaunched food-truck business into a nationwide enterprise. It looked impressive and intimidating and unwanted. I explained to them that while I understood that Korean culture was hurry up and run forward toward success, I wanted to learn how to walk first. I don't know that I'll ever want more than one food truck. Jules seems content with running only one as well.

With five of us, we work through the festivalgoers until the last song is sung and the lights start to wink out. I pull down the service window and we get to cleaning. After everything is put away and the stainless steel counters are shiny once again, the five of us collapse on the curb behind the truck—like five little tired ducks.

Bomi rests her head on Jules's shoulder. Bomi and Jules engage in far more PDA than Yujun and I, and no one bats an eye. Skinship, as they call it here, is acceptable among close friends. Unless the two are passionately kissing each other on the mouth, the sight of the two of them holding hands, hugging, leaning on each other as they are now with Bomi resting her head on Jules's shoulder, is unremarkable.

The two did share their relationship with Bomi's brother and sister. Her sixteen-year-old brother wasn't happy at first. Bomi thought it was because he was against same-sex relationships. Yujun offered to speak with him, and after a couple of weeks of enduring the silent treatment at home, Bomi caved. Yujun took the boy to a batting cage and fed him *hanwoo* and copious amounts of ice cream, which works about the same as soju on the under-eighteen crowd in prying mouths open. The brother confessed he was worried Bomi would lose her job. Yujun assured him that not only was Bomi a valued employee but that someday she would likely run her own department at IF Group. That seemed to resolve the immediate family conflict. As for the rest of Bomi's family, they're not keen on it. A couple of aunts don't speak to her, and Bomi isn't invited to Chuseok this year, which she told me wasn't any kind of punishment.

All in all, they're happy.

"We estimated this pretty well," Jules says with smug satisfaction. She's in charge of supplies and so is rightfully proud.

"You did well." Bomi pats her shoulder.

"I know."

"You sound like Sangki."

"We're both talented in our own ways. I'll take that as a compliment."

"You should," Sangki calls from the other side of Yujun.

"The moms are coming." Yujun points to two women walking toward us. We straighten up. All of us are over twenty-five, with Sangki and Yujun kissing thirty, but when the parents are around, we're children again.

The two women are different in almost every way, from their appearance to their native language. Ellen wears a long colorful cotton skirt with open-toed sandals and a bright green blouse. She's a good four inches shorter and rounder than Wansu, but her colorful presence, Western features, and light brown hair make her stand out. Wansu is tall and slender and hardly ever wears anything that isn't neutral monochrome. Tonight is no different. She's clad in dark gray pants and a matching knit top. Her hair is cut in her trademark severe bob, and due to good genetics and lots of sunscreen, she doesn't look much past the age of thirty.

I once told Yujun that Ellen and Wansu are like potatoes and rice. Ellen's and Pat's families grew up eating potatoes. Wansu and Jonghyung had rice at nearly every meal. No home can be without one of those staples. They ward off malnutrition, have ended famines, provide comfort. You need one or the other in your life, and having both is a blessing. And Yujun and I are blessed.

Ellen and Wansu have become close friends despite the cultural divide. They have more in common than they have differences. Both lost their husbands. Both have raised children that they did not give birth to. Both worry about us endlessly. Both love melodramas. Every night after dinner, they watch one together. It's how Ellen is learning Korean.

My own Korean is better. My accent is terrible and sometimes native Koreans have a hard time understanding me. I have to speak English a few times because my Korean pronunciation is awful, but I'm trying. The walk around the earth is slow, but progress is being made. I might reach a new continent sometime within the next decade.

Yujun is always willing to speak English with me. All of my friends do, but I love hearing them speak Korean. It's a beautiful language and Yujun never sounds sexier than when he's speaking his native tongue. There's something musical and rhythmic in the way that he speaks the language. Oftentimes, when we talk, he'll speak Korean and I'll speak English. It's weird but it works.

"You had a good crowd tonight." Ellen claps her hands together in delight. "Every time we walked by you had a long line. I heard people say it was the best food at the festival and that they were so sad you would be closed until after Seollal." She turns to Wansu. "Did I say that right?"

Wansu nods with silent approval.

"Isn't my Korean getting so good? Wansu says I sound like a native."

She doesn't, but we all bob our heads in agreement.

"I bought these soaps by myself!" She holds up a small clear bag that contains four blocks of soap that look like a slice of Van Gogh's *Starry Night*. "I even haggled a little. Of course, Wansu helped but I did it mostly myself. I think I could go to a café and order alone, not that I would want to, Wansu, but if I had to, I could, don't you think?"

"Yes," Wansu agrees.

Ellen preens with pride. "We wanted to come over and say goodbye. We're headed home now. Don't stay out too late." She comes over and gives me a pat on the face and presses a kiss on my head. She does the same to Yujun.

Sangki taps the side of his cheek. Ellen laughs delightedly and gives Sangki a kiss as well.

"Two moms hasn't turned out all bad," Sangki murmurs as the moms walk away.

"Obviously two moms are superior," Jules says.

"I mean, yeah, if that's all you have, then I guess two moms will do, but in reality two dads are the best," Sangki counters.

"In what world are two dads better than two moms?" Jules shoots back.

As the two bicker, Yujun tilts his head and smiles at me, his dimples deepening. He's happy and so am I. I came to Korea to find my family, to figure out where I belonged, and what I learned was that family has never been about blood. Family is about the people you love and the people who love you back, and in that circle, you are never an outsider, a person with no name. You always belong.

ACKNOWLEDGMENTS

The end of this book is bittersweet for me because I really love Hara and her found family. It will be hard not to revisit them in the future. I want to start by thanking everyone who stuck with me for the second book. The story of Hara and Yujun and all of the others was too big to be told in one book and I'm thankful for the opportunity to be granted so many pages to share the complete story.

Thank you to Cindy Hwang, who believed in me and this duology and who worked so hard to get these manuscripts into publishable works. Ms. Hwang, you do an endless amount of hard work and likely only receive a fraction of the recognition for it. Thank you!

Thank you to Steve Axelrod, who does important work behind the scenes. I appreciate all you and your team does on my behalf.

To Nicole, the novelist assistant extraordinaire, thank you for the work that you do, the creative ideas you generate, and your daily support.

To my friends and daily email and text recipients (Jeanette Mancine, Melissa K., Meljean Brook, Jessica Clare, Robin Harders, Syreeta Jennings, Lea Robinson, Elyssa Patrick, Anne Sowards, Grace House), thank you for your friendship and support. I would not have made it as a writer without you.

Christina, please never leave me.

Diane Park, you are a marvel. I hope you look at yourself every day and acknowledge how fabulous you are. Thank you for reading this, helping me with language and cultural elements, and sharing your friendship.

To the Berkley/Penguin team, thank you for the hard work you do every day: Angela Kim, Fareeda Bullert, and Jessica Brock.

To all the readers, bookstagrammers (Literary PenGwyns, your Instagram messages are so uplifting), Facebook groups, Youtubers, and Twitter friends, thank you for your kind messages and pretty pictures. For the readers who leave reviews on B&N, Amazon, and Goodreads, thank you for the time and effort you put into the reading community.

To the family who found me and the family I've created, I love you. Thank you for all your love and support.

To the adoptees and friends and family members of adoptees, I see you! I hear you. Your stories are important and so are you.

Seoulmates

Jen Frederick

QUESTIONS FOR DISCUSSION

1. What does the concept of "found family" mean to you?

2. Are found families changing the way we observe holidays?

3. Do you think Wansu's choice at the end was the right one for everyone involved, or did you wish for a different outcome for the Chois?

4. How comfortable would you be living in another country whose primary language was different from your own? Or how comfortable would you be living in another country with the same language?

5. What food do you crave when you're away from home? What do you like to eat while traveling?

6. What are some of the landmarks you'd like to visit in Korea?

7. What are some of the foods you would like to try in Korea?

8. Are you a rice or potato person?

JEN FREDERICK is a Korean adoptee living in the Midwest with her husband, daughter, and rambunctious dog. Under the pseudonym Erin Watt, Frederick has cowritten two #1 *New York Times* bestselling novels.

Ready to find
your next great read?

Let us help.

Visit prh.com/nextread